UNBROKEN

JAMIE LISA FORBES

www.pronghornpress.org

For my family

And for ranch children everywhere

Here, on this arc
of grass, sun, and sky,
I will stay and see if I thrive.
Others leave. They say it's too hard.
I say hammer my spirit thin,
spread it horizon to horizon,
see if I break.
Let the blizzards hit my face;
let my skin feel the winter's freeze;
let the heat of summer's extreme
try to sear the flesh from my bones.
Do I have what it takes to survive,
or will I shatter and break?
Hammer me thin,
Stretch me from horizon to horizon.
I need to know the character
that lies within...

—from the poem "Prairie Prayer" by Bruce Roseland
from his volume, *A Prairie Prayer*, recipient of the
2009 Will Rogers Medallion Award.

JAMIE LISA FORBES

1

Gwen Swan stomped her feet on the porch mat. In the gray light, she fretted over the five eggs in her pail, ignoring the icy draft ruffling the dogs. Damnit—now she'd have to buy eggs in town. The door scraped the floor planks as she pushed it shut and the dogs hunkered back down on their beds with soft groans.

Inside, Will, still in his long underwear, drank coffee by the stove. "How cold is it?" he asked.

"Cold enough to stop the hens from laying. You'd better get your pants on. Your father'll be here any minute."

Will moved away, slurping his coffee.

Eggs and sausages sizzled in the skillet by the time John's truck rumbled into the yard. In the pause that followed, she dreaded his every approaching step.

Sure enough, the door flew open and his voice boomed across

the kitchen. "Coffee hot?"

The same damn phrase every morning—as if he'd ever gotten it cold! She'd fed him three meals a day since her mother-in-law had died—barely two months after she'd married Will. Oh, she was so hopeful in those days, so eager to show her new family how much she could do! But after ten years of meals, with a handful of days off for childbirth, John's voice at the crack of dawn zapped her like a cattle prod and just like a cow, she wanted to knock him down as she charged out the door.

"Here you go, John," she said placing the mug in his grasp.

He peered into the dining room. "Where's Will?"

"Don't know. I've been out to get the eggs and I've been here ever since."

"Pretty soon the whole day'll be gone."

John plopped down with a deliberate sigh and before the mug reached his lips, Gwen had arranged the steaming breakfast platters around him. He sank the serving spoon into the fluffy eggs and Will appeared, his sparse hair slicked down on his head.

"I thought you were sick."

Will didn't look at his father. He sat down and grabbed a piece of toast.

"The thermometer says ten below."

Will nodded.

"Want me to chop water holes today, son?"

Will looked up at him. "No. I'll do it."

"Did you check the cows yesterday?"

Will nodded.

"Do we have any early calves coming?"

"No one is showing yet," Will answered.

"Well, you better check 'em again today. Things can change quick." John yelled back to the kitchen, "Gwen, do we have oatmeal today?"

"I'm getting it."

Before John could stimulate more breakfast conversation, his oatmeal and another cup of hot coffee were before him.

Gwen had the dishes cleared and soaking in the sink when she glanced up at the kitchen clock. 6:30. She dried her hands and started down the hall to the children's rooms. She passed the shelves that Will had built to hold her Western Pleasure trophies and her rodeo queen pictures with her cowboy hat set low over her brow and thick curls falling to her shoulders, her gloved hand raised. Smiling. Smiling. She passed the mirror where she glimpsed herself. She'd chopped off those curls long ago.

She entered her son's room. "Rory, get up." Then her daughter's room. "McKenna, get up." She heard reluctant sighs and rustlings of bedclothes. By the hall light, she saw the flannel shirts and jeans on the beds where she had laid them the night before. "Get moving you two."

Will was pulling on his coveralls in the kitchen as John talked to him.

"This afternoon, better start moving hay to the calving sheds."

"I don't see why. We've got another month."

"No point in leaving it to the last minute. What if we get a bad storm tomorra or the day after tomorra? Better move it while we don't have to dig out haystacks, son."

"I was going to service the tractor this afternoon."

"That's not going to take all afternoon, is it? You can at least get started."

Will opened the door to the porch. John was about to follow him when Rory flew through the kitchen and tackled him.

John turned. "Well, young man, good morning to you."

Will took the opportunity to close the porch door and escape.

"Grandpa, can you take us to school today?"

"No," said Gwen, "he's not taking you to school today."

"Well, Gwen, I believe I have time to take them to school."

"The last time you took them they were thirty minutes late because you stopped to talk to the neighbors."

"It wasn't no thirty minutes. All they missed was the Pledge of Allegiance."

"I got a call from the teacher, John."

"Mom, can't we ride with Grandpa? Then we won't have to walk to the bus."

"Stop being so lazy. It doesn't take but a few minutes."

"But it's cold out."

"Cold doesn't hurt. It's good for you." Gwen placed oatmeal and toast down on the kitchen table in front of him. "Eat."

"Mom!" McKenna called from the bathroom.

"It's all right, son," said John. "You can come with me on Saturday morning. Do you want to?"

"Yes, Grandpa."

"All right. I'll see you tonight, then."

McKenna scowled into the bathroom mirror. "I need help."

Gwen picked up the brush and ran it slowly through her daughter's hair, lingering over the silkiness of it.

"You're hurting me!"

"It was just a knot." Gwen swept her hair up into a long ponytail.

"Can't I have it braided?"

"No. There's not enough time. You still have to eat breakfast." Gwen fixed a ribbon over the ponytail holder. "If you want your hair braided, you're going to have to learn to get up earlier." Gwen placed clips along the side of her head then pressed her daughter's face between her two hands. "There. Beautiful."

"It's not beautiful. It's ugly."

"Come have breakfast."

By 7:15, the three of them spilled out the door in their parkas and snow boots. Gwen tugged hats and hoods over the children's heads against their protests. Rory trudged down the road first, followed by his mother and sister. The sky was a pearl blue now and the sun inched over the horizon. Puffs of steam rose from their mouths. The children in their bulky clothes looked like marching snowmen.

"I don't see why we can't ride with Grandpa," said Rory.

"Look at the sunrise," said Gwen. "Isn't it beautiful?"

Rory shifted so as to avoid noticing the sunrise. He kicked at the snow as he walked.

"What are we having for supper?" asked McKenna.

"McKenna, we've just had breakfast. Why are you worried about supper?"

"I just want to know what we're going to have."

"Fish sticks."

"Fish sticks! Yum!"

"I hate fish sticks," said Rory, "Can't we have something else?"

They were at the road now. They stomped their feet while the sun warmed their backs. They turned toward the sound of the approaching bus. It rounded the line of bare cottonwoods, bouncing over the dips in the road, and lurched to a halt.

Warm air mixed with children's chatter rushed over them as the door swung open. McKenna and Rory clambered aboard, then the door shut and Gwen followed the bus' departure until even the sound had dissipated. The cold closed around her again. She envied her children. They were swept up and carried off into a day full of things to do. Ahead of her: a house sunk deep in winter silence.

In the kitchen, she flipped the radio on to the morning talk show—the "Swap Shop." First caller: "I got a Wards washing machine and dryer, a playpen, a couch and a lawn mower."

She listened with half an ear as she started her pie crust. It was all a lot of junk—who'd want a lawn mower in January? But once in a while she'd hear an item they needed. And Will would never buy anything new. She rolled out three crusts, molded them to the tins and pinched the edges. Will came in just as she set them in the refrigerator.

"Ready to feed?"

The sun was high, glittery bright in the ice-blue sky. Diesel exhaust from the rumbling tractor filled the barnyard.

"We're lucky this morning," said Will, raising his voice over the engine. "Not much wind."

Gwen opened the gate while Will pulled through. Then she closed it and jumped on the haywagon. Will waited for her signal and with a jerk, they were off.

Will was right. There was no wind. But a quirk of this country was that the wind didn't blow when the temperature dropped below zero. It felt as if they were submerged in ice. She swung her legs to keep her feet warm.

The cows heard the tractor and drifted out from the willows along the river. They followed it far out into the meadow. He stopped, set the tractor in first gear and aimed it where it wouldn't run into a ditch or a stackyard. Then he joined Gwen on the haywagon. Both of them chopped the bales into sheaves and dropped them in a line. The cows were stampeding now, hungry, hungry. The leaders bumped others out of the line to snatch the greenest, choicest morsels.

After they'd fed a second line, Will stopped the tractor.

"Let's walk through and see if any are close."

Gwen moved down one line and Will, down the other. The cows' sides bulged and their udders were filling, but none showed the last signs of imminent labor and delivery. The cows didn't mind Gwen or Will, they were too intent on filling their empty bellies.

Will shouted to Gwen, "Anything?"

She shook her head.

Will turned the tractor homeward. Gwen tried to ignore the cold by closing her eyes and lifting her face straight to the sun. With that warmth, she could almost forget the numbness in her fingers and toes.

Back in the kitchen, the clock read 10:00. It had been a "Swap Shop" item—a large face with boy and girl figurines in blue gingham. Over time, the background had yellowed but the hands continued to creep over the little boy and girl. She flipped the radio back on and the last phrases of *I'm the Happiest Girl in the Whole U.S.A.* drifted through the room.

She put the pies in the oven and peeled potatoes and carrots for the potroast. Set the table for lunch. She dusted and vacuumed the bedrooms and right as the noon news began, she heard Will and John on the back porch.

Sunlight streamed through the dining room. It was so bright and cheery that it was hard to believe it was cold outside.

"Smells good," said John as he sat down and speared a chunk of meat.

The news blared on, filling the silence between them, though Gwen couldn't say if anyone was listening. But John could never go too long without spouting his own commentary on their daily events.

"Think that ol' Mather is going to show up and feed them calves he just bought?" he said.

"He's not going to let them starve," said Will.

"Driving back and forth from town—that takes effort, more than he's used to," said John.

"He spent money on them and he watches his money pretty good."

"He may watch it while it's under the mattress," John gestured with his fork, "but it don't go too far from there."

"He'll hire someone to feed them," said Will.

"And put them in that rat-trap trailer?"

"What are you so worried about this for?"

"I ain't worried. Those calves are just bawling a lot. I can hear them a mile away. I feel sorry for them. Gwen, I know I smell that apple pie. Do we got any whipped cream?"

As she washed the lunch dishes, it began. A rattling in the highest branches of the cottonwoods. A hissing in the tall grass along the riverbank. And in seconds, the wind was in full roar, shaking the trees with a fury. Gusts smacked the house in waves. From somewhere—where did that sound come from?—came the high whistling shriek.

Gwen dried her hands and went to the living room window. Out in the meadow where they'd fed cows that morning, the wind wasn't driving much snow. Just the dry loose powder across the top. No more drifting snow—until the next storm.

But that sound. It could go on forever.

When the sunlight waned, she glanced at her clock—time to get the children. The air was warmer now, but the wind bit her cheeks. At the road, though she strained hard to listen for the bus, only the wind filled her ears. Even when the bus pulled up, she couldn't hear it.

Rory and McKenna jumped off. Both their jackets were wide open. They were bareheaded and neither one wore mittens.

"Where're your hoods? Get them on this minute!"

"Mom, Rory got in trouble today."

"Don't tattle," Gwen said as she tightened the hood strings.

"McKenna lost her mittens."

"McKenna! Did you?"

"I think I know where they are."

"You don't!" Rory snapped. "You're just saying that so you won't get in trouble."

"Never mind that now," Gwen sighed. "How was your day at school?"

Total silence. Gwen looked at Rory for a long moment. She wavered between ferreting out what had happened or waiting for the teacher's call.

"Livvy brought her guinea pigs to school and we got to play with them," chattered McKenna. Gwen turned—she had to remember she had a daughter, too—but her worries over Rory hounded her.

"How many does she have?"

"A mom and three babies. And Mom, the babies just fit right in your hand. Can we have guinea pigs?"

"You don't play with the dogs and the cats we have."

"Yes I do."

"When?"

"It's hard to play outside with them in the winter. If I had guinea pigs, I could keep them indoors and play with them. Livvy would give me some of her babies."

"McKenna, no, we have too many animals to take care of as it is," Gwen said as she shouldered the porch door. Always—that damn door scraping. When would Will get it fixed? Her heart jumped as she heard the phone and she left the children behind to shed their parkas and boots.

The teacher's voice over the receiver was clipped, cold. Gwen's eyes stung as she watched Rory walk down the hall to his room while Ms. Hart described how he'd shoved the mentally retarded boy on the playground. Another bullying incident. Again. Though she'd talked to him until she was blue in the face after the last time.

When she hung up the phone, the house was hushed. The children had been listening. Rory lay on his bed, fiddling with his GI-Joes.

"That little retard wouldn't let me alone," he said as she stood over him.

"Stop speaking about him that way. You're lucky not to be in his shoes."

"He bugs me. He follows me around everywhere and drools. I want him to go away."

"Knocking him down is not the right way to get him to stop."

"I told him to stop! I said, 'Stop, go away,' but he just wouldn't. It was the only way I could get rid of the retard."

Her disappointment and anger broke loose and she slapped his face. "I told you to stop using that word!"

She left him sobbing. He was sorry he'd been punished, she thought bitterly, not sorry for what he had done.

Now in the kitchen, she could only hear the clock's hum. She flipped on the overhead light. Still another meal to go before she could get out of this kitchen. Will came in.

"There's been trouble at school."

"What?"

"Rory pushed Jonathan down and the boy's hands got scraped."

"Why?"

"Jonathan pesters him. Ms. Hart wants to keep him after school the rest of the week. And she wants to have a conference with us tomorrow."

"I didn't get the hay moved over to the calving sheds like Dad wanted. I gotta start that tomorrow afternoon."

"Our son's in trouble. It can wait one day!"

"I'll go talk to him."

Gwen yanked leftovers in Tupperware from the refrigerator. Why was her boy so mean and wild? What was wrong with her son? What was she doing wrong?

John came in. "Evening, Gwen."

"Evening, John."

"What's for supper?"

"Fish sticks."

She felt John's eyes measuring her. He was wondering why he wasn't drawing more conversation. She wished he would go away. She hated having him in the house when there was trouble.

McKenna ran into the kitchen. "Grandpa!"

John swept her up in his arms. "How's my honey doing?"

"Fine, Grandpa."

"How was school today?"

"Fine, but Grandpa, can I have some guinea pigs?"

"Guinea pigs. They're rodents, ain't they?"

"No, they're not. They're cute."

"No, she can't have guinea pigs," said Gwen. "She always goes to you when she wants something."

Now John knew something was up. "Let's go to the dining room and we can talk about it," he said to the child.

For the first few minutes of supper, everyone was silent. Out of the corner of her eye, Gwen watched John glance from one face to another, trying to figure a way to weasel into the family's troubles.

"More potatoes, John?" she said loudly. She knew her attempt to distract him would be fruitless.

"Why so quiet, Rory?" he asked. "Did you have trouble with the girls today?"

"No," Gwen cut in. "He did not have trouble with the girls."

Will spoke, "He knocked down Jonathan Tate."

"Well," said John, "The boy prob'ly started it first."

Rory hesitated, glancing at Gwen. Then he said, "He was bothering me, Grandpa. He wouldn't let me alone. He always follows me and I don't want him to. He's creepy."

"Well, did you ask him to leave you alone?"

"I told him to go away. I yelled at him to go away and he

just kept on."

"See there, what's the boy supposed to do if the other one won't let him alone?"

Gwen spoke, "Jonathan Tate is a mentally retarded child."

"That don't mean he can't learn to leave other people alone when they ask him to, does it?" He turned to Rory. "Did you tell him you were sorry?"

"Yeah, after the teacher came."

"See there, he said he was sorry! Does he have to stay after school?"

"Yes," Gwen answered, "for the rest of the week."

"I'll pick him up then," said John.

"No, you will not!" Gwen was shocked at her own vehemence. But wasn't it John, always helping the boy to find excuses for himself, who had gotten them into this trouble in the first place?

McKenna crawled into John's lap after supper. "We'll see about your rats young lady," he said.

"They're not rats! They're guinea pigs!"

John stood up and put his arm around Rory's shoulder. Gwen meant to intervene—the child hardly deserved affection—then she relented and sagged back into her chair. The boy threw his arms around John's waist and the old man bent over and hugged him tight.

"It'll be all right, son," he said. They stood there for a long moment.

Beyond the circle cast by the dining room light, the living room was dark and outside the wind still howled.

"Well, I'd better be getting to bed," John said. And he let the boy go.

Everyone else was in bed before Gwen. She'd washed the dishes, checked the school work, kissed the children goodnight and packed their lunches for the next day. She watched the 10:00 p.m.

news and the weather and then went to her bedroom. Will seemed to be sound asleep. She put on her nightgown and eased into bed beside him.

"I'm going to be getting Rory up early from now on," Will said. "He can start chopping the water holes in the morning. Maybe if he's got more to do around here, there'll be less trouble at school."

"That's a good idea."

Will reached over and squeezed her breast. Gwen turned her head to look out the bedroom window. The wind shrieked its long note of winter rage. And in the moonlight pouring down, she watched the tossing tree branches. And tried not to think of this final chore that awaited her before she could slip off to sleep beyond the sound of that wind.

2

Charles Mather turned his head and a wad of tobacco juice arched across the yard. "I see you found the place all right."

Meg had only spoken to her new boss once over the telephone, so she knew she had no right to high expectations. Still, Mather was a shock. Until six months ago, it was Ronnie, her ex-husband, who found jobs for them at run-aground outfits like this one. Now, face to face with this grimy man in overalls splitting at the gut, she churned with doubt.

She reached out her hand bravely and shook his. "How do you do. I'm Meg and this is my son, Jim."

The fat man glanced momentarily at the boy. Jim's existence did not interest him. He gestured behind them to the mobile home.

"This is your house. Didjya find the calves?"

"I heard them bawling and checked to make sure they

had water, sir."

"Keep 'em in the corrals the next five days. Then let 'em out. They can drink at the river, but you'll have to chop the ice."

"I can do that."

"Then feedin'. There's a winch truck at the shed there." He nodded past the mobile home toward a Quonset hut. "I guess you can see the haystacks out in the meadow."

"Yes, sir."

He continued. "Out in the meadow you'll find Sissie, our horse. You can use her to check the calves. You'll find tack in the shed, too."

"Yes, sir."

"I've got everythin' in the shed because the barn burned down."

"How often will you be here, Mr. Mather?"

He spat again, barely missing Jim's toe. Meg gently pushed him backwards.

"I'll be out every two weeks to bring your groceries. I brought you some today. You got anything you want to ask?"

"What about medicine for the calves?"

"There's a fridge in the shed. There's some penicillin in there. Anything more?"

"When do I get paid?"

"First of the month and that reminds me—what'd I say I'd pay ya?"

"Six hundred and fifty dollars a month, plus groceries and meat."

"I've been thinkin' about that. You know I wanted to hire a man, but I couldn't find nobody but you. Now a workin' man, he's got a family to support. He's likely to stay around and pull his load. But you're just a young gal. You're liable to run off and find a husband and leave me high and dry. Besides, I don't know that a woman can do a man's work."

Meg bit her lip. She should have guessed that this muckworm would try to take advantage of her. Yet she'd never spoken up for herself before. She'd never had to. She wanted to be back on a ranch—any ranch. She looked at Jim. She had to have this job.

"I've got a family to support right here," she said quietly. "And I'm not new to ranch work, Mr. Mather. I've been around ranches all my life."

Mather's beady eyes narrowed in his flesh as he examined Jim for the first time. "Where's his daddy?"

Meg hadn't planned on this question. "I left him in Upton," she said quickly.

Mather hawkeyed Jim again. "I see."

Jim blurted, "He's in prison."

The strength Meg had summoned drained out of her. How could she have anticipated that Jim would have turned their lives belly-up for this man to see?

"Prison!" barked Mather. "What'd he do?"

Meg sighed. "He stole from a man we worked for."

"And what about you? You didn't help him?"

"No, sir. I had nothing to do with it."

"Well, I won't want him around here. Just remember that. Like I say, I believe six-fifty's too high when I don't know how you'll work out. I believe we'll make it six and if you're still here next month, I'll raise it."

With her shame over Ronnie exposed, she couldn't argue anymore.

"I'll be goin' if you don't need anything more."

"The groceries, Mr. Mather."

"Oh yeah, think you and the boy can unload 'em?"

"Yes, sir."

Mather reached into the back of the truck and pulled out two cases of cans. He dumped them into Meg's arms.

"Now, I'm not getting you eggs. Gwen Swan down the road. She raises chickens. You can get your eggs from her. And milk. If you want milk, you can get it yourself. Or find a milk cow." He pulled out a sack from behind his seat and handed it to Jim. It was too heavy and the boy dropped it. Mather stared at him again and then looked back up at Meg. "See ya. If you need me, number's by the phone."

One last jet of tobacco juice and he was gone, his battered pick-up truck rattling over the bridge.

"Let's go inside," Meg said.

A musty odor spilled out as she opened the front door. She paused and took in the stained shag carpet, the moth-chewed couch, the light bulb over a kitchen table and two chairs. No surprises here. It was no different from the other quarters where she'd lived with Ronnie in the last six years. She set the cases down. Jim followed her and plopped down at the table. Jasper, their blue-heeler, scurried in behind Jim.

"I saw that!" she snapped, "Out of here!" Jasper slunk toward the door, glancing back for a chance at reprieve. Meg pulled out the other chair and sat next to her son. "Jim, you can't be telling our business to strangers."

"You said to always tell the truth."

"I know. But we don't know anyone here." She stared into her son's blue eyes. He trusted her so, and where had she brought him? "People'll hear your dad's in prison and well, they don't need to know that about you. So if someone asks you where your daddy is, just tell them you don't know. That's all the truth that anyone needs to know."

"I'm hungry."

Meg opened a cupboard, empty except for a box of corn flakes. "What'd he give us cereal for if we can't have milk?" she said bitterly. She rummaged through the rest of the cupboards and pulled out powdered milk, a tin of cocoa and some sugared honey. "I guess whoever was here before meant to help us out a little."

They sat at the table, still in their parkas, and ate corn flakes. Jasper snuck back in and settled under Jim's chair. Jim breathed in the smell of his hot cocoa and watched the steam bead and run down the kitchen windows. Meg looked out the open door to the cartons piled in her truck. The romantic thrill she'd spurred so hard while hanging on to Ronnie had finally played out. Time to turn her back on its carcass.

Jim broke into her thoughts. "These are good corn flakes, Mom," he said.

She reached over and ruffled his hair. At least she'd managed to hang on to this.

Five days later, as Mather had told her to do, she turned the weaned calves out of the corral. Though it was still January, warm sunlight struck her face and traveled all the way down her snow boots. Already, the year was turning.

The calves felt it, too. After the first one skittered through the gate, they fanned out in the meadow like charging buffalo, bucking, kicking, happy to be free. No thought of the mothers they'd left behind somewhere. Now it was just open meadow and sun and air.

With Jim in school, it was time to search for Sissie. If she was going to have to check these calves every day, she had better see what kind of a horse she had on her hands. She threw a halter and lead rope, a saddle and bridle in her truck. Jasper hopped in and together they drove out to the meadow. Sissie had staked out a corner as far away from the buildings as she could get. As the horse loomed larger in the windshield, Meg reckoned with yet another gap between her expectations and reality. She knew she wasn't getting a parade horse, but how had this starving creature lasted out here? The mare hadn't had hay, much less grain in a long while. The wind had twisted her mane into knots. Just a ratty old mare, hardly fit for the killer wagon.

Well, Meg thought as she got out of the truck, I'm no beauty, either.

Sissie didn't linger for introductions. One glance at Meg and she trotted away with her nose straight out.

"When was the last time someone did anything with you," Meg muttered.

Jasper whined from the driver's seat.

Meg followed Sissie with the truck until she stopped and then tried to approach her again. "Easy girl, easy Sissie." She reached to put her arm over the horse's neck and Sissie was gone again at a full tear across the meadow. A lot of stored energy for a starving creature.

After a trip back to the shed, Meg returned with a coffee can full of oats. This time, Sissie's ears pricked with interest as the oats rustled. Meg kept them within her scent, but did not let her have them. She kept shaking the can.

"Not till you're haltered, Sis. You don't get them till you're haltered." Meg and Sissie danced around one another. Then the mare stopped and stretched out her nose as far as it would go. Meg stepped up and put her arm around the horse's neck. Got her! After she fastened the halter, she let Sissie lick the can clean. "I'm sorry you haven't been fed in such a long time, mare."

Meg led her over to the truck. She opened the door, rolled down the window and tied the lead rope around the frame. She prayed that Sissie wasn't so rank as to jerk the door off the truck.

But Sissie stood sensibly while Meg put on the blanket, the saddle and the bridle. Meg led the horse a few paces from the truck and took a deep breath. There was no guessing what might happen next. She took hold of the bridle with her left hand to pull the horse in a circle in case she gave her any trouble while mounting. As she stepped on, the horse followed the pull of the bridle and stepped to the inside. Calmly. No trouble. Meg let go of the bridle and took another deep breath. The horse stood. It was a good start.

Meg nudged her with her heels. Sissie sprang into a brisk walk. When they had covered some ground, Meg nudged her again and she broke into a trot. The ride was rough, but OK.

Meg released her grip on the reins. To her surprise, Sissie exploded into a dead run. She was fast, very fast. Meg saw a ditch coming up ahead and pulled back. There was a stout tug at the other end. The mare had chomped down on the bit and wrested it away from her. Meg leaned back and pulled as hard as she could, but the mare pulled harder. Now the ditch was upon them. Meg clung to the saddlehorn and they flew over it. Meg tried to work her hands down the reins to pull back, but the mare's head was straight up in the air. Now they were approaching the barbed wire fence. Oh God, thought Meg, we're going right through it.

The mare stopped. Meg flew over her head and landed on her back.

The huge expanse of blue overhead went in and out of her vision. Her glasses were missing. Then Jasper was above her, licking her face and inside her ears. She sat up and waited for the world to come back to her. Sissie was gone. Meg saw her in the distance running toward the barn. And I felt sorry for you, you hag, thought Meg.

"Well Jasper, she's probably tore up the bridle and reins by now." She reached for her glasses glittering in the brown grass and limped to her truck. Jasper glanced back as he trotted ahead, not understanding why she was moving so slowly.

"I can be stubborn too, old mare," said Meg when she caught up with Sissie again. Inside the corral, she loped the mare round and round. As they circled, she caught sight of Jim getting off the school bus and crossing the river bridge.

"Mom!" he yelled.

She wasn't stopping. She couldn't stop. Not until she got a handle on this snaky mare.

Jim peered between the railings. "Mom!" White flecks of lather flew off the horse as she loped by him.

"You're gonna have to wait!" she shouted.

"Why?"

Meg gritted her teeth. She needed this horse to make it here. Couldn't he see that?

As she circled again, Jim let go of the rails and turned away with Jasper trailing behind.

When she woke Saturday morning, that image was her first thought. She watched the numbers on the clock flip from 4:59 to 5:00. She dressed and turned on the overhead light in the hall. Though it shone in Jim's face, he slept soundly, his mouth open. She sat on the edge of his bed. I'll make it a better day. I promise.

They ate breakfast silently under the naked light bulb, then climbed into the winch truck and rumbled out to the meadow. Meg held Jim in her lap and let him steer, grinning at his excitement. After she had set the hooks in the haystack, she let him pull the winch.

His eyes widened as the cable lifted the hay free from the stack. "Wow, Mom! That's a monster glob of hay!"

"Pretty neat, huh?"

She pulled away slowly while the calves pressed close to the truck, bawling.

Jim held his ears. "They're making too much noise!"

"They're hungry. You bawl, too, when you're hungry."

"What's that one doing? He's jumping on that calf."

She slammed on the brakes. "Shit! That's a bull!" Damn, she hadn't meant to use that word around him. His pale face registered the shock.

"What I should've said is 'good job, you caught him,' but we've got to get him out of here."

"Why?"

"He's trying to breed that heifer, damnit!"

Jim turned to her. "What's wrong with that?"

"It wouldn't be wrong if she were six months older. But she's just a baby herself. She's too little to have her own baby. Besides, Mather wants to sell these calves. He doesn't want them bred. We've got to hurry and feed this load quick before he gets any more."

She lowered the winch, set the truck in first gear and they jumped out. She handed him a pitchfork. "Now you gotta take your fork and pull some hay off the load while it's moving."

"Why can't we just take the hooks out of the hay?"

Meg glanced back at the bull nosing the calves. "I don't have time to answer all these questions, Jim! If we pulled those hooks out, a glob of hay would be sitting in the middle of the meadow and the calves would tromp it down and waste it!"

She trotted behind the load, tearing into the hay and throwing it to the calves. Jim hopped on the trailing edges of the pile as the truck lurched along, pulling clumps of hay loose with his weight.

"Jim! Stop fooling around! I need you to help!"

Jim struggled to jab his fork into the moving load. I ought to help him, she thought. Some other day, not today. When the load was gone, she knocked the hooks clean, ran to the cab and jumped in.

Jim ran behind. "Mom, wait up!" She grabbed his arm and hoisted him up over her lap.

"What do you want me to do?" he asked as she drove back.

She looked at him. He couldn't ride with her. He'd have to remain behind. Alone. "You've got to stay in the yard. You can watch me from the fence, OK? You'll be able to see me the whole time."

Now, would the mare work, Meg wondered as she threw the saddle on. Sissie sensed the tension in the air and pranced out the gate. But she didn't try to break and run. The calves parted reluctantly around them. Meg looked back to the fence. Jim waved and she waved back. The bull jerked his head up from the hay, glaring at her, daring her to part him from his heifers.

"Get on bull, get out of here!"

At the sound of her voice, Jasper nipped the bull's heel. He bellowed, butted the calves out of his path and threw his head back down in the hay.

Meg followed. "C'mon, bull!" she shouted and Jasper flew at his heels.

The bull broke into a run. Sissie sprang after him and he accelerated toward the dense willows along the river. I've got more speed than you, thought Meg, and she nudged Sissie. In one stride, the mare was even with his shoulder, but then the bull planted his front feet, flipped his hindquarters around and threatened them with his horns. Meg pulled back sharply, fearing for herself and the horse, and the bull wheeled and plunged into the willows.

In the yard, Jim stood as high on the fence as he dared, trying to see Meg. Where had she gone?

"Mom!" All he could see was calves meandering up and down the hay lines. A few stared at him vacantly. Their indifference made him feel even more alone.

He heard a truck behind him and he turned to see an old man leaning out of the driver's window, blue eyes sparkling in his crinkly face. "Hey there, young fella. Are you running this outfit?"

"No, sir. My mother is, but she's out there."

"Oh. You haven't seen a bull, have you?"

Past the old man, Jim could see a boy staring at him, Rory Swan. He had met him at school. Rory was older than he was and until now, hadn't shown much interest in him.

"He's out there, too."

All three of them turned and watched Meg as she flushed the bull from the willows, only to have him whirl and threaten the horse with his horns.

"Well, I see we have some serious misbehavior here," said the old man. "What's your name, son?"

"Jim."

"Would you like to ride with us, Jim?"

"Sure."

Jim climbed down from the fence and slid in next to Rory.

"You boys know each other from school?"

"Yes, Grandpa," Rory answered. "He's the new kid."

"You know his name, don't you?"

"Yeah."

"Why don't you introduce us?"

Rory turned to Jim. "This is my grandpa."

Jim leaned over, "Nice to meet you."

"You sure are a polite fella. Nice to meet you, too. I'd shake your hand, but we'd better help out your mother. Or she might get a little flustered."

They sped across the meadow, bouncing over the frozen manure piles. The bull was spent—he stood there, panting—but he still held Meg and Sissie at bay.

John swung the truck around until it was pointed toward the corrals. He leaned out the window. "You get on home, bull. You get on home right this instant."

The bull shifted his attention toward the truck. His eyes bulged out of his head and a thread of drool ran from the corner of his mouth.

"Yeah, you sonofabitch, you're not used to this much exercise. Hold on, boys." John put the truck in reverse. Then he put it in second gear and slammed on the gas. Jim held his breath. They were barreling straight toward the bull.

Slam. They rammed him broadside. It shifted him a few feet, but otherwise, he seemed undisturbed. He glared back at them.

"I said get on home, you old geezer!"

The old man backed the truck up, put it in gear and rammed the bull again. The bull turned, bowed his head and shuffled toward the corrals, defeated at last. They paraded toward home, the bull, the truck, Sissie, Meg and Jasper in the rear. Without any more fuss, the bull calmly walked through the gate and stood in the yard.

The old man shut the gate, walked up to Meg and held out his hand. "John Swan."

She was slow to extend hers. He'd scooped up her son so easily—too easily. She hadn't even been there to ask him who he was. But it wouldn't do to show ingratitude for such a rescue.

"That's the damndest thing I ever saw," she blurted finally.

"You just gotta learn how to commune with them, that's all. Your boy's got more manners than you, if I don't mind. He says his name is Jim."

She jumped off Sissie. "I'm Meg. Meg Braeburn."

"I'm sorry about the bull, here. I got them bulls in a pasture across the road. If you see one of 'em over here again, you give me a call, OK?"

"Glad to."

"How did Mather find you?"

Meg glanced nervously at Jim. "I answered a newspaper ad."

"Well, you're not from around here, are you?"

"No, sir."

"Where are you from?"

"Hayden, Colorado."

"You're not afraid of snow then."

"No." She started to smile. "Just wind."

"We all hate the damn wind. Rory here curses it every morning before breakfast."

"I do not! You do, Grandpa."

"You never heard me use cuss words."

"You do—all the time!"

John nodded to Sissie. "Mather left you a fine specimen of horseflesh."

Meg laced her fingers through the mare's mane. He had no right to that comment. Sissie had done her job, after all.

"She didn't run from your bull. We're getting along just fine."

"I'll bet. What about the boy here? Does he have a horse?"

"We're fine."

"No," Jim spoke up. "I don't have a horse."

Meg glared at him.

"I've got horses at my place for my grandkids. He's welcome to come over and ride."

"Can I, Mom?"

Meg glanced from John to Rory to Jim. She was trying to think of the answer that would sever the conversation and not commit her to anything. "Maybe. We'll see."

"Meg Braeburn, none of the Swans will bite you or your son. I promise. And unless you like listening to the wind twenty-four hours a day, you'd better start talking to your neighbors. Jim, are you coming with us or staying here?"

Jim hopped out of the truck.

"Get on home, bull," John shouted. He nudged the bull with the truck. The bull plodded forward, crossed the bridge and headed on to the county road.

"Can I go ride his horses, Mom?"

"We don't know these people yet, Jim. Do you know that kid from school?"

"Yeah. That's Rory. He has to stay after school. Every day."

3

The women in their folding chairs turned to stare at the tall late-comer.

Ms. Hart glanced up from her seat and smiled. "I don't know if some of you have met her yet, but this is Meg Braeburn. Her son, Jim, has just joined us in the first grade."

Meg nodded and quickly sat down. Although Ms. Hart returned to the plans for the Valentine's Day party, everyone shifted in their seats to size up Mather's ranch hand.

She's not pretty, thought Gwen. Gangly, with long braids hanging out of her Scotch cap. Owl-shaped glasses, broad cheekbones and a small pointy chin. She wore men's coveralls. Word had spread that she didn't have a husband. None of them had ever heard of an unmarried woman working as a ranch hand. There must be something wrong with her, the gossips had clucked, especially if she was working for that lazy drunk, Mather.

"Now what about refreshments?" said Ms. Hart.

Gwen spoke up, "I'll help with that."

"Yes. And Meg." Gwen turned to see Meg raising her hand. "OK, Meg Braeburn and Gwen Swan—refreshments." She wrote their names down on a clipboard.

The discussion moved to party games. Gwen glanced back at Meg. She sat quietly and stared at her boots, avoiding the others.

"The gal'll be all right," John had said, "She just needs us to pester her a little. You otta take her under your wing, Gwen, teach her how to make some of these pies and she won't need Mather no more."

"Anything else?" asked Ms. Hart. No response. "Okay, I'll see you all on the fourteenth." Women rose and chatted with one another as they folded their chairs. Meg glanced around. They'd forgotten about her. She could bolt and escape these bug-eyed vultures. She'd call Ms. Swan later.

"Meg?"

Meg set her chair down on the rack and turned.

"Hi, I'm Gwen Swan. John's told me about you."

The woman who faced her was as worn as a dishrag, her wan smile weighted with fatigue. Still, Meg remembered what John had said—how she'd better get acquainted with her neighbors—and held out her hand.

"Nice to meet you."

Gwen looked surprised, as if she hadn't expected manners from a woman in coveralls. "Glad to meet you, Meg. Where's Jim this afternoon?"

"He's at home doing his homework."

"My daughter, McKenna, sure enjoys him. She's glad to have another child in her class."

"You have a son, too, don't you?"

"Yes, Rory. He's a handful."

She said it lightheartedly, but Meg caught the undertone of worry.

Gwen continued. "Do you want to talk about the party refreshments for a few minutes?"

"Just a few," said Meg, trying to stick to her plan to bolt. "I gotta get home."

"So do I. There's some coffee in the kitchen. Would you like some?"

What could be the harm, thought Meg. Scrutinizing her didn't seem to preoccupy Gwen, as it had the others. Gwen poured cups for both of them and they leaned against opposite cupboards.

"John tells me you're from Hayden."

"Hm."

"What brought you here?"

Meg shifted from one foot to the other. "I called at the unemployment office and they had the job posted."

"You called here from Hayden?"

There was a long pause as the fluorescent lights hummed overhead. Meg stared into her cup, measuring whether to say—or not to say. This woman meant no harm, it wasn't her fault.

"Upton. I called from Upton."

"Upton," Gwen repeated. "That's a long ways away."

"My folks live in Hayden. My dad's a vet. They raise registered Herefords."

"What do they think of your working here?"

"They don't know I'm here."

Gwen set her cup down. The click of the plastic against the Formica reverberated in the room. Gwen turned back to Meg. Nothing in her face hinted at her reaction.

"I ran off and got married," Meg said with a pinch of defiance, "and here I am."

She's daring me to disapprove, Gwen thought, so it will be

easy to shut me out. I won't be shut out.

She answered quietly, "They didn't like your husband."

Meg grimaced. "No, they didn't."

"When was the last time you saw them?"

"When I left Hayden."

"What about Jim?"

"They don't know about him."

"And Jim's father?"

In the last few days, thought Meg, she'd found the backbone to face Mather, feed his calves in winds that all but flattened her and break his sour mare. Why, confronted only with this woman's sallow face, did she feel like a puddle.

"He's in the penitentiary. In Rawlins." Gwen didn't respond, so she went on. "We worked different places. We were trying to get money together so Ronnie could go professional—he was a bull rider. I thought that's what we were doing. But Ronnie took the money to the bars every night and got different ideas, ideas I didn't know about until the sheriff stopped us. In Upton."

"Doesn't the boy need a family, Meg?"

Now Meg's shoulders slumped. Buried underneath the toughness, Gwen thought, were the memories of a tomboy, a daddy's cowgirl. She knew what she was taking from her boy.

"I'm family enough," she said without conviction.

Yes, John, Meg does need us to pester her a little. Aggravating that he could be right every once in a while.

"You're welcome to have coffee at our house anytime, Meg. It's just right up the road."

"Thanks."

"The hens aren't laying much now, but you're welcome to some eggs when you need them."

"Yeah, Mr. Mather said you had chickens."

"How are you getting along with him?"

Meg shrugged. "There's worse bosses, I guess."

"Is he paying you anything?"

"Not much. But at least I'm back on a ranch. I was waiting tables in a diner before I found this job. I wanted to be back on a ranch—that's enough home for me."

"Why don't you go home, Meg?"

"I got a boy. No husband. No, worse—a husband in jail." Meg shook her head, "They don't want to see me there."

You mean your pride won't let you go there, thought Gwen as she studied the taut line on the girl's mouth. Meg would never understand what true strength was so long as owning up to her mistake was worse than working for someone like Mather.

The two women divided up their responsibilities for the Valentine's Day party.

As Meg turned to leave, Gwen said, "Remember. Come over anytime. And bring Jim. I'm almost always there."

Meg nodded and walked away.

Would she come? With a pang, Gwen realized that she wanted Meg's company more for her own sake than for Meg's.

4

Unlike every other ranching routine, this one thing never got old. Will watched the cow flop to her side. A contraction squeezed her and rippled over her bulk. Moments passed. Then another contraction. Another pause. Then another contraction. Slowly her vulva parted and two white feet glistened. Another contraction. Two white feet, white ankles and a little pink nose. Another contraction. Now the forehead and eyes were emerging. Bigger contraction. Out came the head. Another contraction. Out came the shoulders. One last huge heave and the calf slithered to the ground. The cow leapt to her feet, still dragging the afterbirth. She licked away the sack coating her baby. She cleaned the nostrils and abruptly, the calf's sides heaved. The rest of the sack was cleaned off in moments and then the calf pushed up with his back feet and stood, tottering, surveying for the first time, the world.

It's always a miracle, thought Will, and though he knew that sleepless nights lay ahead and that spring storms just over the horizon would cost him some of the lives so preciously gained, always and every time, each birth was a gift from God.

Will checked the rest of the mothers in his maternity ward. All were quietly munching hay as the daylight drained away around them. It was mild tonight. He'd leave them outside the barn. He checked the calf once more. It had already sucked. Good start—and a good end to the day.

He walked back to the house, eager to announce the first calf of the year. As he crossed the barnyard, there was his father's truck, a red pickup he didn't recognize, and his brother Nick's truck. His eagerness to share the good news dissipated. Nick was here.

As boys, they both had been raised to work on the ranch. But while Will listened to his father and did as he was told, Nick was always in a hurry, racing through his chores, not paying any mind to how well they were done. They'd come to blows a time or two moving cattle because Nick pushed them too hard and then Will would have to gather the scattered ones. They'd jump off their horses and beat the crap out of each other until John came and separated them.

Nick was too simple-minded to figure out how to get along with John. Will didn't always agree with his father, but he'd nod and keep his mouth shut. Nick argued. And when John rejected Nick's various suggestions on how to do things differently, Nick sulked.

He'd mutter, "You're the one he likes. He listens to everything you say while everything I say is worth shit."

Will didn't think he was favored. He just knew how to get along. After all, the ranch would be his some day and he could do as he pleased. But he didn't try to change Nick's view. If Nick thought he was the favored one, well that only served the dumb sucker right.

The showdown had come after Nick had built an alleyway onto their corrals. It was wide at the mouth and tapered inwards so that cattle funneled through the corral gates. He hadn't told anyone about it. He had just done it.

John's jaw had clenched while he surveyed it. "Where'd you get all those posts and the wire?"

"I got the posts from the pile behind the barn. I charged the wire at the hardware store."

"That's about five hundred bucks!"

"Look at how it will work! No more struggling to push cattle through the gates while they mill and scatter. They'll all just trail in! I thought you'd like it."

"Like it? Well, yeah, I'd like it. I'd like it just fine if we hit a few oil wells, like they got all over the rest of the state, so we could *pay* for it! It's not a matter of what I like. It's a matter of what we need. We didn't need this. So it takes a minute or two to get them old cows in the corrals. Until calves start selling for more than sixty cents a pound, the old way was just fine."

Nick's face turned red. The red traveled all the way down his forearms.

"Don't be getting so angry, son. You should have asked me in the first place."

"If I'd asked you, you would have said no. I thought if you'd just see it, and see how it would work, you'd be happy."

"I'll be happy, son, the day you just do as you're told and give me some peace. Now I gotta worry about where more posts and wire is going to come from."

Nick's jaw snapped shut and he didn't say anything more. He finished haying with them that summer and one morning at breakfast, he told them all that he'd found a job at another ranch. He left that day.

They had used Nick's alleyway at every round-up since he'd left. And they never had any more trouble pushing cattle in. Cows filed in and filed out. It had saved them time and manpower.

Horsepower, too. But no one had ever said anything to Nick. Including him.

After a while they got letters from him. He'd married and taken a job managing a ranch up around Casper—where there were oil wells. He came down for their mother's funeral. And they got Christmas cards from him. First there were pictures of one baby, then two. But Will was happy that Nick didn't come to visit much, just as he was happy when the skunks stayed out of the feed bin and he didn't have to shoot them. It was just less stink and trouble for everyone.

Will opened the door to the kitchen and light and noise washed over him. People were talking at the dining room table and kids were playing somewhere in the background.

John noticed him first. "There he is! Will, Nick's here!"

"I saw his truck."

Will leaned against the dining room doorway. A thin woman with long braids sat next to his wife. She wore a flannel shirt and a blue silk scarf tied around her throat. Her eyes darted nervously from one face to another. She looked like a mule deer ready to bolt. This must be Mather's hired hand, he thought.

He faced his brother. "Howdy, Nick."

"Howdy, Will."

"You're getting bald."

"You're getting fat."

"Will, how were they?" John said quickly.

"Good. We got our first calf."

"Which cow?"

"Number 45. That all red cow with the white hind foot."

John nodded with satisfaction. "She's always one of the ones to start it off. How are they?"

"Good."

"Did you put 'em all in the shed?"

"No, it's mild out. No wind. And the forecast's good. I'll let 'em calve outside tonight."

"Suit yourself. You'll regret it later. You'd better put 'em in after supper."

Nick grinned. "Yeah, Will, better put 'em in."

Now Gwen interrupted. "Will, this is Meg Braeburn. She's the new hand at Mather's. She's come over for supper. Her son, Jim, is playing with the kids."

Will leaned across the table. Meg stood and extended a slender hand.

"Howdy," Will said. He dropped her hand to turn back to Nick. "What brings you south, Nick?"

"I'm on my way to Colorado to look at some bull calves."

"How many are you buying?" asked John.

"Twenty for McDaniel. That's my boss, Ms. Braeburn. And two for myself. McDaniel's letting me run my own herd now."

"Well, I'll be…" said John. "How many you got?"

"Twenty-six Angus/Hereford crosses."

Will spoke up now. "What's he charging you for board?"

"Sixty dollars per cow. I buy my own veterinary supplies. And pay my own vet bill."

"Son, why didn't you tell me all this before? I'm proud of you."

Will glared at his father. Now that Nick wasn't around, his value was appreciating in the old man's eyes.

"What kind of bulls are you buying?" he asked.

"I'm looking for shorthorn."

"Shorthorn!" Will replied. "What for?"

"Well, two-way crosses are good. But I believe three-way crosses are going to be even better. I aim to have nine hundred pound calves in the next few years."

"Buyers like those black and white cattle, son. I don't think they're going to be wanting red ones."

Nick shrugged, "I'll try it and see. How much did the calves weigh here last fall, Will?"

"Five-ninety."

"Pretty good."

Will noticed the smirk. "Why? Did yours weigh more?"

"Just a little. Seven-thirty."

Gwen spoke up. "It doesn't seem very fair to me to compare. You've got twenty-six. We've got three hundred."

"But why should that make a difference, Gwen?"

"It's a lot easier to care for twenty-six. Here, Will," Gwen glanced over at John, "and John—have to split care of three hundred among themselves."

Nick slapped a dollop of mashed potatoes down so hard on his plate that the spoon clattered. "Whose choice was that?"

All noise stopped. Will dropped the roll he'd plucked from the center of the table. He knew what he wanted to say, but he didn't want to be the one to start the fight.

"Well, this old man had better be going to bed." John started to rise from his chair.

"You don't want pie?" Gwen asked.

"I don't believe so tonight. Nick, are you staying over?"

"No, dad. I'm going to be off."

"I guess this is goodbye, then." The two men stood up and John roughly embraced his son. Nick hesitated and then put his arms around his father.

Gwen and Will exchanged glances. Neither of them had seen John hug anyone but McKenna and Rory.

"You need to come more often, son—and bring your wife and kids. I'd like to see my grandchildren."

"Well, Deborah works full time in Casper. But we'll see what we can do."

"We'd better be going, too," said Meg. "Jim!"

A pale red-haired boy came running into the circle of light followed by Will's own children.

Meg lightly tugged at her son's collar. "Get your coat."

"Are we going?"

"Yes."

"But we were just starting to have fun."

"If you hurry up and go to bed right now, you can have more fun tomorrow."

Chairs squeaked against the floor as everyone rose from the table.

Nick turned to Meg. "Nice meeting you, Meg, and good luck working for Mather. You've lasted longer with him than any old hand I know."

"I've only been there six weeks."

"Uh-huh. Will," Nick stuck out his hand, "glad to see ya."

Will paused and then took his brother's hand. "Yeah, Nick. Come back." Will watched Nick and John leave. A brief trickle of regret ran through him. He didn't know when he'd see his brother again.

He turned around. Jim had put on his coat and Meg was standing behind him with her hand resting on his shoulder. Was it the hand, the braids, or that rail-thin body that made her appear so painfully vulnerable.

"Nice meeting you," she said.

"Same here."

She turned to the kitchen. "Gwen, are you sure I can't help with the dishes?"

"No, no. You go on home. You can do the dishes when I come to your house."

Now everyone was gone. Gwen was at the sink, scrubbing away at a mountain of pots and pans.

"Rory," Will called, "let's go get the cows in."

Rory came into the kitchen. "Do I have to? We're playing."

Will gestured to the porch. "Go get your coat and boots on."

They stepped out into the dark and silence. No wind tonight. Will clicked the flashlight button and illuminated the path to the yard gate. The only sound between them was their footsteps on the frozen ground.

First, they checked the heifer barn. Will had already shut the heifers in and when he turned on the overhead light, they wheeled. Their eyes blinked and their nostrils flared, trying to peg their intruders.

"Okay," said Will to Rory, "you go through them."

Rory walked softly through the heifers. He looked at each hind end. But none of them seemed distressed or in pain. All of them were on their feet.

They walked down the river to the cow barn. Will stopped before they got to the gate. "Hear that?"

"What?"

"Listen."

"It's just the river."

"That's it! The river's thawing."

"Does that mean I don't have to chop water holes anymore?"

"No. It means maybe in a week or two, you won't have to. The river's fast here. It's slower where those water holes are."

Will flashed the light around the pen. Cows were standing quietly or lying down. None of them were in labor.

"Oh, to heck with it," said Will. "We'll leave 'em out tonight."

"Won't Grandpa get mad?"

"Yeah. He'll just have to add this to his list."

"What list?"

"Nothing. I didn't mean anything by it."

"But why don't you want to put the cows in?"

"Because on a night like this with no wind and no snow,

they're better off undisturbed. They can choose any old corner in this nice wide pen to have their babies. In the barn, they're kinda cramped. They can't get away from the other cows like they want to. The more we fool with their way of having babies, the more we risk breaking that bond that starts the moment they feel that first contraction. Those babies' lives depend on that bond being there. This whole ranch depends on that bond being there. So we should only risk it if we have to. Not when it's not necessary."

"Did you tell Grandpa?"

"No, I didn't."

"Why not?"

"He doesn't agree."

"What's he going to say in the morning when he sees all the cows out?"

"I'll worry about it tomorrow. Let's check the new baby."

They found the pair in the corner of the pen, pressed up against a willow to keep off any wind. Will shone the light in the calf's eyes and it jumped to its feet. The cow snuffled the air anxiously.

"Well, he's a lively one," said Will.

"Can I touch 'im?"

"No, his mother wouldn't like it. Your mother doesn't let you talk to strangers and to her, you're a stranger."

They walked home and took off their coats and boots quietly on the porch. The kitchen was dark except for the light over the stove and it cast an eerie glow on Rory's face.

"Night, Dad."

"Night, Rory."

Every hour of a Wyoming night the stars rotate closer, closer. More and more of them appear, and by two a.m. they're so thick and close a body could reach up and grab them like diamonds. The shooting stars are always thick at that hour, leaving paintbrush trails across the sky.

At midnight, Will had found a heifer in labor. Now he was back out to check her. He flicked the light switch and blinked, waiting for his eyes to adjust.

She was still lying on her side, still straining. Will thought about getting her up and putting her in the stanchion himself to pull the calf, but it was easier to have someone's help. Plus, it was a comfort to have Gwen there to share the deep night, the cold, the glaring overhead light, the heaving of a warm animal pushing forth life.

He went back to the house and shook her awake. "Heifer in labor," was all he said.

5

John lifted Jim up and plopped him in the saddle. "There. How does that feel?"

High, Jim thought. He gripped the round smooth horn between his hands and looked down at the horse's feet far below. Rory and McKenna were on their own horses, trotting round and round the small meadow in front of John Swan's house.

"Grandpa," Rory shouted, "Can we go outside the gate?"

"No. You can't go without me and I'm helping Jim here. How does that feel, Jim?"

"Good."

"OK, now take a hold of the reins."

Jim looked to his mother for reassurance. She was standing next to John with her arms crossed. Jasper sat next to her with his ears up and one paw raised, ready to spring off the moment the horse moved.

Jim slowly let go of the horn and picked up a rein in each hand.

"OK," said John, "now let me show you how to hold the reins with one hand so you can have the other one free." John stepped over to the horse, took Jim's left hand and worked the reins between his fingers. With his free right hand, Jim gripped the saddlehorn again.

"Now, give him a nudge with your heels and go."

Jim nudged. Nothing happened.

"Harder."

Jim nudged again.

"OK. Give him a great big kick with both your heels."

Jim raised both legs straight up in the air and slammed them back down on the horse's sides. The horse plodded forward.

"Mom!" said Jim.

"You're doing fine." He looked down. Jasper was pacing at his side, looking up at him.

"How do I stop?" he yelled back.

"Sit back in the saddle! Pull back on the reins!"

Jim sat back and jerked on the reins, but nothing happened. The fence was straight ahead and Jim knew they were going to run into it.

"Mom!"

The horse stopped.

John placed a hand on Jim's knee. "Your mother's here on the ground. She can't help you. You have to do it all yourself. Now start back to the gate and this time when you want to stop, do it a little smoother. Don't jerk."

John pulled the horse around and pointed it back to the gate. "OK, go."

Just then, Rory went flying by. His horse nearly hit the gate before he got it stopped.

"Rory," said John, "you need to stop working that horse so hard."

"When are you going to come with us, Grandpa?"

"I'm not coming today. I'm helping Jim so he'll be able to ride with you."

"When is he going to be able to ride with us, then?"

"Well, not today. In a day or two prob'ly."

Rory jerked the horse away from the gate. "I don't see why he has to ride with us."

"You needed help getting started. Let your old grandpa help someone else. There'll be plenty of time left over for you."

Jim had been plodding forward toward his mother during their conversation. She was still standing in the same spot where he'd left her. He leaned back in the saddle and pulled the reins. The horse stopped.

She grinned. "Good work!"

By the end of the session, Jim could stop and turn to the right or left. He hadn't let go of the saddlehorn the whole time, but John said that was OK. One day, he would.

"How would everyone like some hot chocolate?"

"We couldn't," said Meg, "we've got to be getting back."

"Getting back to what?"

Meg stared at him for a moment. "I just don't want to put you out."

"Jim doesn't think he's putting me out, do you, Jim?"

"No. Mom, let's stay."

John Swan's house was built of logs. Like Gwen's, it was surrounded by cottonwoods and backed up to the river. They mounted the steps to a sagging, wrap-a-round porch strewn with busted rocking chairs and various machine parts.

John opened the door to the living room. The floor was covered in stained linoleum with cowhide rugs thrown here and there.

There was a couch, a chair, a TV. Hanging on the wall was a huge black and white photograph of a young woman. She sat sideways to the camera, dressed in slacks and a Western checked shirt. Her smile was broad, as if she was looking at someone who made her happy. Her lipstick was thick and shiny. Braids, with ribbons woven through them, encircled her head.

Jim and Meg stared at the picture.

"That's Anna," John said. "She was my wife."

"She's very beautiful," said Meg.

"Yes, she was."

Anna's been gone a long time, Meg thought, as she stepped into John's kitchen. The table was covered with stacks of newspapers and magazines and several packages of half-eaten powdered donuts. The top of the wood cook stove was dirty and dishes were stacked up to the faucet in the sink.

"Sit down," said John. "You can have some donuts while you're waiting."

Meg would have stopped Jim, but Rory and McKenna were already rummaging through the packages.

John took a pot and several mugs out of the sink and rinsed them. "As you can see, I don't do too much cleaning up. That was Anna's job and I figure it can wait until she gets back."

"But Grandpa," McKenna spoke up with her dusted with powdered sugar, "Grandma's dead. She's not coming back."

"Well, McKenna, it looks like the kitchen is never going to be cleaned then."

"I could clean it for you, Grandpa."

"That's all right. I believe it can stay like this for a little longer."

John stoked up the fire and set the milk on top of the stove. He handed them all mugs almost half filled with cocoa.

"I don't know about you," he said, "but I like mine with lots of chocolate." When the milk was ready, he poured it into each mug and milk slopped over the sides. Meg rose and looked around the sink for a rag to mop up. All the dishrags were frayed and greasy. She looked around for paper towels.

"What'cha looking for, Meg?"

"Some paper towels to wipe up the milk."

"There aren't any. Just grab one of them dish towels beside the sink."

The stack of dish towels was surprisingly clean. Meg picked up the top one and stared at it.

"Don't worry about dirtying it up. I'll just to take it to Gwen with the rest of the laundry."

Meg imagined Gwen unloading bags of laundry from John's truck.

"So, what's Mather going to do with the calves you've got?"

Meg set her cup down. "He's keeping them until fall."

"Tell me, what does a young woman like you want to stay here for?"

Rory jumped up from the table. "Grandpa, can we go outside?"

"Sure."

This was her opening to escape, Meg thought. "We better be going."

"Hold on just a minute. I want to show you something."

"Can I go outside with Rory and McKenna, Mom?" Jim asked.

Meg glanced at him nervously. "OK, but don't wander too far. We're going soon."

"OK."

"And don't go on the ice. It's too thin."

"Same for you two," said John.

John went to his bedroom and brought back two over-stuffed scrapbooks. "I'd like to show you a few things about me." He opened one book to a photograph of a younger John leaning against a corral. He had one heel up on the railing and his arms were extended on either side. Four young women perched on the rail above him.

"In high school, I bull-dogged steers," he said. "It wasn't any kind of way to make money, but it was a great way to meet women. You could walk into any kind of arena and inhale 'em.

"Now, here's where I met Anna."

Meg looked at a photograph of the two of them dancing. Anna's back was to the camera and her head was turned, looking over her shoulder. John was facing the camera. His cowboy hat was pushed back on his head. He had a sheepish grin on his face. The camera had caught him by surprise.

"A couple of days after that dance, I drove all the way to Virginia Dale to see her again. I got out of the truck and there was a pretty paint horse in the corral. About that time, her father stepped out the front door. I could see he wasn't too interested in some young fool chasing his daughter, but I thought I could butter 'im up a bit.

"I stuck out my hand. He kept his in his pocket. We both stood there staring at each other and I started to fidget. I offered him my chewing tobacco. He just shook his head. I took a pinch and looked around the yard. 'Nice horse,' I said.

"'You can have the damn animal,' he said, 'if you never come 'round here again.'

"I said, 'Well, then I guess I won't ever be owning that horse.' He turned around and stomped inside and I stomped in right behind him. I got that girl, but the horse cost me a thousand bucks."

Meg smiled. He had drawn her in and made her forget that she had to leave.

Outside, McKenna, Rory and Jim were throwing stones into the river to break the ice. Rory made explosion noises every time his stone hit. Jasper sat and watched them.

"I wish Grandpa'd rode with us today," McKenna said.

"Yeah, he didn't because of the retard here."

"I'm not a retard."

"No," said McKenna, "he didn't go with us because he likes to be with Meg."

"What he does like her so much for? Kabushshshsh."

"Maybe she reminds him of Grandma."

"She doesn't look nothing like Grandma."

"Where do you go riding when your grandpa rides with you?" asked Jim.

"Out in the meadow and all around," McKenna answered, "and Grandpa tells us stories about Indians and cowboys. And sometimes he lets us run. And sometimes we sing songs. '*Whoopee-ti-yi-yo, get along little dogies, it's your misfortune and none of my own. Whoopee-ti-yi-yo, get a long little dogies. You know that Wyoming will be your new home.*'"

Rory twirled his finger around his temple and pointed it at McKenna.

Jim nodded as if he agreed, but he wanted her to sing the song again. "'Dogie?'" he said. "What's a 'dogie'?"

"It's a word for calf. It's about driving calves to Wyoming."

"Let's cross the river and go exploring in the woods," said Rory.

"But Grandpa said not to cross the ice."

"We don't have to cross the ice. We'll find another way."

They walked down the bank and found a fallen log crossing the water.

"Here," said Rory, "here's a way." He jumped on the log and slowly put one foot in front of the other to cross.

"Hope you don't FALL-L-L," shouted McKenna.

Rory paid no attention to her and leapt off on the opposite bank. "Let's see you do it."

McKenna started to cross, sliding first one foot and then the other. Halfway, she dropped to her hands and knees and crawled.

"Ha, Ha," shouted Rory. "Sissy!"

Now Jim started. The log felt rough under his feet. He could feel the long fissures running into the wood. Like McKenna, he slid one foot and followed with the other. He understood what had scared her. The water was deep and gurgling loud at the midway point. He sucked in another breath. First one foot, then the other. Over and over until he saw the grassy bank beneath him and he jumped down.

"Good job, Jim," said McKenna.

"Thanks."

"At least he didn't do it sissy-style, like you."

Here, unlike the meadows, the grass had not been cut during the summer. It was tall and dry. They had to pick up their knees to wade through it. All around them were fallen logs and willow thickets and deer paths. They played they were Indians, hiding in the forest.

They found an old cottonwood hollowed out by lightning. The lower limbs were thick and easy to reach. Rory and Jim climbed up. McKenna crouched in the hollow part of the tree.

"Let's make this our fort," she said.

"Indians don't have forts," said Rory.

"Let's make it our clubhouse, then."

"What kind of club?" asked Jim.

"A place where we can come and do things and no one can find us."

"A club is a girlie thing," said Rory.

"Can't it be our hideout?" asked Jim. "Indians have hideouts."

"But girls," said Rory, "don't have hideouts."

"They do so," said McKenna.

"I know," said Jim, "McKenna can be our scout. Indians have to have scouts to tell them where to go. And to look for danger. So we need McKenna in the hideout."

"What's that noise?" asked McKenna.

They sat still. A plopping sound came from the river.

"Just ice breaking," said Rory.

Plop plop plop plop. It kept a constant rhythm.

"That's not ice. Ice cracks," said McKenna. "I'm going to go see what it is."

"You do that. You're the scout," said Rory.

They watched her swish through the thick grass.

"You want to stay over at my house tonight?"

Jim looked at Rory, then leaned back and looked up at the sky. "I don't know. I'll have to ask my mom." How deep the sky was, Jim thought, just like an ocean. Depths and depths of blue. And what made him think of water was the constant plopping noise, plop, plop, plop.

"Jim! Rory! Jimmmm!"

The boys jumped out of the tree and ran toward the river. The same thought flashed through both of them—McKenna had fallen in.

But McKenna was standing on the bank. In the river was Jasper, trapped. His front legs were on the ice and his hind end had fallen through. The plopping they had heard was his back feet as he struggled to keep afloat. Now the noise that had seemed so gentle before turned sinister. "Jasper!" screamed Jim.

"He can't get out," said Rory. "The ice is too slick."

"Let's get Grandpa," said McKenna.

"How are we going to get back across?" said Jim.

They looked up and down the riverbank. "I don't remember where the log was," said McKenna.

Jim didn't remember either. He watched in horror at his dog struggling.

Rory stepped off the bank into the river. "What are you doing!" shrieked McKenna. He ignored her and waded toward the dog. Jim knew it must be cold. Deeper and deeper Rory went: first his ankles, then his knees, then his waist, then his chest.

"Rory!" McKenna kept screaming, "Please don't."

The ice around the dog started to sink as Rory broke through and finally, Jasper floated free into Rory's arms.

Now both McKenna and Jim were screaming. "You did it! You did it!" Rory looked back at them as he pushed the dog to the opposite bank.

McKenna and Jim found the log bridge, crawled back across and ran to meet Rory. They found him sitting on the bank.

"Are you OK?" asked McKenna.

He was shivering. "I'm cold."

"I'll go get Grandpa," McKenna said and she ran toward the house, shouting "Grandpa! Grandpa!"

Jim looked down at Rory. The fear he felt for this bigger, rougher boy was mingled with a new respect. "You saved my dog."

Rory reached out to pat the wet dog's head. "Can you tell my Dad? And Mom and Grandpa, too?"

6

Where the hell was Gwen, thought Will. He and John had fed
the cows in a blizzard and he'd expected Gwen to come along and
check them. The cows were clustered up and down the rows of hay
and it was the best time to get a good look at them before they broke
for water. Once they scattered, it would take the rest of the day to
find and check them all, especially since you couldn't see ten yards
in this white-out.

Three weeks into the season and they'd lost seven calves. Two
hadn't survived delivery. Two had bloat. An abscessed belly button.
One was born outside in the last storm and froze to death. One fallen
in the river. And none of that diarrhea—scours—yet, but that would
change after today. There was such a thing as will to live, but why the
hell all of them weren't born with it, he didn't understand.

When he'd returned to the barnyard, he checked the barn

where he'd left the two horses. They had finished their grain and were fidgeting in the stalls. Neither one of them had been saddled. Damn it, where was she? Will tacked them up. By the time he was done, Gwen still hadn't arrived.

He didn't bother to remove his coat and boots on the porch, but walked straight into the kitchen, dripping muck.

She was on the phone. "Ms. Hart," she mouthed to him.

"We need to get going."

Gwen held up a finger to shush him. Will sighed heavily and leaned against the sink.

"Yes, I look in his book bag and check his homework every day." Pause. "No. I didn't see that." Pause. "It was worth one hundred points." Pause. "Well, can you make a list of his homework every day? I'll check it off here at home." Pause. "I've got to go. Thanks for calling." She hung up the phone.

"Rory flunked a spelling test last Friday. When I asked him about spelling last week, he said they weren't going to have a test. Then he had a social studies project due today. They were supposed to do a report about a foreign country. He never brought the assignment home."

"Gwen, I'd like to talk about it, but I've got three hundred cows and a hundred calves to check. I can't worry about Rory right now."

"He's our son!"

"And this is our life, our ranch, our cows! I've got your horse saddled up! I'll see you at the barn!" Will strode out and slammed the door behind him.

Gwen swallowed the lump of hurt at the back of her throat. Her son's failures. Her husband's callousness. And the burden of this ranch that could suffocate a person.

She put on her outerwear and followed Will to the barn. He had taken his horse and left without her. Buck was pawing the floor, annoyed at being left behind. He tossed his head as she tried to bridle him.

"I don't know why you're in such a hurry to get out there today," she said.

With all her extra clothing, she could hardly lift her leg to the stirrup. At least Buck stood quietly while she heaved herself into the saddle. Not quite as nimble and elegant as in her Queen days. For an instant, she heard the roar from the crowds in the stands as she made her gallop around the arena. Then the snow engulfed her.

Gwen couldn't see anything except the tire tracks. She followed them out to the feeding ground. The cows were already breaking for shelter in the willows. Some had left calves behind in the scraps of hay that remained. She dismounted and pushed each calf to its feet. Had they eaten that day? Did they have scours? She watched Will cut a full-term cow, a "heavy," off the feeding ground. She thought about helping him, but he wouldn't want her to. He'd want her to check all the pairs.

After she checked the feeding ground, she followed the cows to the willows. It was hard to maneuver Buck through so many bunched cattle and still get a good look at them. The calves stood, wet and shivering, with their backs hunched against the driving snow.

She hated these storms, hated them for the misery they brought on all of them. The ground around the willows was churned to muck from hooves and manure. If the calves tried to lie in that, they'd all get scours. Well, no matter how hard they worked, scours couldn't be too far off.

Will rode up to her. "Find anything?"

"No, they look all right, so far."

"I'll finish up here. Why don't you check the rest of the meadow?"

She crossed back over the feeding ground out into the white void beyond. There were no tracks now and Buck broke his own trail through the knee-deep snow. When she rode in white-outs like this, a cold fear wove through her thoughts, a fear of losing herself in this landless, skyless realm of wind and snow. She pushed it away; there was work to be done.

At the last haystack in the farthest corner of the meadow, she spotted tracks on one side. She followed them to the east side, away from the wind, and found a cow in labor.

Gwen sighed. Bringing in this cow would mean turning her into the wind and trailing her back through a mile of blizzard. Now Will's annoyance with her for the morning's delay seemed justified. If she had not spoken with Ms. Hart, she and Will would have been on the feeding ground earlier and they would have caught this cow before she had traveled all this way to have her calf.

A current of anger surged through her. "Stupid bitch! How do you think your baby is going to survive out here!"

As she cut the cow away from the haystack, the smack of wind and snow in her face took her breath away. At the pace they were moving, they had at least a forty-minute ride ahead—if the cow didn't turn back, or head for the feed ground.

John was watching for her at the shed and threw the door open. Gwen pushed the cow in and the door slammed behind her. As her eyes adjusted to the gloom, she saw cows all around and vapor rising from their bodies.

"Will," said John, "you about done yet?"

"Yup." Just as he spoke, Gwen heard the squish of a new wet baby landing in the straw. She walked over to the stanchion just in time to see the cow nose the wet mass before her. One more alive. So far.

Will scooped up the bloody pulling chains. "Did you get a good look around the meadow?"

"No. It took me all this time to bring in one in labor."

"One of us is going to have to go back out there."

"It's nearly noon," John whined. "We got to eat."

"We can't eat if there could still be cattle out there."

"One of us could take the snowmobile out," said John, "then the other two could go eat."

"That's no help, because you can't bring in a cow with a snowmobile. The snowmobile would just have to come back and get a rider. We'd still lose time that way."

"I'll skip lunch and go back out," Gwen said.

The men stared at her.

She read their thoughts. "I haven't fixed anything, if that's what you mean. There's leftovers in the fridge, but if you eat those we've got nothing for supper tonight."

"Are you sure you can go back out now?" asked Will.

"Yes, I'm sure."

"Then we'll go in and put together something. We'll leave a plate for you."

The three of them stepped back into the storm. In a moment, Will and John had vanished and she could no longer see or hear them. Buck pawed at the snow, nosing for grass underneath. Good weather or bad—it was all the same to him. Gwen dusted the snow off her saddle and headed back out.

With the wind driving through her, she couldn't sit in the saddle any longer. She dismounted and trudged through the snow. At least this way she could fight off the cold in her hands and feet. Every few moments she glanced up to gauge where she was. A haystack loomed in the snow. A few more steps and she saw a cow standing next to it. The cow wasn't restless and twitching her tail as a cow in labor would do. She was quiet. A few more steps and Gwen knew the cow was no longer pregnant.

As Gwen approached, the cow's nose dropped to the ground. Oh God, she's lost one. The snow around the crib had drifted deep and now Gwen was up to her hips trying to get to the calf. She broke through and there was the calf lying in a pool of diarrhea. Damn, scours. Gwen glanced up at the cow's udder. The calf had not sucked today. He would not make it through the night out here. He was too weak to walk in. She could hardly walk much further herself.

She got back on Buck and galloped back to the calving shed. She hoped one of the men would be there so she wouldn't have to waste time searching for them.

Will was there, checking the cow Gwen had brought in earlier. Thank God, she'd calved without any trouble. He got the snowmobile and the sled and Gwen followed him out into the blizzard.

Damn, damn, damn this weather! It would not let up! She wanted to scream with frustration, but why, when there was no responder?

Will picked up the calf and Gwen trailed behind with the cow. By the time she reached the shed, Will was standing outside, waiting for her.

"How is he?" she asked as Will reunited mother and baby.

"I don't know. We'll see. I've done all I can. Are you finished out there?"

"Yes."

"I'm going back out to check the main bunch along the river before dark."

Gwen nodded. She was too exhausted to speak. She led Buck to the barn and unsaddled him. In the kitchen, she found a cold plate of baked beans. She wasn't hungry. She was cold, all the way to her bone marrow. She started some coffee and slumped in a chair by the kitchen table.

Now that she'd shut the door on wind and snow, her son's problems swamped her and she felt as uncertain of her bearings as when she'd picked her way through the blizzard. Throughout the struggle to make a life on this ranch, she'd turned to her children for comfort, for her justification. But at nine, her son was a baldfaced liar and a bully. He was failing school. When had that wind breached her door?

And what to do with him? Her own father would have belted her, but she already knew beltings would not work on Rory. She thought of horses she'd known who responded to beatings by becoming more resistant, more obstinate. The beatings meant nothing. They were simply events to be endured. The same attitude prevailed in her son, the same unwillingness to be directed by outside force. If he was to succeed, the force had to come from within.

But how?

She wiped the tears off her face and looked at the clock. Four p.m. Time to meet the bus.

By the time Will had completed his final check and returned to the shed, the scouring calf had died. He sighed as he took in the glassy stare and the hide, sunken between the hip bone and ribs. He picked the calf up and dumped it outside. He kicked its mother out of the shed, then out of the calving pen. She stood at the gate, bawling for her baby.

Tomorrow there would be ten more with scours.

The storm was lifting. Out in the meadow, he saw what looked like a lone fence post. Abruptly, it spread wings and rose into the air. Up, up through the dwindling snow. Then it circled, glided over the shed and turned to follow the river.

A blue heron. It must be spring.

7

"Mom."

"What?"

"I don't want to eat oatmeal anymore. I don't like it." Jim was speaking to Meg's back as she stared out the kitchen window.

"That's all we got right now. Mather'll bring some more groceries today. Put some sugar on it."

"I did."

"Put on some more."

How much had the snow drifted in the night, she wondered. She hadn't heard the wind, but once the sun tipped the horizon, it would start.

Jim dipped his spoon in the oatmeal and let the globs drip back out.

Meg turned around. "Quit playing with it and eat!" She set

her coffee cup down. "When I get back in here, you'd better have finished that." She walked out of the kitchen toward the bathroom.

Jasper scooted closer to Jim and their eyes met. Jim put the bowl down quietly on the floor and Jasper lapped up the oatmeal. Jim heard the toilet flush and snatched the bowl back up.

"I'm going out to start the truck," Meg said as she reached for gloves. Jasper turned and followed her out the door.

Jim put the bowl in the sink. He'd gotten away with it, but his stomach was growling. He pulled a chair up to the cabinets.

Meg came back in. "What are you doing?"

"I'm still hungry."

"We've got to go. Go get your coat on and get in the truck."

While he was getting ready, Meg popped a slice of bread in the toaster. She handed it to him as they went out the door. In the truck, Jasper silently pleaded with Jim as he sunk his teeth into the toast. Both of them glanced at Meg to see if she was paying attention. Her mind was on the roads, the snow, the bus.

Meg looked down the road to the Swans' turnoff. It didn't look too bad.

The bus pulled up. The driver stepped out and Meg rolled down her window.

"Meg."

"Morning, Steve."

"I can get them all to school this morning, but it's deep everywhere. If the wind starts up, I don't know about this afternoon."

"I can come get him at school."

Jim had already gotten on the bus. She looked after him. "Love you, too, son."

Jim looked back at her through the window and slowly lifted his hand.

By the time she'd warmed up the winch truck, the wind was driving sheets of snow across the meadow. Calves, with clumps of ice sticking to their sides, crowded at the gate. They fanned out behind her as she drove to the haystack.

Six foot drifts surrounded the stack. She looked back at the hungry calves around her. There was a Caterpillar tractor in the shed and she could plow out the drifts, but the calves would be left waiting. She looked for another stack that was more accessible. Snow drifts were piled around all of them. If she got the truck stuck backing up to these stacks, the calves wouldn't get fed before nightfall.

She drove back to the yard. The calves milled in confusion. Plumes of blowing snow soon obscured them.

She climbed into the Caterpillar and pulled the starter. Nothing. She rummaged in the drawers and cabinets, looking for battery cables. She found empty beer cans, rusted nails, bolts, hammer heads with no handles. The battery cables were on the floor under a heap of barbed wire.

She felt only a moment's relief once the Caterpillar roared to life. Its highest gear was a crawl. At that speed, it would take her twenty minutes at least to reach the stack. Then another twenty or thirty minutes to plow it out. And in the seat for that long, exposed to the wind, she'd freeze.

The wind blasted her so hard she had to lower her head. She stopped every hundred feet or so to jump off and run around the machine to get the blood moving in her feet and hands. Many of the calves gave up and drifted back toward the willows. She watched them go as she plowed and jumped off, plowed and jumped off. In an hour she was done and the calves were all gone.

They thundered back when she returned in the winch truck. The wind still stung her cheeks, but the air had warmed some. Patches of meadow here and there had been swept clean of snow. A new wet sheen glazed the drifts. This snow and wind wouldn't last. They couldn't. The sun had tipped past its zenith by the time she'd returned to the yard and turned off the truck. Then she realized there'd been no sign of Mather. He was supposed to have brought salt, groceries and her paycheck. Was he stuck somewhere? Should she go look for him?

As she walked into the house, the telephone rang. The ringing jarred her after hours of listening to wind. She grabbed the phone.

"How's the calves?" It was Mather.

"They're fine."

"Where ya been? I've been calling for two hours."

"The stack was drifted in. I had to plow it out."

"With the Caterpillar?"

"Yes."

"Did it start?"

"After I put battery cables on it."

"Well, I called to tell you I'm not coming out. The weather's too bad."

"We're about out of groceries. And I need my paycheck."

"You can come into town if you're that bad off. I'll give you a check for the grocery store."

Meg got directions to his house and hung up the phone. She thought about what to do with Jim. She couldn't be back in time to meet him when he came home from school. She picked up the phone and called Gwen.

"Gwen?"

"Meg. How are you?"

"I'm OK. Listen, I need a favor."

"Sure."

"Can Jim go home with Rory and McKenna?"

"Well, yes, but why?"

Now Meg balked. She did not want to admit that there was no food in her house. "I got to go to town."

"You can't go to town in this, Meg. Do you need something?"

"Yeah. The calves are out of salt."

"That can wait a few days. And if it can't, I'm sure we've got some blocks we can spare here."

"Mather wants me to get it today."

"Then why isn't he driving? Are you sure there isn't something else?"

"No, that's all."

"Meg, I guess I don't know what it's like where you're from, but here you don't play with this weather. You're a fool to drive in this."

"Can Jim stay with you?"

In Gwen's pause, Meg heard her weigh whether or not to continue arguing.

"Yes, but call us when you're headed back from town."

"All right."

Her truck churned through drift after drift. Snow sprayed and sifted through a crack she'd left open in the window. She wasn't too worried because there were tracks to follow and the drifts hadn't hardened. Still, when she rolled over the final drift on to the highway, she sighed with relief—until she realized the blowing snow had turned the highway into a ribbon of graveled ice. She crept from mile post to mile post.

After she passed the airport, the wind dropped and the highway cleared. The afternoon sun bounced off the Laramie rooftops. It had snowed here, but there were no signs of the blizzard that had battered the range. It may as well have been Arizona.

Mather's house was on the outskirts of town at the end of a dirt road. The siding, which had once been blue, was blackened where the wind had ground the dirt into it. The white trim peeled around the windows. A number of tireless cars sat in the yard. Mather's truck was parked in front of an open garage stuffed with junk.

She walked up the steps and rang the doorbell. The door cracked open and a woman in a stained apron peered out. Her frizzy hair was a drab gray and her shoulders slumped.

"You must be Meg."

"Mrs. Mather?"

"Gladys! Get out of the door. You're letting all the heat out of the house."

Mather pushed his wife aside. "So you got all the calves fed today, did ya?"

Meg nodded. "It's not so bad here," she offered, wondering why Mather hadn't tried to come out.

"No, it's not. But I knew it'd be bad out there. So you must have needed your check awful bad. Or are you out hunting boyfriends?"

"Jim and I need to eat."

Mather leaned over the porch railing and spit out his chew.

"You came to town alone?"

"Jim's in school."

He stared at her while he slowly pulled his wallet out of his hip pocket. He handed her a paycheck and forty dollars for groceries.

"Don't forget the salt."

"I won't." She turned to go back down the steps and the front door slammed behind her. As she got in the truck, she saw a hand lift the curtain and Mrs. Mather's pale face stared out at her.

Melting snow slid off the shiny hoods of the tractors for sale in front of the feed store. Meg pushed open the door and a cow bell jangled. The store smelled of grain in gunnysacks and new machinery and engine oil. A big fan overhead blew out warm dry air. Just standing there was a reprieve from the elements.

Customers—ranchers, she guessed—stood at the counter. They turned and stared at her. She was an unknown here. Their eyes said, what was a woman doing here alone?

The man at the counter smiled at her. His Scotch cap was pushed back on his head and his parka was open.

"Can I help you?"

"Yes, sir. I need some salt blocks."

"A truck load?"

"A truck couldn't get out there right now. I just need some to get by."

"Where's this at?"

Meg glanced around nervously. Everyone was listening. "Charles Mather's."

"Are you the new hand out there?"

She nodded.

"How do you like it?"

"It's windy."

The man laughed. "You're not from around here, are you?"

"No, sir."

"How do you like your boss?"

"He's OK."

The man's eyes fixed her for a second. He smiled. "I hope you're tough, Miss. . ."

"Braeburn."

"Braeburn," he murmured. "What else can I get you besides the salt?"

Meg thought of Sissie. "A fifty-pound sack of oats." And Jasper. "And a fifty- pound sack of dog food. I'll pay for the dog food myself."

"And the rest on Mather's account?"

"Yes, sir."

"OK, pull your truck around and I'll load this up for you."

She walked back to the front door. All eyes were on her, she knew, as she pushed the door open and the cow bell jangled, marking her departure.

After she deposited her check, she felt like a kid skipping school. She'd fed the calves, Jim was taken care of and she wasn't expected anywhere. It seemed like a corral gate had swung open and she was free to romp out and do as she liked. The sun was bright and the mounds of snow were melting into slush at the curbs. She parked the truck along Second Street and began to walk.

She passed clothing stores, antique stores, restaurants, a Western wear store. Behind the glass, people were busy buying or selling or making small talk. They moved from warm stores to warm cars to warm homes. Weather to them was an annoyance, not an opponent. What could she talk to these people about? She could murmur the "pleases" and "thank-yous" and "how do you dos." She could pretend that she belonged, but how could she tell them of the emptiness that she felt here? She was an alien, though she only lived twenty-five miles away.

A patron opened the bakery door and the odor swept out into the street. She caught the door handle and went inside.

She stood with her hands in her coat pocket and stared at the display cases. Cakes and leprechaun cookies with green frosting and breads and donuts. The smell alone was a luxury. She ordered half a dozen of the leprechauns. Jim would like the treat.

"Anything else?" asked the man behind the counter. His long hair, streaked with gray, was tied back in a pony tail. His smile was friendly, but he couldn't hide his curiosity. You're new here, that's what he was thinking.

Meg glanced up at the beverage choices. "A cup of hot chocolate," she said.

She sat down at one of the little tables and opened the cookie bag. She bit into the green frosting and sipped her hot chocolate. Delicious. She stared out the window at the parked cars and passersby, at all these people who didn't share her good fortune of a soft sugary cookie and a scalding cup of hot chocolate.

She became aware of the man behind the counter watching her. Women at the other tables were dressed in nice slacks. Their leather gloves lay beside their paper plates. She was the odd one, that's why she was being watched. This baker wasn't used to seeing a woman in Carhartts, overshoes and a Scotch cap. She wolfed the rest of her cookie and stood up to leave.

"Thanks," she said to the counter man.

"I haven't seen you before. What's your name?"

"Meg Braeburn."

He held out his hand. "Nice to meet you. I'm Gene."

"Nice to meet you, Gene." She moved toward the door.

"Come again," he shouted quickly.

She grinned. "I will. It was good."

The door closed behind her. He watched her go, the steam on the windows obscuring her image as she walked away.

By the time Meg had bought groceries, the sun was getting low. She stopped at a pay phone and called Gwen.

"Where are you?"

"In town."

"Meg, you can't get back out here. All the roads are drifted shut now. We had to get the kids in the snowmobile."

Meg paused. Gwen had been right. She should not have left in the first place.

"I've got to get back."

"You can't drive back. Will can pick you up at the highway with the snowmobile."

"What about my groceries?"

"Will will bring a sled."

After she left Laramie behind, the wind and ice reappeared on the highway. She'd been stupid to make this trip and it was wrong to put Swans to the trouble of picking her up. She'd been damn selfish, but how could she have asked them for food?

She pulled off the highway onto the dirt road. She shut off the truck and the sound of the wind enveloped her. Cold air seeped in through the windows. She could see the snowmobile headlight moving toward her across the dark prairie.

When it pulled up alongside, she jumped out of the truck. Will was in his coveralls with his hood pulled tight over his head.

"Gwen was worried about you."

"I know. I'm sorry."

He glanced at the groceries in the truck bed. "She would have shared whatever you needed."

"I couldn't ask."

"But you could head out on roads like this?"

"I'm sorry. I don't know what else to say."

Will lifted the grocery sacks from the truck bed. "I know you're young and on your own, but maybe you won't be such a damn fool next time."

She stuck the leprechauns underneath her coat and climbed on behind him. She pressed against his back to avoid the wind. Soon they were away, flying across the drifts with the stars swirling above.

8

The spring air whooshed through the open window as Meg drove to the Swans. She thought of the dream that had awakened her—Ronnie again, when they were happy, before the jolts. In the windshield, a shooting star arced through the sky. By the end of this day, her hair and clothes would reek with sweat and singed cattle hide. Swans had asked her to help them brand.

"There's coffee," said Gwen, smiling, as Meg came through the door.

Gwen was dressed like she was going to a party. She wore a ruffled Western shirt and her blue jeans were starched and pressed. Meg had never seen her with makeup and mascara before.

"Is there room in the refrigerator for this?" asked Meg, gesturing with the hamburger and macaroni casserole in her arms.

"Sure. Put it in there."

"You look nice."

"There's a big crowd coming and I'd like to look something like I used to look." She poured Meg's coffee. "We've got a few minutes. Let's sit outside."

They sat on a porch swing in the front yard and watched the eastern horizon pale, then turn pink, then red. The air sparkled with dew. Above them, the red-winged blackbirds, high in the cottonwoods, trilled, one after another.

"What a lovely morning," Gwen said.

"No more wind," said Meg.

"Oh, it's not gone. It's just forgotten us for now."

"Mornings like this I used to go irrigating with my dad."

Gwen looked over at her. This was the first time she'd heard Meg speak of her family.

"He'd irrigate before dawn so he could get to his clinic on time. He got me a pair of kids' hip boots and I'd wade out, catch frogs and put them in a pail. Then when he was done, we'd eat breakfast together in the kitchen, just the two of us, right about this time."

"What about your mother?"

"She didn't get up early. I'd bring her her coffee after Dad had gone and she'd look at me and say, 'No young man is ever going to marry a girl who plays with frogs.'"

Gwen smiled. "But one did. And one will again."

Meg shook her head. She looked as if she were going to say, no, I'm not a girl any man will ever look at, when a familiar voice boomed across the yard.

"Gwen! Is there any breakfast?"

Gwen didn't turn around. "It's on the table, John."

Meg looked over her shoulder and waved.

"Hey, Meg. Aren't you going to eat?"

"I'd rather sit out here."

"If you don't get in there and eat, you'll drop in your tracks before ten o'clock."

"I'll be fine."

John shrugged. "Well, suit yourself." The door to the porch slammed behind him.

"That man's entire life revolves around his gut. And my whole life's about keeping it filled."

Meg didn't know what to say. She hadn't realized the depth of Gwen's bitterness. And her own fondness for John made her want to defend him. Was it so hard cooking for one extra person?

"You've got your own place here," Meg said quietly, "your own cattle. And the children."

Birdsong filled the pause in the women's conversation. Then Gwen responded.

"The worst thing that can happen to you, Meg Braeburn, is to watch your dreams come true and then reckon with how shallow they were all along."

The porch door slammed again and both women turned at the sound of footsteps running through the grass.

"McKenna! Go back inside! You'll catch cold out here."

McKenna, in her nightgown, bounced into her mother's lap.

"I want to be with you." She pressed herself against Gwen's body.

Sunbeams fell on her face and bare arms and she wriggled with delight. Gwen nosed her daughter's hair.

"Are Jim and Rory up yet?"

"Yes. Grandpa told them he would put their heads under the faucet and turn on the cold water if they didn't get up."

"It must be time for work then."

Will and John came out of the house. They were engrossed in their own conversation, but John turned long enough to shout, "C'mon and help load the truck, Meg."

"You go on," said Gwen, "I'll bring Jim."

Meg let Jasper out of her truck and joined the men. As she caught up, she heard Will say, "It's not going to take three of us to load the truck."

"You and Meg can load it, then, and I'll saddle the horses."

They left John at the barn and went to the Quonset shed.

"I don't 'spose you can load the branding stove yourself, can you?" He sounded as if a negative answer would inconvenience him.

"I haven't seen it, but no, I don't 'spose that I can."

"Let's get that first then."

Women as ranch hands, what a ridiculous idea, thought Will. No way this fence-pole of a woman could do in three hours what he could do in one. No wonder Mather was underpaying her.

He grabbed the handle of the branding stove and she grabbed the other side. He expected her end to sag, but she bore the weight evenly. He jumped on to the tailgate and lifted his end up. Again, he expected to have to pull up most of the weight, but she picked up her end and the stove slid over the tailgate.

"You're pretty strong."

"For a girl?"

"No, for a woman that's so… slight."

"Is that a compliment?"

"Get those branding irons against the wall, will ya?"

Meg loaded the irons while Will loaded pails, ropes, vaccine, penicillin and syringes. He pointed to a dozen plastic jugs and told her to fill them at the river. As she made trips back and forth, Will spread out several pocket knives on the side of the truck and sharpened them one by one.

John came in. "Horses are saddled, including yours, Meg. Got the truck loaded?"

Will nodded.

John had a stocky palomino and Will rode a smaller sorrel with a white blaze down its forehead. John looked back at Meg as she put her foot in the stirrup.

"Sooner we get through, sooner we eat!" he shouted and with one slap of the reins, the palomino was off at a dead gallop out toward the pasture.

Will grimaced, as if he was embarrassed by his father. "Ready?" he asked.

"Sure," Meg answered.

Will nudged his own horse into a brisk trot and Meg followed with Jasper at Sissie's heels.

Now that there was green grass, cows and calves were scattered all the way to the fence line. The palomino streaked down to the farthest corner and set them in motion. Will and Meg separated and Meg rode down the center of the pasture, turning cows and calves as she went. Sissie, out of her home pasture and sensing the commotion around her, tossed her head and stamped. Not today, thought Meg. Please, not today. The last thing she wanted was a horse wreck in front of the Swans.

One slick fat calf veered away from Meg's bunch and vaulted over a small ditch. Sissie sprang after him without even a nudge, but the moment she cleared the ditch, she threw down her head and bucked until Meg hit the ground.

Meg pushed Jasper away as he wriggled up to comfort her. She was too annoyed that what she had feared had happened. She lunged for the reins dangling in front of her before the mare thought to run off.

"You all right?" Will rode up and dismounted. Meg didn't look up. She knew she had just confirmed his opinions of her.

"Yeah."

"Give me your hand."

"I'm all right!"

Will held out his hand. She put her palm in his and was surprised at the strength of his grip. He yanked her to her feet.

"Are you sure you're all right?"

"I'll be OK."

"That man oughta be shot, leaving you a rank horse like that."

"She's all right. It's my fault. I should have worked her out before we started off."

"If you got to work 'em out every time you go to do something, what the hell good are they? Dad and I can get the herd in from here. You can leave the mare in the corrals if you want."

"I'm fine!" She took up the reins and stepped into the stirrup. Realizing how harsh she had sounded, she turned back to him. "I can ride. The mare'll be OK now."

Will shook his head. "Suit yourself. Between you and that mare, it's hard to tell which one's more mule-headed!"

Meg whirled Sissie toward the cattle. Now that the old rip had had her say, she was perfectly calm.

As the cattle filed into the corral, Meg saw Gwen arrive with the branding supplies and the children. Another five pickup trucks drove in behind her. Meg recognized the four Wilcox boys and their dad from school. The other pickups were full of older boys and their girlfriends. Everyone parked in the corrals. The men and boys huddled together, shook hands and spit tobacco. The girls climbed up on the fence and chewed bubble gum. The children gawked at each other. Rory grabbed Justin Wilcox's cap and ran away with it. The boy chased him, tackled him to the ground and promptly began pounding him.

Will lit the branding stove and the roaring flame sucked up all sound, so that for an instant, there was a vacuum of silence. Meg took Jim's hand and led him over to Rory. She put her arms around both boys and knelt down to talk to them.

"Rory, can you wrestle calves with Jim?"

"I don't want to wrestle calves with him. He's too small to hold 'em down."

"Why don't you give him a try? If it doesn't work out, you can switch."

Rory regarded her skeptically. "OK."

"How do you wrestle calves, Mom?"

"I'll show you." She walked behind a small calf and grabbed its back leg. She pulled it away from the other calves out to the center of the pen. Rory crossed over to the forequarter, grabbed the calf's front leg and together they lifted him off his feet and set him down. Rory jumped on the calf's neck and held the front leg tucked behind the shoulder. Meg sat down and slid her feet against one back leg, while holding the other leg back with both hands. "See, now he can't get away from you. Here, you sit where I'm sitting, so you can see how it feels."

Jim sat down next to his mother. He put his feet next to hers and grasped the calf's leg with his hands.

"Hold on tight. Don't let go." Meg let go and the calf jerked free of Jim's grip. Meg quickly caught the leg again and handed it back to Jim. "You've got to keep a tight hold because once his back leg is free, Rory can't hold him by himself. And if you lose your grip on his leg, he could kick you in the face."

Jim nodded and tightened his grip.

"Now you have to hold on while everything gets done. Each calf has got to have a brand, an ear notch, a shot and if he's a bull calf, he's got to be castrated." Meg picked up the calf's leg and pointed to a little pouch. "See that? That's his testicles. Heifers are not going to have that."

"What's 'castrated' mean?"

"Will is going to cut the testicles out."

"Why?"

"Because it's easier to castrate two hundred some calves when they weigh one hundred pounds than when they weigh four or five hundred pounds."

"But why?"

"A male animal's gotta have testicles to breed. And the Swans don't want these calves breeding. What ranching is all about is deciding which ones will breed and which will be sold. We don't want the animals deciding.

"Now, John, Mr. McCullough and Mr. Wilcox will be doing the branding. Justin Wilcox is ear-notching," Meg explained. "Me and the McCullough girls are doing the vaccinating. Everyone else is wrestling calves. Remember, everything has to be done before you let the calf go. Can you remember everything?"

"What's Mrs. Swan doing?"

"She's taking Will's horse and going home to get dinner ready. What are the things that have to be done?"

"Branding...ear notching...vaccinating...and castrating if it's a boy."

Meg watched while the boys held on to the calf.

John stepped over with a branding iron. He looked down at Jim. "Are you ready, son? You have to hold tight."

Jim nodded. John planted the brand down on the calf's shoulder near where Rory was sitting. The calf kicked and Jim turned away as the smoke covered his head, but he held on.

"The smoke's stinging my eyes, Mom!"

"It's all right. Good job holding on."

Then Will knelt down beside them. Without a word, he slit open the calf's scrotum, squeezed out what looked like two shiny sausages and cut them free. He stood up and threw them in a bucket by the branding stove.

Rory turned to him. "Ready to let go?"

Jim nodded. They both let go. The calf leapt to its feet and thrust itself into the mass of calves crowded against the fence.

"All right," said Meg, "it looks like you're ready to be on your own."

"OK, now pick another," said Rory.

All around Jim, the older boys were grabbing and flipping calves. It was a whirling chaos of smoke and people moving every which way around the pen. Boys on the ground shouted: "Brand!" "Shot!" "Mr. Swan!"

"Are you just gonna stand there, or are you too scared?"

Jim looked back at Rory. "I'm trying to decide which one."

"Well, then look down at them, not all around the pen."

Jim shuffled through the calves, searching for one that was not too big. He reached down and grabbed an ankle, as he had seen the others do, but the calf kicked him off.

"You're going to have to hold on better than that, wuss."

Jim reached down with both hands this time and grabbed an ankle. The calf kicked, but he held on.

"Pull him outta there so I can grab the front!"

But Jim couldn't pull. He couldn't even talk. It was all he could do just to hold on. Rory pushed the other calves aside and ran to the front. He grabbed the front leg and tried to yank the calf over, but Jim wasn't ready for the flip. He lost the back leg and the calf kicked him as he sped away. There was a stabbing pain in his shin. He glanced at Rory. He knew better than to show pain.

"Serves you right. You shoulda flipped him over when you saw me grab his front leg. Let me do the back this time."

Rory dove into the stream of calves and pulled one out.

"Quick, quick, get around to his front!"

Jim tried to get to the front, but the calf side-stepped away from him, although Rory held the back leg tight.

"No, stupid. Reach over his shoulder, grab the front leg and flip him."

Jim grabbed the front leg and pulled up. Nothing happened.

"Harder!"

Jim felt Rory pull the calf up just as he did, and the calf went to the ground. Jim scrambled on its neck and pulled the front leg back against the shoulder, as he'd seen Rory do. Everyone appeared at once, the brander, the ear notcher, one of the girls with the vaccination gun.

Rory pulled up the back leg. "Heifer," he said.

They let the calf go and stood up. Jim was tired. And that was only the second calf!

"I'm going with someone else," said Rory and walked away.

Jim looked for his mother. She was helping one of the girls reload her vaccination gun at the table next to the branding stove.

"Wait until the air bubble rises to the top," he heard her say, "then just squirt it out." Out came a bubble and a thin stream of liquid from the needle.

"Mom, Rory doesn't want to wrestle calves with me anymore."

"Why not?"

"I can't do it."

"What can't you do?"

"I can't throw the calves. I can't hold on to them."

"Yes, you can. You just need a better partner, that's all."

Jim straightened up at the words, "better partner." So his mother did not think Rory was so great.

Meg walked up to the big girls sitting on the gate. "Would one of you like to wrestle calves?"

A girl with blue eye shadow and braces slid down. "I can do it," she said.

"Hi, my name's Meg."

"Mandy," she replied.

"This is my son, Jim. He needs a partner."

"Hi."

Jim didn't reply. These older girls were a mystery to him. Why did they wear all that stuff on their faces? His mother never wore makeup. And if they had come with their boyfriends, why weren't they wrestling calves with them? Jim thought boyfriend and girlfriend meant that you spent all your time together. What did it mean to have boyfriends if all these girls had come to do was to sit on the gate and blow bubble gum?

But Mandy had more patience for him than Rory did and they wrestled calves together for another hour until Jim was too tired to stand. He crawled underneath the table in the center of the pen and found McKenna there, too. Her face was grimy with smoke and her hair had fallen loose from her ponytail.

"Did you wrestle calves?"

"No. Dad says I'm not big enough."

"What have you been doing then?"

"Carrying water to the wrestlers. And watching." She picked up a rock and scraped manure off her boots.

"Are you guys OK?"

They looked up at Meg bending over them.

"Just a hundred more. And then we can go eat."

Jim stared ahead as wrestlers, calves and the branding crew rotated in and out of his vision. Next to the branding stove, two wrestlers had just tackled a big calf. He saw Will squat down and reach between the calf's backlegs.

But the wrestler on the back end looked away. The calf kicked and the wrestler lost his grip. Will's knife flew up in the air and just as when the branding stove had been lit, all sound stopped.

Shiloh McCullough's screaming pierced the silence. She was staring at the knife stuck in Will's palm.

Meg pushed the girl aside and looked down. "Where's the first aid kit?"

Will was staring down at his hand. "Check the glove box in the truck."

Meg rushed away. Jim watched Will gingerly pull the knife out. Blood pooled in his upturned palm.

McKenna got up and went to her father. "Daddy?"

"It's all right, McKenna. Go sit down."

Wrestlers all over the pen shouted, "Mr. Swan! Mr. Swan!" Over the noise and smoke, they couldn't see what had happened.

John came over. "What's holding you up?" Then he saw Will's hand. "Give me the knife," he said.

John dipped it in alcohol and hustled off to castrate calves.

Shiloh yelled, "Aren't you going to help him?"

"Wrestlers can only hold down a calf for so long, hon. 'Specially when they're tired. Got to get these calves cut before they give up."

Meg grabbed a wad of cotton off the table and pressed it into Will's palm. "I couldn't find a first aid kit."

He looked up at her sheepishly. "Looks like I'm the one who needs help now."

Meg grimaced at his reference to her mishap. It did even the score.

Mr. McCullough set his iron in the stove and came over. He wiped the sweat off his forehead with his arm.

"Problem, Will?"

"Little one."

He stood for a moment watching Meg staunch the blood. "Why don't you wrap some gauze around that?"

Meg replied, "They don't have any."

"You didn't bring a first aid kit?"

"Forgot it," said Will.

"Good thing that it's just you that's hurt. So far. I've got some duct tape in my truck."

He went for his duct tape while Meg dropped the bloody cotton and grabbed another wad. Once Meg had taped the cotton to his hand, Will went back to castrating, although Jim could see blood oozing from under the tape.

At last, the wrestlers shouted that they couldn't find any more slick calves and John shut down the branding stove. The silence that settled over the pen was weighted with exhaustion. Cows and calves drifted away from the corrals. The wrestlers sat down, or leaned against the fence posts. Will rubbed the irons in the dirt before loading them back on the truck.

John pulled Jim and McKenna up off the ground. "Well, what did you think of branding?"

"It was long," said Jim.

"Grandpa, I want to go home."

"Sure, we'll go home. And there'll be fried chicken and baked beans and mashed potatoes and gravy and ham and at least four kinds of pies."

"How do you know?" said McKenna.

"'Cause I can smell it all right from here."

"No you can't. It smells terrible here."

"You gotta sniff beyond it. When the day gets too cold or too hot or too smelly, I just think about what's waiting for me at home."

Will nodded toward the other pickups headed up the road. "If we keep talking about it, there won't be any left for us."

At the house, the men and boys stood in a circle in the front yard while the girls sat Indian-style in the grass, tearing up dandelions and rubbing them on each other's faces. There was a steady crack and swish of beer cans being opened. Gwen and the other wives passed out platters of deviled eggs and Ritz crackers.

Gwen looked at the three children as they staggered through the yard and said, "Go in and wash up, all of you, and you can eat."

When Jim stepped back outside, he noticed that what John had said was true. There were two big picnic tables covered with food. And just as John had predicted, there were four kinds of pies: apple, peach, banana and chocolate cream. Fat clouds cruised overhead and fat green buds on the cottonwoods unfurled.

Will and John came into the yard. John carried a full bucket that sloshed with every step. He shouldered his way through the men and set the bucket down. "There's your oysters!"

"Oysters?" thought Jim. Jasper squirmed through the men's legs and snapped something white and stringy from the bucket. The testicles!

"Jasper, you scamp, get out of here!" John shouted at the dog. "Meg, get your dog before he eats up these boys' wages!" Then he saw Gwen and shouted at her. "Can you get me a plate?"

"What do you want?"

"Everything." Will looked tired. He sat down heavily next to Rory and McKenna, who already had plates.

"Aren't you hungry, Daddy?" asked McKenna.

"Nah, just a little thirsty, that's all. Go get me a pop, will ya?"

Meg brought Jim a plate and sat down. "How are you doing, son?"

"OK."

Meg smiled. Her face was as grimy as the men's. But she wasn't talking with anyone. She was not standing with the men around the beer bucket. She was not sitting with the other mothers around the picnic tables. Her owl glasses had slid down to the tip of her nose and she ducked her head while she picked at her potato salad.

"Will, what's wrong with your hand?" Gwen was standing over him.

"Calf kicked the knife."

Gwen knelt and removed the duct tape and soggy cotton wads. When the final layer was gone, she stared down at the open lips of the wound.

John came up to them. "I wouldn't fuss, Gwen. It's just a little cut."

"Why didn't you tell me about this?"

The tone in her voice made John stiffen. "'Cause it's nothing to worry over. Clean it up and it'll be fine."

"Do you know when his last tetanus shot was?"

"Tetanus shot? That knife had been dipped in alcohol before he sank it into his hand."

"What's the matter? Are you afraid he's going to miss a few hours of slaving for you?" Gwen snapped.

All the chatter and laughter stopped. Grins fell from sunburned grimy faces.

"We're going to the hospital," Gwen announced. "Meg, would you look after the children?"

"Sure."

They all turned to watch her as she grabbed Will by the arm and steered him toward the pickup. No one said a word as she drove away.

One of the men by the beer tub broke the silence, "She coulda let him get something to eat. It coulda waited another hour or so."

A woman at the table spoke up, "You hush up. Don't you pick on the woman behind her back while you stuff her food in your mouth."

Meg looked down at her plate. She wished she'd had the guts to say that.

9

"You complain that he won't mind, won't listen to you and picks on McKenna, but you won't let him take on some responsibility. If he's got a job to do, he'll stay out of trouble."

"If he won't listen, how does he have the maturity to be on a tractor ten hours a day?"

John listened to Will and Gwen bicker while he worked through his pancake stack. He sighed loudly and let his fork clatter on the plate.

"Gwen, you know I'll watch him. He won't get into any trouble."

"The last time you watched him he ended up nearly froze in the river."

"You know damn well that we all started haying at his age."

"That doesn't make it right for him."

The light warmed Rory's eyelids and he opened them in time to see the sky pale, then blush. The voices from the dining room were muffled, but he knew that his parents were arguing about him. Grandpa's voice broke in every few moments. He got out of bed and opened the door.

"All right. Keep him home. But I'm not going to listen to you complain about him the rest of the summer when he has nothing to do," Will said.

"Are you saying that we should start him on heavy machinery because we can't find anything else for him to do?"

"Gwen, let the boy go," John said. "He's going to learn who he is by doing, not by you reining him at every turn."

"He's my son and I'm entitled to decide what's best for him!"

His father was the first to see him. Then everyone fell silent.

"Good morning, young man." Grandpa reached out with one arm and hugged him.

"Mom, I want to go haying."

His mother's lips compressed into a tight line. The dawn light streaming in the windows illumined tiny lines scratched at the corners of her eyes.

"You'll get hot and tired."

"No, I won't. I want to go with them. Please."

Gwen rose and gathered the plates. "I can't fight you all," she said, retreating to the kitchen.

"You heard her. Go get dressed," said John, and then he whispered, "before she changes her mind."

Out in the meadow, the morning air was chilly and dew beads sparkled in the grass. A falcon's cry rent the silence—the spring birds had stopped singing weeks ago. Above, them, the sky domed, violet and immense. Somewhere the ranch ended, bounded by roads or fences, and the rest of the world began. But nothing enclosed the sky.

His father and grandfather murmured and tinkered with the machinery.

"There's too much dew for you to rake yet," said John. "We'll let the hay dry an hour or two and in the meantime, you can ride with your dad on the swather."

Rory swelled with excitement. The swather was the closest thing he knew to the dinosaur hulking in front of the geology museum in town. He clambered up the ladder behind his father.

"Can I start it, Dad?"

"No, you just hold on to the bar here." His father pointed to the bar around the deck. "And don't touch anything."

The machine roared to life and Will sank the header into the quivering stems. It rotated, sweeping the grass into the sickles. Birds flew up, terrorized, in front of them. The air smelled of cut hay and gasoline.

"This is fun!" shouted Rory.

His father glanced up at him and started to smile, then turned his attention back to the machine.

Rory was getting hot by the time they saw John speeding across the meadow to intercept them. Will cut the engine down and stopped.

"He's coming to pick you up," he shouted and Rory reluctantly climbed down and joined his grandfather in the truck.

"Are you ready to learn to handle the tractor?"

Rory nodded.

John pulled up next to the tractor. "First we're going to try it without the rake. Get yourself situated in the seat there."

Rory reached for the steering wheel to pull himself up. His grandfather stood on the back and talked over his shoulder.

"See that little switch? That's the ignition. Turn it to 'on.' Now see that knob there? That's the starter. Pull it."

The engine sputtered. The lid on the exhaust pipe joggled until the engine steadied and then it stood straight up. The foot plates vibrated beneath him and Rory thrilled at the power. He looked back at his grandpa and smiled.

"Do you like that?" John shouted.

"Yeah!"

"OK, see that pedal on your left? That's the clutch. See if you can push it all the way down."

Rory tried, but it only went half way. "Okay, you're going to have to shut 'er off so we can fix that."

"Why, Grandpa?"

"'Cause you got to be able to push the clutch all the way in."

Rory felt disappointed as the motor puttered out.

"Don't let that lip sag. It ain't no good if it can't go anywhere. Let me get in the driver's seat and we'll take it back to the shop."

They switched places and rode home.

"What we need," said John, "is blocks."

They went out to the junk wood pile and found some scraps of lumber. Then John measured them and marked some lines.

"There, now you saw them down."

He handed Rory the saw. Rory put the blocks on the work table and tried the saw, but it stuck in the block and wouldn't move.

"Let me help you now. Start the saw on the edge of the wood, here, until it bites and then move your whole arm back and forth."

Rory felt wonder, then pride, as the sawdust flew off the work table. He was one of the men, now. He sawed out two thick blocks: one for the clutch, one for the brake. Once John had lashed them to the pedals, they drove back out to the meadow.

"Now, you're going to push down the clutch, put the tractor in first gear and let the clutch go very slowly until you feel 'er start to move and then let the clutch go out all the way. Got it?"

Rory pushed the clutch, ratcheted the gearshift into the notch and lifted his foot. The tractor bucked hard enough to make his neck snap, then it stalled out.

"You can't just let go of the clutch. Take your foot off it slowly, just until the tractor starts to move. Then you can let go."

Rory released the clutch, slowly, slowly, just as his grandpa told him. But nothing was happening. It was taking too long. He let it go and the tractor bucked to a standstill again.

There was silence for a moment.

"You didn't let it go slow enough," John said.

"I did, Grandpa, but it won't do it."

John reached in the tool box and pulled out a canteen. "Here, have a cool drink."

Rory gulped down the tepid water. John took the canteen from him. He tilted his head back into the sunlight and his Adams' apple bobbed up and down as he swallowed.

"There." He wiped his mouth on his sleeve and screwed the cap back on the canteen. "Back to the matter at hand. Don't think of the tractor moving this time. Just think of your foot lifting slowly. Try to see how slow you can lift it. Put all your mind to it."

Rory restarted the tractor. The engine rumbled while he stared at the clutch. He smashed it down, then inched his foot away. He willed it to barely move. His thigh trembled from the effort of moving so slowly. As the tractor began to pull, his excitement overtook him and he let go. The tractor bucked and stopped.

Rory pounded the steering wheel. "I did what you told me. And it didn't work."

"You want to quit and go home?"

"No. But why won't it work?"

"Son, nothing in life comes easy. Nothing. Try it again. And remember. Don't think about the tractor. Keep your mind on your foot and don't stop until your foot is all the way off."

Rory tried again. The engine began to pull. He glanced up at the meadow ahead, but didn't move his foot. Only when the tractor was completely in motion did he let go.

"Grandpa! We're moving!"

"Better watch where you're going. You're about to hit that ditch ahead." Rory gripped the steering wheel and turned away from the ditch.

John yelled in his ear. "Now, how does that feel?"

"It's great! Thanks, Grandpa!"

His father was approaching them in the pickup.

"OK. Put your foot on the clutch and put your other foot down on the brake."

They halted abruptly. Will leaned out the pickup window. "Lunch," he said.

Rory let go of the clutch and the brake and the tractor bucked again before stalling.

John squeezed his shoulder. "Son, you got to take it out of gear when you're stopped, or you're going to shake your grandpa's brains out of his head."

After the first week, Rory was on his own. Will, or John, drove him out in the morning. They filled his tractor with gas and checked the oil. They sifted through the hay, checking to see if it was dry enough to rake. Then they drove away. Rory started his tractor, put it in gear and followed the rows of hay. Behind him, the rake wheels flipped the rows over, exposing the green underbelly to the sun.

For the first week, the prestige buoyed him. He liked marching in behind Will and John, smelling of sweat and oil and washing his hands at the sink with them. He liked ignoring McKenna and Jim, who was over at his house now that Meg was haying. He liked the money that his grandpa gave him at the end of every week.

But in the afternoons, the sun stood still and he hated the

pounding heat. Sometimes, when he swung by the river, he saw McKenna, Jim and Jasper wading. McKenna waved. He didn't wave back. That was beneath him now, but he wanted to join them.

John had told him that he could only run the tractor in second gear. One day, he snuck it into third. He looked over his shoulder to make sure John was gone. The engine surged and the rake wheels spun in a frenzy, churning the hay so hard it flew into the air.

And he was finishing so much faster than normal! He would be done way before lunch. Then maybe Will would let him ride the swather. He saw the stackyard straight ahead. He tried to turn to go around it, but he couldn't turn fast enough. The rake wheels caught the stackyard fence, hit the posts and tore off the barbed wire. By the time he'd slammed down on the clutch and brake, the rake wheels were twisted and bent.

He shut the tractor off. Panic boiled up his throat and he wanted to run away. Off in the distance, he could hear the swather and the baler. His father and grandpa would be furious. They would never let him run the tractor again. Then they would tell his mother. He could already see the twist of disappointment in her mouth.

With one last look behind him to see if anyone was watching, he tore down to the river. It pattered over the mossy rocks, mindless of his plight. Slivers of light rippled through it. He bent down and peered across to the other bank. Trout undulated where the willows arched over the water.

The pickup was approaching. Was it Dad or Grandpa? He held his breath and squatted down low, willing himself to become part of the river.

"Rory!"

It was Grandpa. There was a worried edge to his call.

"Rory!" Then silence. Then, "Rorrreeee!" His grandpa was getting scared.

He stood up.

John saw his grandson's head poke over the riverbank. "Rory! Are you all right?"

"Yes, Grandpa."

John knelt down and looked him in the eye. "What happened?"

"I was going down the row and I saw the stackyard and I turned, but the rake hit the fence."

"Let's go back and look at it."

Rory stood at the tractor while John inspected the rake and the stackyard fence. Without a word, he plucked his canteen from the truck and sat down on the tractor tire.

"What really happened, son?"

The sobs bubbled out. Rory tried to suppress them, but they surged out of him like vomit. "I had it in third gear!"

"Why didn't you tell me that the first time?"

"I thought you'd be mad and you wouldn't let me hay no more."

"Why'd you put it in third gear?"

"To see how it felt."

"Why didn't you tell me you wanted to put it in third gear?"

Rory wiped his nose on his sleeve. "I don't know."

"Yeah, you know. Because you thought I wouldn't let you. Here, take some water."

"I'm sorry, Grandpa."

"If you want to try something—anything—like put the tractor in third gear, or ride broncs or chew tobacco or drink liquor, or whatever it is, tell your Grandpa, because if you do it with me, you'll always be OK. I'm not so worried about the mess," he said as he surveyed the wreckage around him, "as I feel bad that you didn't tell me what you wanted to do. Hell, I'd have let you do it, but I'd have been with you."

Rory watched John get up and rummage through the tool box. His grandfather's absorption in the clanging metal broke him and he ran up and threw his arms around his waist.

"Please don't hate me, Grandpa!"

"Hate you? Who said anything about hating you? Where'd you get such a notion?"

"Everyone hates me!"

"Whoever said such a thing?"

Rory hiccupped back a sob. "Dad, for one."

"Did he ever say such a thing?"

Rory paused. "No. He just won't talk to me."

"Well, what do you want him to say?"

"I don't know."

"What about your Mom? Did she ever say she hated you?"

"No. She just yells at me."

"What about McKenna and Jim and Meg?"

"No. They never said it."

"And you know I never did. Because you know I love you very much."

"Yes."

"So this idea that everyone hates you—it's what you *think* they think."

No response.

"Your dad said you done a good job yesterday. I heard him. Right?"

Rory sniffled. "No."

"No? We were sitting at the same table. And what kind of pie did your Mom make three days ago?"

"Apple with ice cream on top."

"I thought that was your favorite. The only one around here who's used the word 'hate,' as far as I can tell, is you. Right?"

"Yes."

"And that was 'cause you don't like what you did. Right?"

"Yes."

"So the next time you think everyone hates you, come get me and we'll sort it out again. OK?"

"OK."

"Now help me fix everything up."

Gwen knew something was wrong when the three of them came in at dinner. John wouldn't meet her gaze and all three looked grim. Paul Harvey blared from the radio.

"Well?" she said.

"There was an accident," said John.

Gwen stared stonily at him.

"Rory ran into a stackyard."

She looked at her son. There wasn't a scratch on him. She looked back at Will and John.

Will spoke this time. "The stackyard fence will have to be fixed. The rake wheels are wrecked. We'll have to stop haying and straighten 'em back up before we can go on."

Gwen wrestled with her response, swallowing back the bitter words that flew to her tongue. But as she stood to pick up John's plate, she said, "He's learning by doing. That's what you wanted."

They watched her as she collected the rest of the dishes and carried them to the kitchen.

With relief and half a prayer, Meg spotted dark clouds boiling over the mountain tops. She'd mowed, raked, swept and stacked hay for ten-hour days over the past twenty days. At nights, when she picked up Jim from Gwen's, she was too tired to speak to him. I'm ready for a rain day, she thought.

She'd met Ronnie on a hot afternoon like this when he'd come looking for a job in the hayfields. He was twenty-five. "I aim to be a bull rider," he'd told her father, "and I'm just trying to get some money together to go out on the road."

She smiled at the memory of him striding across the fields in a white t-shirt—so sure of himself. With his broad shoulders and big smile, she had believed him, even if all her father had said was "hmm."

She'd avoided him at first. She still hadn't been on her first date and he had to have a dozen girls hanging on him every night when he went to town.

But one day after a heavy rain, her father had sent them to check cattle together and that's when it started. They'd spent the whole day riding and talking and they'd had so much to say to one another that she was surprised when the day wore out on them.

Ronnie stopped going to town at night and instead she snuck out of the house. They walked down to the riverbank, spread a blanket in the cool grass and listened to the crickets. That's where she'd first learned about her body.

They came in from the fields one afternoon holding hands just as her father came back from sewing up a horse. He saw them. And he told Ronnie to leave.

"Why?" They'd both asked.

"Just get your things and go."

Ronnie had started to his truck without a word..and without a backward glance at her.

"What are you doing?" she had screamed.

Her father looked away. "He doesn't want you, Meg."

"What do you mean?"

"What does a two bit dandy want from a straight A student with a room full of 4-H trophies? What can there be between two people like that?"

"He loves me."

Again, her father looked away. He didn't believe her. All

along he had thought what she felt about herself. She wasn't pretty enough. She wasn't feminine enough. She wouldn't draw a man's eye.

"No, Meg," he'd said. "He wants all this." He gestured to the barns, sheds, corrals, fields. "This is what he wants. You'll make me happier and you'll be doing more for yourself if you don't see him anymore."

But she'd skipped school to meet him at the gas station and soon, every day after school, they'd scavenge for empty bedrooms. Then her parents came home early from Stock Show in January and found them. Her father had thrown Ronnie out in his underwear into the twenty below and Meg had scooped up his clothes and started for the door.

"If you go after him, don't bother to come back."

Her hand cupped the cold doorknob.

"Is he worth giving up your life for? Giving up me and your mother? The ranch?"

"Yes!"

Meg jumped as lightning crackled on the mountainside. The wind had picked up and fat raindrops splatted her. She ran for the truck. Once she slammed the door and the rain poured down, she smiled. She'd gotten her day off.

Since there was no haying in the morning, Meg kept Jim with her. She'd work on the machinery a few hours, she thought, and then maybe they could drive up to the mountains and have a picnic.

"What are you going to do, Mom?" he asked as he climbed in the truck.

"I'm going to fix a cracked sweep tooth. You can help. And then I can be with you the rest of the day."

They unloaded the toolbox and a new tapered wooden pole, a sweep tooth. She showed him which wrench to pull from the toolbox.

She tried to loosen the bolt on the old tooth, but it stuck. She struggled for a while and then realized that Jim was gone. She looked around for him. He had climbed on a tractor and was pretending to drive.

"Jim, get off of there."

"Why?"

"It's not a toy. Get off."

Reluctantly, he slid off the seat. She rummaged in the tool box for a wrench with a longer handle, or a pipe—anything to give her more leverage to twist the bolt off. Nothing. She tried the bolt again, throwing all her strength in it. Damn Mather. Damn his hide and this rusty equipment that was no better than junk.

She heard a creaking noise and looked up. Jim was back in the tractor seat. She leaped to her feet, yanked him off and slapped him over and over.

"I told you to stay off of there!" He pulled away from her and raced home over the meadow.

Why did it always come to this? She could be a mother, or she could be a ranch hand, but not both together. At this rate, she wasn't teaching Jim to love this life, as her father had done for her. She was teaching him to hate it. During those years when her focus was on Ronnie, she'd never seen these sinkholes ahead.

A couple of months later, she confessed the incident to Gwen while they were gathering Swans' cattle in the mountains. Gwen was riding ahead of her on the rocky trail. For a few moments, she said nothing and Meg became fearful of judgment looming against her.

But when Gwen turned, she said, "I know you can run a ranch, Meg. When it comes to raising children, grit alone won't do it."

"What are you saying?"

Gwen pulled Buck off the trail. "What I'm trying to say is the wall you're building around yourself might take you down with it when it falls."

Meg bristled. "I'll just try harder next time."

Gwen smiled sadly. "I know you'll try." She urged Buck on up the hill and his shoes clattered on the rocks.

10

It had snowed an inch or two the night before, but the morning was not all that cold, just snappy. The calves rose slowly and shook the snow from their hides. If they thought ahead at all, they were looking forward to another warm fall day where they grazed in the morning and drowsed at the riverside all afternoon. But today was goodbye.

Meg, John and Will fanned out from the gate. All the horses knew something was up. They tossed their heads and threw out their feet, leaving hoofprints behind in the snow. Jasper streaked down the fence line, sending the fat calves flying. By the time the sun peeped over the horizon, the herd had reached the gate.

John rode ahead to make sure they didn't all crowd in at once. He thinned the leaders and they fed through the yard, over the bridge and out onto the county road toward Swans' corrals and scales where the trucks would come to pick them up.

A sense of loss pinched Meg as the last calf passed through the gate. She'd shepherded this group for almost a year now. She remembered how scared both she and they were when they'd all arrived. But she'd gotten them through and hadn't lost any. And now they were going on. What about her?

She closed the gate and looked back at the meadow. Empty. And quiet.

On the road, she could see John way ahead. He'd stretched the line so they wouldn't bunch up at any point. The calves were quiet; the only sounds were the beat of hooves against the road and John's steady encouragement.

"All right, get up there now. Don't stand and stare, honey. Hey-yah. Hey-yah. Hey-yah. Move, move." He released his rope from the saddle strings and slapped it against his thigh.

Will rode the middle. He swept back and forth, pushing calves out of the borrow pit, back onto the road. He kept glancing back in Meg's direction, gauging how far behind the stragglers were.

John trotted ahead and rode past the Swans' corral gate and waited so he could turn the leaders in and prevent them from pushing past him and charging down the road, losing precious pounds in the process.

John's horse pawed as the cattle cautiously approached. A truck, Mather's, pulled alongside him. Mather lumbered out and stood in the borrow pit. Good. A second person to turn them.

The leaders turned in without a fuss and the rest of the herd filed behind them. The trucks were coming. They glittered in the sun: huge silver boxes on wheels. Dust billowed up behind them and though they were still a mile away, Meg could hear them.

The trucks pulled around to the chute and behind them came the brand inspector, the vet and the buyer in an emerald green Lincoln. She expected him to be well-dressed, but he was wearing coveralls like any regular rancher. He was a tall man with a lined face and he carried a buggy whip.

Mather puffed out his chest and strutted up to the buyer.

"Glad to see ya, Emmett. This is John and Will Swan. They're helping us out today. We're using their corrals and scales. And Robert Gonzales, the brand inspector. And my hired hand, Meg Braeburn. And..." he looked around for the vet, "there he is...Dr. Hom."

Dr. Hom, eager to be on his way, was already sifting through the calves.

The buyer also didn't seem inclined to chat. He shook hands, nodding curtly to each one, and then looked over their heads at the idling trucks.

After the introductions, the pace quickened. Groups of calves were herded into the chutes, then onto the scales. Mr. Gonzales leaned against the fence, eyeing each calf as it skitted past him. The vet signed his papers, certifying the cattle free from brucellosis, and left.

John operated the scales with Mather and the buyer peering over his shoulder. As group after group crossed the scales, Meg wondered, what were they weighing? The truck drivers turned the calves off the scales and pushed them up the chutes. Hooves clattered against the metal and truck doors slammed shut.

By 10:00 a.m., it was all over. Mather, John and the buyer came out of the scale house. Meg studied their faces, trying to read the outcome. The buyer was impassive. Mather looked smug, but he would look that way no matter how the cattle did. John's face didn't give anything away, either.

The trucks rolled past her, the trailers creaking under the weight. There they go—a whole year of her life. It had been a comfort, after all, to have them to care for.

Will and Meg, each leading horses, followed the others to the gate. Meg strained to hear what they were saying.

"You're all welcome at the house for coffee," said John,

"I believe Gwen's got some pie, doesn't she, Will?"

"No, thank you," said the buyer. "I'll be going with the calves."

"Where?" asked Meg.

"Hyannis, Nebraska."

"Long way," agreed John, "Sure you couldn't stay a minute?"

The buyer shook his head. He extended his hand to Mather. "Charles, best cattle you've ever raised."

Mather's chest puffed out again. "Appreciate it, Emmett. Hope to do business with you next year."

Meg got bold. "How much did they weigh?"

The three men turned to look at her. Did they think she was being impertinent because she was a ranch hand? Or a woman?

John smiled. "The steers weighed seven hundred, and the heifers, six-forty. That's the highest weights you've ever had, ain't it, Mather?"

"We've had one or two higher."

"When?"

"I'll be going," said the buyer. He strode off to his emerald car.

"The rest of you coming?" asked John.

Everyone nodded. "Will, lead my horse, will ya. I'll ride with Mather."

The sun felt warm on their backs. The snow had melted away. The fields were straw-colored. The hillsides were brown, and snow dusted the peaks.

Will turned to Meg. "You did a good job."

She smiled, remembering his earlier impressions of her. "Thanks."

"Will you be leaving?"

"Guess so. Mather hasn't asked me to stay."

"Where will you go?"

"Another ranch, I guess. Now that I've had this job, it should be easy to find a place."

"Let me know if you need a reference."

"You wouldn't have given me one when I first came."

"I was wrong."

Will did not say anything more. The day stretched out before her like the sky over her head—wide, empty.

John and Mather were still talking in Mather's truck when they rode into the barnyard.

"Park that hellcat horse of yours in the barn," John said to Meg, "and come on in."

"Why'd you say that?" asked Mather. "She gets on just fine with that horse."

"Yeah, if she works her to death before she gets on."

"I haven't heard anything about that. That horse was just fine the last time I rode her."

"When'd you say that was?"

A cool draft blowing through the barn smelled of hay, manure and old logs.

"Tie her in that stall over there," Will gestured, "and I'll get her some grain." He led the other two horses to the back of the barn.

"Can I help?" she called out.

"No, you go on."

Meg could hear John and Mather arguing when she walked in the kitchen door. The room smelled of fresh-baked pies.

Gwen was putting on her jacket. "Meg, I'm helping out at school today. There's coffee on the stove and pie in the dining room, OK? Help yourself. I'll see you later." And she was gone.

Meg poured herself a cup and sat down at the dining room table. She wasn't listening to Mather or John. She was watching how the sun streamed through the bay windows and spilled over the floor. There was time now to notice these things.

"Meg, stop gawking out the window and eat some pie." John shoved the pie dish in front of her.

"I'm not really hungry."

"Then pass it over," said Mather. "What are you planning on doing with your calves, John?"

"I haven't heard a price I like yet. If they're not gone in another month, we'll just go to the sale barn."

"You're taking your chances there."

"We'll be all right."

The men slurped their coffee.

"Think we'll have much of a winter?" asked Mather.

"I haven't heard anything that would tell me one way or another," John answered. "I know one thing. We haven't had enough snow in the mountains this fall and that spells trouble. If it don't pick up here shortly, there'll be no late water next spring."

Mather snorted. "Why do you care about that? You got the best rights on the river. You can shut everyone else off."

"I'll tell you the trouble with that. First, everyone hates you for it, second, you got to be worried all the time about who's stealing it from you."

Mather grinned, revealing the tobacco wadded in his lower lip. "I don't begrudge you anything, John. I'm a law-abiding citizen."

"Everyone is. Until they need water."

"Isn't Will coming?"

"He's probably gone on to check the weaning pen."

"Well, I guess it's time to be getting on." Mather stood up. "Thanks for the use of the scales."

"No problem."

"I don't think it would have been so easy to get you to lend them if it hadn't been for Meg."

"I won't lie to you. You're right about that. We're fond of Meg. We're glad she's here."

It pleased Meg that John had spoken up for her. She knew he meant it.

"She's the best hand you've ever had."

"I don't know about that."

"You will when she's gone and you gotta find someone else."

Meg followed Mather out the door. It was time to make her break with this man. She imagined the cattle trucks, with the sun glinting off them, as they rumbled toward Nebraska. She needed to be off, too.

Mather opened the pickup door and reached for his flask. He took a long swig. "Where will you go from here?" he asked as if he'd read her thoughts.

She looked east, toward where the trucks had gone. "On to another ranch, I guess."

"You like being a ranch hand?"

"Yeah. I do."

Mather took another swig. "Strange woman."

"No stranger than Gwen."

He spat. "She ain't strange, just a frazzled old Jezebel, that's all. I'll be getting more calves in a couple months."

"Black ballies again?"

"Yeah. I'll have to get someone to watch 'em."

"Maybe you can find a man this time."

"It's a lot of trouble. Paying for an ad. Getting all the phone calls. Weeding through the drunks. It'd be a helluva lot easier if you'd just stay."

The words surprised her. "All you've ever done is complain that I'm not a man."

"That is your worstest fault. 'Cause one of these days—and I don't know why it hasn't happened yet—you're going to hitch up with some old tom and leave me hanging. But the trouble with it is I could get some drunk s-o-b who'll do the same thing. When I look at it that way, I'd rather stick with you."

Did she want to stay? She looked past the cottonwoods, stark in the bright fall sunlight, to the haystacks with bales stacked sky high. Looking at it now, you'd never imagine the wind driving snow across these meadows, the cattle huddled and shivering against the stacks, the Swans in their coveralls with their heads bowed against the wind. And the wind rattling her mobile home night after night. The dishes in the cupboard rattling from the gusts. At this moment, it was hard to imagine it could be that way.

This country would as soon kill a person. Yet how lovely it was just now.

"You don't pay me enough."

"Hell. I pay you a fortune."

"I want seven hundred dollars and groceries. And I want to buy them myself."

"That's just taking advantage. That's pure ingratitude for the free roof over your head and a chest freezer full of beef."

"Mostly hamburger."

"It keeps you fat and snug all the same! Six seventy-five and a hundred dollar grocery allowance."

"That's one bag of groceries."

"If you're buying ice cream and frozen foods it is. If you're buying spuds and a few cans of corn, it'll last you and the boy just fine. Take it or leave it, Meg."

She held out her hand. Mather's meaty palm met hers. It wasn't noon and he already reeked of alcohol.

11

Icy air blended with party anticipation in the entryway of the Plains Hotel as the Swans arrived for the annual Stockmen's dinner dance. They'd brought Meg with them, and her date, Gene, from the Gem City Bakery. Will grumbled about Gene's long hair.

As she greeted friends she hadn't seen through the year, Gwen caught the excitement in Meg's face. She wasn't swept off her feet like Meg appeared to be. This was just another part of the ranch year, except it was less laborious and at least you were out of the wind. She should have looked forward to stashing her worries for a few hours to eat, drink and dance.

But coming here year after year, it seemed the short hours telescoped together between leaving the kids at the babysitter and bundling them back up into the car, with Will and John both too drunk to drive and five a.m. rocketing toward her like a locomotive.

Tomorrow, the sun wouldn't rise before eight and great plumes of snow and dust would blow across the range. This night would be like a scarf dropped in the wind.

It didn't help that Nick had come with them this year. Oh, he'd given them fair warning—he'd called several weeks ago. John had grown more and more excited while Will got more and more sulky. And why hadn't Nick's wife come? That woman hadn't accompanied him since their wedding. There were always excuses, the kids were the most common one, but it was strange, thought Gwen.

Her kids had been thrilled to see Uncle Nick and his truck bed loaded with gifts for them. John, his voice nearly trembling, had asked, "Can you stay for Christmas, son?" and he'd sagged like a kid who'd gotten coal in his stocking when the answer was no.

Already a knot of people were clustered around Nick. She felt Will's frown without seeing it. He took her elbow, steering her.

"C'mon. Let's sit down."

Long banquet tables traversed the dining room. Each table was decorated with evergreen boughs, sprigs of holly, candles and decorated Styrofoam balls. It was more color than they'd seen all together in one year. People carried in their drinks and the room smelled of pine, tobacco and liquor.

Meg glanced over the sea of faces. The only people that she knew were people from the school. She nodded at them. But the rest didn't seem any different than the ranchers she'd known at home. There were the same weary, rugged faces.

The man at the podium was bald, but the gray hair on the sides of his head hung to his shoulders, Ben Franklin style. He wore a dark purple shirt and his stomach spilled over his silver belt buckle. He leaned into the microphone.

"I know you came out on this dark freezing night to eat steak and not to listen to me, but there're just a few items of business we have tonight. For those of you who don't know me and those who'd like to forget, I'm Sean Haggerty, president of the Albany County Stockgrowers' Association."

There were whoops and applause.

"Before I get down to business, I'd like us all to take a moment and reflect on why we're here." He bowed his head and clasped his hands in front of him.

Everyone bowed their heads as well.

"Lord God, we thank you for another year. We thank you for letting us all be here together tonight in fellowship with one another to celebrate your season and the end to another year. We thank you, O Lord, for holding off on your blizzards so everyone could get here safe. We thank you for your bounty, the good calves we all had this year and the hay crop that'll see us through another winter. Lord, we'd all like cattle prices to be a little higher, but we know, O Lord, everything in its due time and season. For the delicious and plentiful food that we are about to eat, thank you. And help us to continue to seek your Holy Light through Our Lord Jesus Christ, Amen."

A rustling of "Amens" ran through the crowd. Then Mr. Haggerty announced some awards to ranchers who'd donated money, or animals, for 4-H and FFA. He thanked the Plains Hotel for hosting the event and the flower shop that had made the table decorations.

He concluded, "Now, in keeping with the season, we've done a little something to encourage romance. There's mistletoe hanging over one lucky couple here tonight, so I want you all to look up at the ceiling and figure out who it is and as soon as that lucky young fella gives that lucky young gal a kiss, this dinner/dance is officially started."

Meg looked up. The mistletoe was hanging over her table. She looked around nervously. She and Gene had only been dating a few weeks and she wasn't ready to kiss him in front of a bunch of strangers.

The man sitting across from them shouted, "Hey, Sean! We

can't tell who it's over, whether it's them," and he pointed to Gene and Meg, "or us!"

"Well, Leo, you don't have any objection to kissing your own wife, do you?"

Leo glanced around the crowd, feigning shyness.

"To get this show on the road, I suggest you both kiss your gals." The crowd roared approval.

Gene grinned at Meg, waiting for her to lean over, but she had difficulty looking back. She meant to look back at him because these people expected her to, but her eyes darted all around. She saw Will sitting at the next table down. He was leaning forward and watching her, wondering if she would go through with it. This was getting too uncomfortable, thought Meg. She closed her eyes, leaned in and kissed Gene to the Stockgrowers' applause.

Salads of iceberg lettuce, red cabbage, shredded carrots and ranch dressing were already on the table. Meg glanced around. Everyone seemed to have forgotten about her and had dug into their salads.

She looked across the table into Leo's face. "I'm sorry," he said, "I didn't catch your name."

"Meg Braeburn."

He extended his hand. "Leo Saunders. And this is my wife, Louey."

Leo was a wiry man with sandy-colored hair. He wasn't that much older than Meg. Louey was plump, with a pale, but cheerful face.

"Nice to meet you. I never heard of a Braeburn before. Where's your ranch?"

"I don't have one. I work for Charles Mather."

"Ain't he the one west of town along the river?"

Meg nodded.

"You cook or…" Leo was politely attempting to understand her role.

"I cook for myself and my son, but I don't get paid for that. I get paid for doing ranch work."

"Oh."

He'd been dissuaded by her tone, Meg realized. She hadn't meant to sound so harsh, but wasn't her face as reddened as his?

With a forkful of lettuce in his mouth, Leo glanced from Meg to Gene. He was wondering at the connection between the two of them and how they'd been invited here when neither one was a local rancher. But he clearly felt too whipped to ask any more questions.

Louey spoke up. "I know Mr. Mather's sister. Is he here tonight?"

"Not that I know of," answered Meg. To steer the conversation out of the pothole it had fallen into, she added, "We're guests of the Swans."

Louey's eyes widened with recognition. "Gwen Swan?"

"Yes."

"Where is she?"

Meg gestured toward the next table.

"I'll have to go talk to her later on. My cousin was one of her attendants."

"Attendants?"

"Frontier Days attendants. Don't you know? Gwen was Frontier Days' Queen back in 1962."

Meg glanced down the table. She caught Gwen's profile as people shifted in their chairs. She'd noticed Gwen's pictures but had never thought to ask. She couldn't reconcile the images—the young woman flying into the arena with sparkles glinting off her white gloves and the Gwen she knew. It surprised her that people knew a different Gwen.

The kitchen doors opened and the waiting staff hefted platters of steaks, baked potatoes and dinner rolls. Leo felt up to more questions.

"What's Mr. Mather got on that place now?"

"We just got in two hundred black bally calves. Where do you two live?"

"Up north, off of Tick Creek. Ever been there?"

The conversation between Meg and the Saunders smoothed out during supper. Gene glanced around the room, clearly bored. It had been a mistake to ask him along, Meg realized. Coffee was poured and the excitement lulled a little as people pushed their chairs back. For a few moments, there was a collective relief of not having to be anywhere, especially not having to be outdoors.

Gradually, chairs emptied. Louey stood up and said, "We'd better get upstairs."

"Is that where the dance is?" asked Meg.

"Yes. It's always in the ballroom."

The ballroom? Meg had never been in a ballroom.

It was huge, about the size of a gymnasium, with a wood floor. The band had set up at one end and round tables encircled the dance floor. In the middle was a giant Christmas tree glittering with lights. Long ropes of tinsel wound from top to bottom. The band was starting and a few couples dribbled out onto the dance floor. Meg stopped in the entryway, just to drink it all in.

She turned to her date. "Let's find Gwen and Will."

"That'd be all right."

The Swan family was squeezed around one table. Extra chairs were pulled up for Meg and Gene. Meg sat down, expecting all of them to share her excitement, but the faces around her seemed strangely glum.

John leaned over. "Do you want a drink?"

"Yes, please. Beer'd be good."

John nodded and went to the bar.

Meg turned to Gwen. "Thanks so much for inviting us. This is great."

"Glad you're enjoying it."

Nick looked at her for a long moment and then turned to Gwen. "Gwen, let's dance."

"All right."

He took her hand and they walked to the dance floor, just as the band struck up *Blue Moon of Kentucky*. He grabbed Gwen and swept her close. She laughed at his gesture and her skirt flipped and twirled. Out there on the dance floor, she looked ten years younger than she had an hour ago.

Gene turned to Will. "How's ranching been this year?"

Will shrugged. "Can't complain. Good fall. Not much snow. The calves weighed good. They didn't bring what we thought they would, but that's always the case. We have a ninety-five percent pregnancy rate, so we're set to dive into another year."

The men glanced away from one another, as if embarrassed by the lack of common ground between them. Will couldn't talk about bakeries. Meg doubted if he'd ever been in one.

Will turned to Meg, relieved that someone present spoke his language. "How are the new calves doing?"

"Good. They'll be ready to turn out of the corrals in a couple of days."

"Where are they from?"

"Mather says New Mexico."

"New Mexico? You'd better hope the weather holds off for another month."

"They're fine so far, and I would have expected them to get sick when they came off the truck."

Will looked at her skeptically. "You've got a long winter ahead of you, young lady."

John plopped her beer down in front of her. "Get some foam off of that and let's dance."

They stepped out on the dance floor. Meg felt awkward

because she was taller than John.

> *"Corrina, Corrina,*
> *Where you been so long?*
> *Haven't had no lovin'*
> *Since you've been gone."*

John spun her around until the awkwardness had drained away. She felt as giddy as if she'd been on a carnival ride. He spun her around one more time as the chorus wound down.

Applause broke from the dance floor.

"Thank you, Miss Meg."

Meg stepped back, noticing beads of sweat on John's forehead.

"Are you all right?"

"Just a little warm. That's all." He wiped his head with a handkerchief.

They worked their way through the crowd back to the table. Gwen and Nick had returned and everyone sipped their drinks to avoid speaking.

As the band struck up *Your Cheatin' Heart*, Will leapt to his feet. "C'mon, Gwen. This is a beat I can handle."

Meg watched them go. Will's arm circled his wife's waist and his feet shuffled into the beat. He looked over Gwen's shoulder at nothing in particular. It was impossible to tell if he was having a good time. They circled around the dance floor and soon Meg lost them in the crowd.

John turned to Nick. "Am I ever going to see those grandkids?"

"You're welcome up there any time. You know that."

"It's a long drive, son."

"I do it."

"Well, your brother can't manage that ranch alone. He needs me."

Nick looked hard at his father before slurping a long draught of beer. "You've got it exactly the way you wanted it."

"What's that 'sposed to mean?"

"Nothing."

"I never asked you to leave. You made your own decisions."

"Sure, I made my own decision. The same way a fella losing an arm wrestling match decides to say 'uncle.'"

John snapped, "Don't give me that. Nothing's stopping you from coming back."

"C'mon, Meg," said Nick. He lifted her from her seat to the strains of *Faded Love*.

When they squeezed onto the dance floor, he pulled her close, as if they were intimate. Meg felt threatened and pulled back. He whispered into her ear.

"What are you doing with that guy?"

"He's my date!"

"You know what I mean." Nick pulled her close again. "He's not for you."

"You don't know anything about me."

"Yes, I do. I know you're a woman driven to live out-of-doors. That's something he won't ever understand. How'd you end up with him anyway?"

"I met him at the bakery. Jim and I go there every Sunday morning for donuts."

"And what are you going to get out of this?"

"None of your damn business."

Nick laughed. "Meg, I've got you figured out better than you think."

"How's that?"

"I understand you. That's all."

The song was ending.

"Understand what?"

"Understand how you want to be accepted where you're not."

The singer's voice came over the microphone:

Black-eyed Suzie went to town, all she wore was a gingham gown.

Couples whooped as they recognized the song. They hustled onto the dance floor.

I may get drunk, I may get woozy, but I'm comin' home to Black-eyed Suzie.

Nick twirled her so hard it took her breath away.

Up red oak and down salt water, some old man's gonna lose his daughter.

The dance floor was so crowded they could hardly move. Still Nick found room to swing her round and round.

Hey, ho, Black-eyed Suzie! Hey, ho, Black-eyed Suzie!

Out of the corner of her eye, Meg saw Gwen dancing with John. He had his arm around her waist and they promenaded on the outermost edge of the floor. Gwen was looking into John's face. She was smiling and there was a sparkle in her eyes that Meg hadn't seen before.

As the crowd applauded, Nick held on to Meg. She felt uncomfortable under his stare. He was still appraising her. What for? She twisted her shoulders away from him.

"You're something," she heard him say.

"You're married."

"Doesn't mean I can't admire from afar."

Around midnight, people were leaving and only a smattering remained on the dance floor.

Will crossed the floor to Gwen. "Better be getting home," he said.

The sparkle Meg had seen in her earlier sputtered.

"Meg, are you going to follow us to the babysitter's?" Gwen asked.

"Sure."

Cold air swept into the lobby from the door. It didn't bother Meg. She was still warm from the food, the beer, the dancing. The cold seemed refreshing.

On the sidewalk, Meg and Gene dropped behind the Swans.

"Look up," said Meg.

Gene's gaze rotated heavenwards. "Wow."

Millions of stars, frozen hard, glittered down on them. The sky was so close it was sucking them into it. The wind wasn't of earth, but of the vast spaces beyond, a range of no horizons. If you stared up long enough, the ground beneath you gave way and you were drifting among those stars.

"Come home with me tonight," Meg said.

He looked down on her. "Are you sure?"

Nick's words filtered through her thoughts, but the longing for a warm body next to hers washed them away.

12

Meg climbed on the back of the feed truck to get a better view of the calves milling around her. Five cases of pneumonia in five days and she'd lost three. They'd dropped when she'd tried to bring them in to treat them.

"You've got to be careful," the vet said. "Don't stress them. Don't push them. Don't rope them. Don't set the dog on them."

"What if I don't try to get them in at all?"

"You're taking your chances there."

Mather stared at the carcasses grimly. "If you don't stop killing 'em, I'm going to take it out of your pay."

She fed another load. The wind flattened the calves' winter hair against their sides. She counted one, two, three runny noses. She fed her last line straight into the corrals and went to get Sissie. Hopefully, the sick ones would drift in.

Sissie was not wintering well. In spite of all the hay and grain Meg stuffed into her, she was nothing more than hide stretched over bone. It wasn't helping to have to ride her so hard every day.

She corralled three calves easily. By the time she'd found a fourth, the herd was breaking for water. She'd have to push this heifer back toward the feeding ground against the drift of the others. Should she leave her for tomorrow? She didn't want to take the chance.

Meg tried to turn the heifer, but she exploded and tore for the willows. Meg dropped back, followed her, found her in a knot of calves and began to push her out. The entire group thundered out of the willows back toward the meadow. The heifer trailed behind, then stumbled and collapsed.

Meg dismounted and knelt by the animal's head. The wind was roaring in her ears. The heifer struggled for her last breaths while her legs flailed in the air. With one last groan, she was gone and her tongue lolled from her mouth. Sissie pawed the snow. The other calves stared at them for a moment, then wandered back to clean up the last wisps of hay. Meg's feet were numb.

After Jim was in bed that night, she put on her overalls again and stepped into the yard. She leaned against the corral railing, watching the stars that had seemed so entrancing the night of the dinner dance.

The affair with Gene had fizzled. At first, the rediscovery of how exquisite it could be overtook her: the warm tingling of fingers on skin, the taste of another mouth, the crest of desire that swept her up as he entered her. But each morning, she had to confront how flat their partings seemed. When she'd dated Ronnie, every minute without him ached. She waited to feel that way about Gene, but it didn't come.

One night, he'd turned on the lamp. She thought he was beginning another round of lovemaking, but he sat up and said, "I don't think I'll be coming out anymore. I've got to be at work early and this is too far from town."

She knew what the excuse really meant. But if she didn't love him, then why did it still hurt?

Could she go home? She imagined sitting down with her father. "I'm managing a herd now," she heard herself say, "and I'm having trouble with pneumonia. What would you do?"

The differences that had pushed her out of the house would be forgotten. They'd be father and daughter, pals again.

She called Gwen at dawn the next morning. "Can Jim go to your house after school?"

"Sure. Are you going to town?"

"Yeah. I won't be back until late, though. It might be nine or ten."

"Date with Gene?"

"Uh-huh."

"Well, have fun."

Meg hung up the phone. She didn't know why she'd lied.

No wind that morning, but the temperature was twenty below. Just walking across the yard made her cheeks sting. She found the water holes frozen solid. She hefted the axe and ice chips sprayed around her. As the blade bit deeper, she grew alarmed because no water bubbled up out of the hole. Finally, there it was, a bare trickle on the river bed. She broke up the ice back to the bank so they'd have some footing. At least now she was warm.

The sun was high when she saddled up to ride through the calves, but it was too cold to stay on the horse. She walked through the feeding lines, leading Sissie. No runny noses or coughs today. Maybe the bug had been frozen out of them.

It was one o'clock when she got in her truck. She'd planned to leave Jasper behind, but as he sat by the steps watching her, she decided it was easier to cart him along than tussle with the guilt for the next three hours.

She opened the door. "All right." He was in over the gear shift and plopped on the floor before she could draw another breath.

Johnny Paycheck on her radio sounded puny over the whine of the tires. She wove up through the dun hills dusted with snow. Below, in the draws, the crowns of bleached aspen clawed at the air. Now evergreens rose up around her. Plumes of snow blew off the boughs, dropping slush in the road. It would be icy coming home.

She lost the radio station at Mountain Home. She let the static carry her past Fox Park and on to the "Welcome to Colorful Colorado" sign. She swooped down into North Park, a high corridor squeezed between two mountain ranges. The wind didn't clear the snow there, as it did down at Mather's. She looked off to the side and watched wind-driven crystals snake over the glaring surface.

She fiddled with the tuner and found another country station. In Walden, the snow was piled high on either side of the street in dirty mounds. She gulped some coffee out of a Styrofoam cup and went on to Rabbit Ears Pass. The music faded to static again. Once she crested the pass, the wind stopped. The snow was ocean deep here and even without stopping the truck, she sensed the stillness.

She nearly cried to see the Yampa valley expand below her again: the white meadows and the shaggy draft horses lining the fences, cows in the plowed trails settling down to chew their cuds for an afternoon. And no damned infernal wind.

She shut off the radio. She crawled through Steamboat Springs, glittery with its tourist traps, and then accelerated again in the open country, speeding through the quiet plains and the clusters of cottonwoods and willows along the spine of the river. She began to worry. Would anyone recognize her? The truck had Wyoming plates and she'd been gone so long that no one would think to look for her here. She could probably drive right through the middle of her town, unnoticed, like a ghost.

Why not spy on her hometown?

She swallowed hard as she passed her own turn-off and slowed at the thirty-five mile per hour sign. There was the Ranger Motel. The parking lot was empty and there was a tarp over the pool. Her mother used to have her birthday parties there. And Shaeffer's Drug Store. And Hungry Amy's Café where she'd devoured platters of French fries and onion rings. And Robinson's gas station, where she used to pull up and say, "Charge it to my dad." And just on the outskirts of town, before the speed limit changed back to sixty-five, there was a brand new Burger King. The parking lot was full.

She was a ghost. She saw the place that she remembered, yet Hayden was no longer that place. It had ripped loose from her and drifted on. She could stop in any of these places and maybe someone would recognize her, but no one would know her.

She turned around, drove back to the turn-off to her ranch and stopped. Her heart was pounding in her ears. She rolled the window down and the icy air whooshed over her face.

In front of her, the road ran straight across the pasture. Beyond, and out of sight among the cottonwoods, would be the log bridge that crossed the Yampa. Then the road would wind up the hillside to the house. She could see it from where she sat. The sun, in whose wake she had traveled all afternoon, dropped and gold light splashed over the hillsides and tree-tops and settled in the wisps of grass that poked out of the snow.

She was not who she used to be.

Jasper watched the doors, as if he expected them to get out. "No. We're going back home," she said. She shifted into reverse and backed out on the highway.

It was twilight now. Yard lights glittered across the valley. She left the window open and the frigid air sucked the sobs out of her.

13

The shed door banged open and Will blinked in the twilight. He'd been up since four a.m. with a heifer and now the mother was licking her new baby's head. He was surprised to see puffy snowflakes falling, hissing as they hit the ground. When he'd walked over from the house, the sky had been clear.

Cows lumbered to their feet and calves pressed to their sides, backs hunched against the cold, bracing their tiny frames against the day to come.

On his way back to the house, Will checked to see if Rory had opened the water hole. It was open, but the thawing and refreezing of the last few days had left a slick sheet of ice along the bank. The boy needed to open it all the way up.

Everyone was seated at breakfast when he came in.

"Rory, you'll need to go back out and chop all that ice

away from the bank."

"He just sat down," said Gwen.

"The water hole's open, Dad. They can get water."

"Cows can break through that ice, but a calf? A calf might slip and fall and not be able to get back up. Or a leg or two might break through and he might not be able to lift himself out."

John spoke up. "I'll take care of it."

"It's his responsibility."

"He'll miss the bus," said Gwen.

"Not if he leaves right now."

"But I won't get any breakfast."

"Where you're concerned, the cows come first. We're here because of them."

John started to open his mouth again, but Rory left the table.

"Hurry, or you'll be late," Gwen called after him.

They heard the door slam.

John turned to Will. "What's got into you?"

Will poured a mound of sugar on his oatmeal and reached for the milk. "It's exactly what you would have told me to do."

"Not on an empty stomach." Will glared back at him and John felt a prick of doubt. Had he done that? He riffled back through his memories for the one he could hold up and say, you're wrong, that wasn't me. But it was all a blur now, really. He recollected a pretty wife and two little boys, but how they had lived day by day, he didn't remember. The calves had been branded, the fields irrigated, the hay put up, the calves sold. Those things he remembered clearly. Drought years, flood years, bad market years, killer blizzards, he remembered all those, but what his boys had said and done as children, or what kind of a father he'd been… no, he didn't recollect.

"It's getting late," said Gwen. "I'm going to have to take McKenna to the bus."

"I'll take Rory to school," John said.

Rory had put on his coveralls and walked to the water hole. Snowflakes blew into his face and melted on his nose and lips. Just a day or two more and he wouldn't have to worry about ice. Just a couple of weeks more and there would be a mat of green as far as the eye could see.

He had cleared several yards up the bank and was working his way down toward the water hole when he saw John striding toward him. He swung the ax over his shoulder and smashed it down. Chunks of ice split and spun in the river's eddy.

"Good job," said John. "No calf'll get into trouble here."

Rory didn't look up, but continued to bust the ice. "I don't care about them."

"You don't care about them? Why not?"

Rory shrugged, "They're just stupid animals."

"You're mad at your dad."

"He cares more about them than me."

"That's not true. He just can't say the right words to you, is all."

"Then why did he send me out here without anything to eat?"

"'Cause he's been up all night with a heifer and he's not thinking, Rory. While you were sound asleep under your cuddly quilt, he was out in the shed hour after hour. And maybe he won't get to sleep tonight either. It wears a man down. It wears him down. And he forgets to think about those he truly loves."

"I don't ever want to be a rancher when I grow up."

"Fine. You don't have to be. It's a lousy job."

"I want to be a jockey."

"You know how they start out, don't you?"

"No."

"They got to muck out stalls for years just to earn the chance to ride. Are you going to do that?"

Rory scrambled up the bank. "Yeah, Grandpa."

"Well, you still need to go to school first, so let's go."

They got in John's truck. John pulled out a package of sugared donuts from the glove box.

"Here. You can eat the whole thing."

"Are you sure, Grandpa?"

"You worked harder than I did this morning. You deserve it."

By the time they'd pulled into the schoolyard, the donuts were gone.

"I love you, Grandpa," Rory said as he slid off the seat.

"Me, too. I'll see you at supper."

John watched Rory in his rear view mirror. He'd be OK. By tonight, he'd forget all about this.

The snow was several inches deep and falling fast. After he fed the bulls, he'd sneak over and see how old Meg was doing. Gwen said her fling with the baker had ended and maybe that had left her a little down because she hadn't been over at all. Last thing that girl needed was to shut herself up. Last thing her boy needed, too.

When he drove into her yard, she was just stepping on her old black nag to check calves. She looked like the Michelin tire blimp with all the clothing she wore. How the hell could she reach her leg up to the stirrup with all that on?

He rolled down his window. "Howdy, stranger."

A big smile spread under her owl-shaped glasses. "Where've you been?"

"Where've you been? We haven't seen you in ages!"

"It's just been a couple months. I've been busy, that's all."

"Busy doing what?"

"The calves all got pneumonia and I had a helluva time

getting it stopped."

"Did you lose any?"

"A dozen." It had beaten her pride down, he could tell.

"Baxter Black says you can't kill 'em all. Why didn't you call for help?"

She stood there for a moment while the snow blew in her face.

"There wasn't anything that anyone could have done."

"I could have dragged off some carcasses for you."

Meg smiled grimly. "I did that myself."

"Do you have any coffee in that house?"

"Instant."

"Why don't we have a cup or two?"

"I can't, John. I've got to look at these calves. Mather's coming out today."

"In this weather?"

"That's what he said at five this morning."

"You got five or ten minutes. Let's go inside."

He knew she was only relenting for his sake.

"Five minutes is all I got."

Meg piled her outer clothing on a chair, but kept her overshoes on. Muddy snow dripped on the floor. She had her back turned toward him as she boiled the water. There was something girlish about the way her two braids hung straight down her back. She was just a girl, he thought.

"Milk? Sugar?"

"Just black," he said as he slid into a chair.

She sat down next to him. Her chapped hands encircled her mug, as if she was warming them.

"How's calving?"

"Almost all of the heifers have calved. Of the cows, we've got about fifty on the ground. We haven't lost any so far. 'Course, that'll all change after today."

"I hope I'm done with losses."

"How did Mather take it?"

"He threatened to cut my pay for every one I lost, but I said I'd quit, so he didn't. I know it wasn't my fault. I didn't buy the cattle."

"But you took it like it was your fault."

Meg eyed him over the top of her mug. "All they've got is me."

"There'd have been a lot more of them with four legs in the air without you." He paused to slurp his coffee. "Gwen says the baker won't be out anymore."

Meg set her mug down.

"Did you think we wouldn't have any use for you after he was gone?"

"No."

"Well, I couldn't picture you as a baker's wife, anyway." He paused for a moment and they listened to the snow hitting the roof. "You know, my boys think I was a horrible father."

Meg looked startled. "Why do they think that?"

"Damned if I know. I think they turned out pretty good. But children are the orneriest critics. They peck at you over things they don't know anything about."

She shifted in her chair and he knew he had her attention.

"Twenty years from now, if we plunk Jim down right here—a young man just getting started in his life—how'll he rate you? What will he say about you hiding him in this shack away from his grandparents?"

She stiffened.

"Before you put on that holier-than-thou-pout, just hear me out. Would you be the kind of woman you are, the kind of woman who could go out in this every day and care about those animals that aren't yours, if you hadn't grown up with your people? You blame them for throwing you out, but everything they done for you got you to where you could get up and leave and stay gone. Think about what you had and ask yourself why shouldn't he have the same."

"He has me."

"And you can give him everything he needs." He could see it—oh, he'd hit a nerve all right.

"I've done it up till now."

"You're a lot like Will, Meg."

"What do you mean?"

"Neither one of you can put your boys ahead of your conceit."

"I've got to go." She stood up abruptly.

He reached over and grabbed her wrist. "Don't be sore at me. I don't have to see that boy every day to know how he needs a family."

"What do you want me to do?"

"Call your folks up and tell 'em that you need them. That your boy needs them."

Meg collected the mugs. "I tried. It didn't work."

His windshield was covered with snow. He started the truck, then stepped back out to brush it off. The wind was up now. He realized that he'd better get back and help Will. But he waited and watched as Meg mounted her horse and rode away. In an instant, the blizzard swallowed her.

John drove over to the calving shed. Inside, the overhead light was on, but it was too dim and all he could make out was shifting cow shapes.

"Will?"

"Here," came from the stanchion.

"Are you pulling one?"

"No. Trying to get one to suck."

The heifer's head was locked in the stanchion. Will had tied one hind foot back to the rail. He was kneeling at the heifer's side, squeezing the calf's jaw open with one hand and squirting milk into its mouth with the other. The heifer's tail swished furiously.

"It's getting on close to lunch."

"I don't know that that will mean much around here. I haven't been out of this shed except to feed and Gwen's still riding."

"Did she find anything?"

"She brought in some heavies. We turned ten pair out. She's doctored two for bloat. She brought in that pair down there..." Will gestured to one of the pens, "She says that one's not sucking. She said she found a dead calf, one of the first ones born, out by a stack. And she's still out there."

"What happened to the dead one?"

"She says she doesn't know."

"God, I hate that."

"I'd hate it, too, if I had a minute to think about it."

"Maybe I'd better take him for an autopsy."

"It was prob'ly bloat."

"It could have been blackleg."

"Dad, I shouldn't have to tell you not to go to town today."

"By tomorrow, it'll be too late."

"There's enough going on here today. I can't go out looking for you, too."

"You won't have to, son. I've been driving these roads since before you were born."

Will let go of the calf and stood up. "I'm asking you not to."

"I'll be fine. Hey, look, you just worked yourself out of a job." The calf was sucking on its own.

"One less job."

John drove out to the meadow. The haze had lifted and he could see a good hundred yards ahead. This wasn't any killer storm. He'd be fine.

It was easy to spot the calf because the mother was still there. She nosed it as he approached.

"I'm afraid he's not coming back, Momma."

The calf was big, a good hundred pounds. To lose one like this was a punch in the gut. He picked it up and loaded it in the truck. The cow bawled, more like screaming, really. He could hear her bawling all the way back to the barn.

The drive to town wasn't too bad. The snow had lightened to a fine spray. And the plows had been through. By the time he'd be returning, the sun would be out and it would be a fine afternoon.

He dropped the calf off at the Animal Science lab and went to Katy's to grab a burger. It was already two p.m. The place was empty except for a bored waitress and the cook.

"Burger and fries," said John as he sat down.

"Coffee?" said the waitress.

"You bet," said John and winked at her. She brightened right up and hustled to the coffee machine. The cup she set in front of him was steaming hot. He took a sip and nodded up at her in gratitude.

"This place is kind of quiet today."

"The lunch crowd is already gone." She looked out the window and John pitied her. He couldn't have tolerated being penned in this gloomy place day after day, waiting for people to come and go, waiting to go home, fix supper, watch TV, go to bed. If you couldn't have the wind and sun in your face and the next day's weather to worry about, then you were living like a zombie. As he looked up in her doughy face, he wondered how this could be life at all.

They chatted while he ate his burger and fries. Turned out she was married to one of the Maddocks. They had a ranch at Laramie Peak, but her husband, Glade, worked at the auto parts store.

"What about you?" she asked. "What kind of family have you got?"

"Well, I got one son and daughter-in-law at the ranch and two grandkids."

"That's nice."

"And my other son manages a ranch around Casper. He's

married and has two kids."

"How often do you see them?"

"Not often. But after calving, I think I'll go up there and surprise them."

"What about your wife? Will she go with you?"

"No. She's been dead almost a dozen years now."

"I'm sorry."

"Ain't nothin' to be sorry about. With how sick and miserable she was at the end, she lived several months too long."

The woman bridled like a green horse smelling a dead cow. It amazed him how town people thought you should want to keep your loved one with you, no matter how much they were suffering. What Anna went through, no horse or cow of his had ever endured.

He hadn't had one day of contentment since Anna had gone. But he wasn't going to share that with this biddy. Better for her to chew on her indignation.

She got friendly again when she eyed the fat tip he'd left her. She thought that she'd received it for her conversation. But it was just pity, really.

Back on the highway, the storm had returned. The snow blew so hard that he could only see a reflector or two ahead of him. That's all right. As long as he could see from one reflector to the other, he'd stay on the road just fine.

The radio was playing *I'm Walkin' the Floor Over You*, and what drifted into his head was a vision of dancing with Anna, not the woman he'd lived with for forty years, but the young girl from the photograph. Every time she twirled around, her eyes were back on him.

Out of the haze, a vehicle drove straight toward him.

He swerved to the right, missed the reflector pole and dove into the borrow pit.

The truck landed with a thud. John gripped the steering

wheel. His heart was racing. He took a deep breath. Who was that? Whoever the hell it was he had to be some drunk son-of-a-bitch to run him off the road and leave him there.

It was Mather. He thought about the shape of the truck, the shape of the driver. It was Mather.

He sat still until his heart slowed down. Then he shifted into first and tried to drive forward. The tires spun. There was soft mud underneath the snow.

He got out of the truck. The wind nearly knocked him flat. He struggled through the snow to lock the wheel hubs into four-wheel drive.

By the time he got behind the wheel again, he was out of breath and his face was sweaty. He waited until he could breathe then gave it another try. And spun. He rocked the truck, backwards, forwards, backwards, forwards. He was just digging in deeper.

He looked up the slope to the road. It was so steep that no one would see him. He got out and tried to climb it. He slipped, dropped to his knees and crawled to the top.

He looked in both directions. There was no way to tell if anyone was coming or not. All he could hear was the wind. And he couldn't see anything. If he kept standing there, he'd freeze to death.

There wasn't anything else to do but try and wait in the truck. He turned up the radio. He wouldn't be able to run the engine too long, or he'd die of carbon monoxide poisoning. He'd have to shut it off. He felt hot again. He slumped against the door frame. It felt cool on his forehead. He closed his eyes and tried to shut out the wind.

Summertime soon. Green grass. Calves basking in the sun.

14

The pallbearers, all dressed in Western suits, advanced toward the grave while Meg willed them to turn back. Ranching families she'd seen at the Stockgrowers' dinner dance stood quietly now, their reddened faces expressionless. All that remained of the blizzard were patches of snow, puddly around the edges. They'd be gone by noon. The wind was still sharp, but Meg could hear the blackbirds trilling miles away. John would be out riding on a day like today, with his jacket open and his head tipped back to take in the sun. How could he be gone, now that the world was healed of winter?

She squeezed Jim's hand and their eyes met. It startled her how intensely blue his eyes were, just like his father's. No tears, but his face was pale. In the glance they exchanged, they asked one another, are you all right?

After Gwen had called, she'd sat down next to him at the kitchen table.

"Jim."

He heard the gravity in her voice and his pencil stopped.

"John's dead."

"How?"

"He ran off the highway coming back from town. He tried to get out, but he had a heart attack and died."

"We'll never see him again."

"We won't see him again here."

"Will we see him in heaven?"

Meg wiped tears away with the back of her hand. "I don't know."

"Is there a heaven, Mom?"

"There should be."

"He would be there, if there is one."

Mather was among the mourners. His wife stood next to him, shriveled as a winter leaf. Five kids pressed around them. Mather angled to the side of the crowd to spit his tobacco.

Her last conversation with John poured over her like ice water. She'd been so sure that he did not understand. Now that she would never see him again in this lifetime, she wondered if it was her own understanding that had fallen short.

The preacher shut his book and no one stirred until he turned to the family. But as couples started toward their cars, a shriek stopped them.

It was Rory. The child had dropped to his knees, screaming. A murmur rose among the gathering. Some ignored him and walked away. Some approached the Swans. Gwen bent and tried to lift her son off the ground, but he leaned against her arm, pulling her down with him. Will looked at his son and grimaced.

Nick squatted next to the boy. He stroked his head as he cried, the sobs wracking the seamless sleep of the dead.

"More pie, Nick?"

"Yes, ma'am. I'll have another piece."

Gwen served him another slice of blueberry pie and stood up. "I'm going to check on the children."

The two men sat in silence. Will reached for a toothpick and leaned back in his chair. He looked at a spot over Nick's head. He could half-way see Nick's jaw work as if words were tumbling over themselves, ready to spill out, but instead, he sunk a fork into his pie.

He cleaned up the plate, licked the fork and reached for his coffee. After he swallowed, the words stampeded from his mouth, as Will had expected they would.

"I know what Dad wanted. He wanted us to work this place together."

Will's eyes dropped to Nick's face. "Think so?"

"He was hoping that if he split everything between us like he did, you'd see you couldn't do it alone. We'd have to work together."

"Why would he want that when we've never worked together in our lives?"

"Maybe now is the time to start."

"You haven't been here in over fifteen years."

"That's not my fault."

"What do you mean it's not your fault? You had one fight with him and you've been pouting over it for fifteen years. You think he treated me any different than he treated you? As far as he was concerned, I could never do anything right. The difference is I stuck it out."

Nick shook his head. "No, it was different for me. Because both of you were against me. He'd criticize and you'd gloat."

"The point is you never even tried to come back. Never sat down with either one of us and told us that was what you wanted. You

made your own life somewhere else. Fine. But now you want to go
back to the beginning when you've put nothing in here for the last
fifteen years. After all this time, I think my family and I are entitled
to live here in peace."

"What are you going to do, then?"

"I'll have to buy you out."

"Do you know what the place is worth?"

"We'll have to get it appraised."

"How are you going to come up with that kind of money, Will?"

Will's jaw clenched. "I was hoping I could pay you off
over time."

Nick snorted. "With interest?"

"I was hoping you'd cut me some slack on that."

"Why the hell should I?"

"Look, you can take your half of the cattle now. I'll let you
pick out whatever you want."

"Yeah? And how are you going to make an income and
pay me with what's left?"

"We'll manage."

"How?"

"Gwen's going to get a job in town."

"And you're going to run the place alone?"

"I can hire help if I need it."

"What will you pay them with? Eggs? Hay? Is this all
easier than just giving me a chance?"

"Maybe not. But at least when I'm gone, the ranch goes
to Rory and McKenna. And they don't have to worry about splitting
it with their cousins."

"All right. You can buy me out. But we both have to agree on
the appraiser."

"Fine."

"And I want Dad's house."

Will started to object, but then reconsidered and said, "All right. Are you going to move in?"

"No. I'll just use it when I'm down here."

"That'd be fine."

"It oughta be fine. The place is half mine."

As Gwen and Meg hesitated at John's front door, McKenna peered through the windows.

"Are there ghosts in there, Mom?"

"No, it's just an empty house, that's all."

"Do you want me to open the door?" asked Meg.

"No. I'm all right."

The living room looked as if John had left only minutes ago. Dust motes rode the sunbeams streaming through the windows and the light slanted across Anna's face—happy and young, forever.

Gwen handed McKenna a carton. "Honey, can you go to the bedroom and start putting clothes in here?"

McKenna nodded and walked down the short hall to the bedroom.

Meg hauled in a trash can. She threw away newspapers, magazines, donut boxes. One drawer in the china cabinet was full of old gloves, holes in every one of them. Anna smiled down over the dreary scene while the dust whirled about her face.

Gwen gestured toward the picture. "She ran off on him one time, you know."

Meg looked up from a bookshelf of yellowed westerns. "She did?"

"She took the boys and ran off with a ranch hand one year."

"Why?"

"I never talked to her about it, but people say he told her he had a rich family in California and that they'd live in a house on the beach. John fired him one day when he got suspicious and she took the boys and followed him out there. Turned out he was already married."

"How old were the boys?"

"Young. Not school age. If they remember it, they don't speak of it."

"Will's never mentioned it?"

"No. And I've never asked him. It was a huge embarrassment for the family."

"How did she and John get back together again?"

"She just came back. No one knows what she said or he said or how they worked it out. They just went on."

"He loved her so much."

"Why wouldn't he have? She came back. Ran his household. Raised his children. Helped with the ranch."

Meg stared at the portrait. "You're not the first woman in history," Gwen said, "to have made a mistake."

"But you'd never do it."

"No. But I'll make different mistakes. When are you going to start dating again?"

Meg shrugged. "Don't know."

When McKenna opened the bedroom door, odors of moth balls, musty blankets and cow hair swept over her. She opened the closet. Men's clothes hung on one side, women's on the other, with a row of shelves between them. She pulled a cigar box from a dusty shelf. Inside were dozens of buttons, all different colors and sizes. She sifted through them: brass buttons, horse-head buttons, buttons made from coins, leather buttons. She wondered if her mother would let her keep them.

Next came a shoebox stuffed with photographs. The top one was of her grandpa, but he was much younger, Dad's age maybe. Trees in full leaf filled the background. Summertime. Grandpa stood in the hayfield, wearing a straw cowboy hat. He was laughing at something.

What was so funny, Grandpa? Outside, McKenna could hear the muffled voices of Meg and her mother as they opened up drawers and cabinets.

The next day, McKenna sat down on her bedroom floor and spread the buttons out. She sorted them by size and shape. The horse-head buttons were special. Her mother said she'd sew them on a shirt for her. She was encircled by neat piles of buttons when Rory burst in the room.

"What are you doing?"

"Nothing."

"What are those?"

"Buttons."

"Where did you get them from?"

"Grandpa's house."

Rory's face darkened. He was not allowed in his grandpa's old house.

"Let me have some."

"No. Mom gave them to me."

Rory sat down, picked a few buttons and cupped them in his hand.

McKenna screamed, "Daaaadyyy! Rory's taking my buttons!"

Rory jumped up and kicked the buttons across the room.

McKenna wailed louder. "Daaaadyyy!"

Will came in the room. "Look what he did, Daddy!"

Will grabbed his son by the arm, dragged him through the living room, kitchen and porch and shoved him out the door. The door slammed behind him.

Now Rory screamed. He screamed as loud as his lungs would allow. But when he stopped, there was no one to answer him. It was late in the afternoon. A tart breeze rattled the willow branches and Rory, in only a t-shirt, shivered. Beyond the wind, the river babbled to itself, as it did always and forever, no matter what happened. Why did it keep on when his grandpa was gone?

Rory wiped the tears off his face and ran along the riverbank toward his grandfather's house. The lights were on and the door was open. He leaped up the steps, ready to scream all over again.

Except the house was empty. The furniture and cowhide rugs were all gone. The dining room table was bare. Even the smell of his grandfather was gone.

He ran into the kitchen. Gwen stood on a chair, scrubbing out cupboards. All around her were cartons, packed and closed.

"Mommy!" he cried.

Gwen went to hug him. "Oh, Rory!" When he pushed away from her, he saw that she was crying.

"I'm sorry I can't make this any better for you, son, but look what I found." She reached in her pocket and pulled out a Western wallet tooled with roses. "I'm sure Grandpa would have wanted you to have this."

Rory turned it over in his hands, then threw it as hard as he could against the cupboard and watched it fall into the sink.

"I hate it!" he cried.

15

Jim glanced over his shoulder as the horse beneath him tore over the prairie. Jasper had fallen behind, though he was running as fast as he could. Over the hoof beats, Jim heard his yelps of frustration.

It had been Rory's idea to race. The Swans and Braeburns had spread out over the pasture to move cows and calves to the mountains. Will and Gwen rode to one corner, Meg rode up the middle and the children had been sent to the other corner.

After they were out of the adults' sight, Rory shouted, "First to the fence line wins," and with a whoop, he took his reins and smacked his fat bay.

McKenna was falling behind. Jim sensed that she was pulling her horse in. She didn't want to race. Jim leaned over his horse's neck jockey-style. The sensation of rocketing through space overtook him and he rode it like a wave, intent on catching Rory.

Something caught his eye and he looked over his shoulder. Two baby antelope raced alongside him. Where had they come from? They matched him stride for stride, their brown eyes wide open. This is what it felt like to be wild!

Below him the horse's legs reached for the next expanse of earth and then the next. They were closing in on the fence line. Rory abruptly turned aside and Jim's horse dropped his pace. He looked to the side again and the antelope were gone. McKenna was closing behind them.

"I won!" yelled Rory.

Jim caught his breath. Was it already over? It felt as if it should go on forever.

McKenna snapped, "I didn't want to race, Rory!"

"So… you didn't have to."

"But you made Gopher run so then Babe wanted to run, too."

"Why didn't you stop her?"

"I couldn't!"

"Oh, go home, sissy!"

"Did you see the baby antelope?"

Rory and McKenna stared at him. "What baby antelope?"

"They were right beside me and now they're gone."

"Why didn't you stop us? I could have roped them!" said Rory.

"You don't know how to rope anything," said McKenna.

Jim looked around once more, but all he saw was Jasper panting hard. Beyond Jasper, the prairie was speckled with olive sage and the butter yellows, lavenders and mauves of tiny wildflowers.

Meg and Sissie jogged up the center of the pasture. Meg was annoyed with herself for not making Jim ride with her. She didn't like the children to ride alone. But Will had sent Rory and McKenna off by themselves and Jim said he wanted to go with them. She started to say no, but as she did, she glanced at Will. She read his judgment in the lines on his face—Jim was a momma's boy. She had yielded. Why should his approval matter after all these years? She was managing just fine without anyone's approval. She didn't need anyone else.

Well, that was a lie. The days and nights piled on top of one another and what ached was the longing to share. Sharing—she'd never had that. It seemed that she never would.

At the school programs and potluck suppers, she felt even more isolated than she did on the ranch. Husbands and wives had each other for props, regardless of how they felt about one another. She could talk about children with the wives, but she hadn't tried the latest recipes, or picked up yarn to knit Christmas sweaters.

And the men regarded her as they would a jackalope. "You managing that place on your own?" they'd say, and step back, amused.

Gwen, if she was in hearing, always came to her rescue. "Meg Braeburn does a fine job out there," she would say. "Mather's never had cattle that looked so good."

There was no draw in moving on. Jim had friends and was making good grades. They had the Swans if they needed anything. Now that Gwen was working in town, Meg helped them out for extra money. After each day, Will would stuff a wad of bills into her hand and she'd say, "This is too much."

He would take the money back without a word and tuck it in her coat pocket.

She missed John. She thought of him hanging out of the pickup window on the day they'd first met. She imagined him sitting at her table with his hands around his mug and his Scotch cap pushed back on his head. Funny, the one man she'd felt the closest to was dead.

As Gwen and Will rode along the fence line, she turned to him. "Are you sure that was a good idea, letting the children ride off together?"

She wasn't asking a question, Will thought, she was making a statement.

"Rory's been running hay machinery for the last two years! Are you saying they can't ride to the corner of the pasture and come back with a few cows and calves?"

"I'm saying it would have been just as easy to send one of us with them."

"Between you and Meg, those kids are never going to do anything for themselves."

"No one was doing anything for them, Will. It just would have been sensible for an adult to have ridden with them. That's all."

How could the day be turning sour when it was just beginning? Gwen used to love to ride when she worked at home, even when John was along, critiquing everyone's cattlemanship. Now that she worked in town, ranch work had become just another chore.

She didn't miss John. But his absence hadn't improved her family life the way she hoped that it would. She and Will talked even less than they had before. When the men used to come in at lunchtime, she'd had a finger on the pulse of the ranch. Now, Will summed up the day in five minutes at supper and she felt shut out.

Wordlessly, Will and Gwen split up to gather separate groups of cattle. Will watched as she loped off. Her curls bounced underneath her cap. She still looked like a rodeo queen. That's what John would say if he were here: "By God, she still rides like there's a crowd watching."

Will lost his hair after John died. It could be age—or heredity—but he believed it was because the burden of the place now fell on him. All his adult life, he'd resented his father's domination, but once he was laid to rest, there was no one to blame. The decisions: whether to put out money for fertilizer, how much of the excess hay to sell, whether to sell calves in October, or see if the market climbed a little higher in January, whether to put money back into the place, or pay down interest to Nick—he owned all this now.

Before, he'd wait for John to say: "I believe we'll keep over another twenty heifer calves this fall."

"We don't have enough hay."

John would nod, stare out the window. "It'll be all right. It's not going to be a bad winter."

And when there wasn't enough hay, cattle and men would all suffer together. Will wouldn't say anything, but he'd mutter to himself, at the second May blizzard with nothing to feed, "Damn fool got us into this."

Now he was the damn fool.

He'd tried talking to his dad. No one answered. The shop and barn were cavernous and silent. The river looped the same refrain.

For six months after John's death, Will had cursed his father for leaving the ranch the way he had. Or he'd curse his brother's existence. Why couldn't Nick just have walked away from it and left them all in peace? Well, who would walk away from that kind of money? But wouldn't somebody do it if it was for the good of their family? Would he have done it had he been in Nick's place? Hell, no.

During that time, Nick hadn't stopped at the house. On weekends, Will would see his truck going in and out of the driveway to their parents' old house and he'd curse the son-of-a-bitch who must not have to work all that hard if he was down here hanging around.

The year had passed. The day of John's death came and went just like any other day, with a fresh crop of calves to tend to, calves who'd never see the old man. The next day, a Saturday, Will had had errands in town. He pulled onto the highway and looked over the plains. They were that funny color: not winter-bleached, not green, but smudgy like pea soup.

He glanced in his rearview mirror—Nick was behind him. He focused on the road again—on the white lines whirring past. Suddenly, Nick pulled alongside him, gesturing for him to pull over. Will sped up. Nick sped up, still gesturing for Will to pull over. Will stomped on the gas pedal. Nick caught up. They were barreling down the highway at eighty miles an hour. If Will didn't pull over, someone was going to get killed.

He pulled over. Nick slowed down and parked behind him. As Will rolled down his window, he watched Nick get out and walk to the driver's door. A blast of wind smacked his face and Nick said, "When does this stop?"

"What?"

"This."

Will gawked at him for a moment.

"He was my dad, too."

"Yeah, I know."

Neither of them said anything while the wind continued to howl and suck the heat out of the cab.

"I got to go to town," Will said, finally.

"Me, too. Gwen's invited me to supper."

"See you then."

Nick got back in his truck and they both pulled away and went on. It wasn't his brother's fault, after all.

Will snapped out of his thoughts and booted his horse into a jog. Where were all the cattle?

Most of them were on the children's side. But despite Jasper's best efforts, the drive was not starting well. Rory had pushed the cows too hard, separating them from their calves. The calves bawled and turned, sprinting in all directions. McKenna and Jim tore after them, but there were too many to chase down.

Rory realized he was all alone and turned to see what had happened. "Why didn't they keep 'em pushed up?" he grumbled.

He picked up his reins and smacked the horse, charging after one of the runaway calves. It bounced over the prairie like an antelope, leaving little puffs of dust where its hooves hit the ground. The calf was determined to outrun him. Even though he pushed right up next to it, it wouldn't turn back. He reached for the strap holding his rope. If he could rope this calf, Will would be proud of him. But by the time he'd undone the strap, they'd reached the fence. The calf sailed through the barbed wire and Rory pulled up.

"Shit," he said as the calf flew on eastwards. He trotted down the fence line, looking for the gate. Every few moments, he glanced anxiously over his shoulder. The distance between them widened. If he lost it, what would he say to his father?

He found the barbed wire gate shut tight. He dismounted and reached overhead for the top loop of wire over the gate post. No good. The loop bit so deeply into the wood that it had left a groove. He leaned hard against the post with his left shoulder, wrapped his arm around the fence post and pulled. He looked up at the loop. It had loosened. He reached up with his right hand to push it off, but then his tension against the gate post eased and the loop sunk back into the wood. He tried again and again. With every moment, he imagined his calf running farther away. It was probably on the highway to Laramie by now.

He had to open the gate. He took a deep breath and hugged the post until his shoulder ached. He reached up with his right hand and inched the loop up the post. Then he had to stop and rest. He tried again, inching the loop up, up until it was just on the lip. Then he had to rest again. He braced the post against his sore shoulder and hugged it one more time. He jabbed upwards with his right hand. The loop slipped off and the gate crumpled at his feet.

He galloped over a slope and there was the calf below him, a brown and white speck in an ocean of prairie grass. He pulled back on his reins. If he chased it, it would start running again and he might never catch it. Better to move up on it slowly and then try with his rope.

He jogged down the hill. The calf slowed to a walk, doggedly headed in a direction where it would never find its mother. Rory readied his loop and twirled it over his head. The calf heard him and began to trot. Rory kicked his bay and trotted, too, twirling the loop faster and faster. The horse sidled near the calf and Rory flicked the loop. But he didn't pull up fast enough and the calf skipped through it.

Rory stopped and coiled the rope. It was late and he was getting hot. His father would kill him if he didn't get back with this calf. He trotted until he was next to the calf again. It was almost under the horse's belly. Rory kicked loose from his stirrups, slid off the saddle and tackled the calf to the ground.

He slipped his rope over its neck and front shoulder. He did it! Grandpa would have said, "Son, it don't have to be pretty. It just has to work."

He looked back uphill. How far was he from the gate? If he had to lead this calf, it might as well be a hundred miles. And once he got back through the gate, how would he find the rest of the herd. The calf was too tired now to do anything but walk. And why hadn't anyone come to look for him? He sat next to the calf and they both gazed out at the emptiness around them.

He jumped up with relief when he saw Sissie trotting over the hill. "Meg! Meg!" he called and waved his arms.

Sissie eased into a lope and they were nearly on top of him before they stopped.

Meg jumped off. "Are you all right?"

"Yeah."

"What happened?"

"This calf got away and went through the fence. I chased him and caught him."

"Good job."

He swelled at her praise, but didn't know how to thank her. "Where is everybody?"

"They're all waiting for us at the gate to the road. But this calf's in no shape to go to the mountains today."

"What do we do?"

Meg smiled. "You asking me for help? That's a first."

"There's no one else here."

Meg took off her cap and wiped the sweat from her forehead. Like his dad, her forehead was white while her cheeks and neck were leather red.

"I'll take the calf and you go on and join your dad."

"How will you catch up?"

"I won't. You'll have to go on without me. I'll take the calf home and your dad can trailer him up tomorrow."

Rory's lip gaped for a moment. His parents liked Meg. They wouldn't want him to leave her behind.

"Go on. Your dad's waiting. Those cows aren't going to stand by that gate too much longer."

He galloped through the gate that had given him so much trouble and then over the pastures, empty of cattle and riders. He sensed how annoyed his father would be at having to wait. He thought about smacking the bay to speed him up, but the horse's head was dragging and they still had the whole day to go.

He stopped at the lip of the plateau. Down below, the herd waited by the gate. Will, Gwen, Jim, Jasper and McKenna were positioned to try and contain them, but the cattle milled restlessly. Calves that had lost their mothers were testing the riders and trying to break back.

Rory loped down toward his father. He knew his mother

would want to talk to him first and see if he was all right, but he ignored her and rode straight toward Will.

"Where the hell have you been?"

"A calf got away. He went through the fence."

"Where is it now?"

Rory regretted that he hadn't brought it back so he could show his father. "I roped it, but Meg's got it now."

"Where is she?"

Rory pointed. "Way back there. She says to go on without her. She'll take the calf home and we can trailer him up tomorrow."

Gwen rode up. "Are you all right, son? What's wrong?"

"He's fine. He lost a calf through the fence. How'd you lose the calf in the first place?"

"It just broke back."

"'Cause you pushed the cows ahead and left the calves behind."

"Don't yell at him!" Gwen snapped, "You're the one who insisted that the children ride alone. If you want him to drive cattle your way, you ride with him next time."

"He's been on cattle drives since he could walk. I don't understand why he hasn't learned yet that you can't push cows ahead of calves."

"Mom!" wailed McKenna. A group of calves stampeded past her, followed by a line of bellowing mothers.

"God damn it, the day's shot to hell!" said Will.

Jim took off after the cows and calves, followed by Jasper. That Jim was a steady boy, even if Meg did baby him too much. But what to do now? Try to round up the herd, or give up and try again tomorrow? He knew what John would have done. Make them round up every last cow and calf and head up. Even it if took 'til midnight to get them up there. Maybe it was force of habit, but that's what he would do, too.

It wasn't midnight when they got there, but the sun had set.

They'd run into swarms of mosquitoes so thick that they'd all nearly suffocated. McKenna busted out crying and swallowed a gob of them. Then the bridge was out over the Crayden ditch and they'd spent an hour there chasing calves up and down the bank until they could be coaxed, heaved, roped or wrestled into the muddy water. But now the gate was shut. Cows and calves bedded down by the creek and none of Will's family was speaking to him.

They all turned to listen as a pickup crested the hill. It was Meg with their truck and horse trailer. From the commotion inside the trailer, she'd brought the missing calf.

Gwen and the children were overjoyed to see her. They ran to open the gate. Will hung back. He didn't want to show her how glad he was.

16

The hawks' nest was empty. For three weeks, it had been Jim's secret, the hawks' nest in the cottonwood crown along the river. While the hay machinery rumbled in the meadows, he had hidden and watched the hawks bring back carcasses for their nestlings. But today, there were no hawks perched on the nest, or in the tree. He'd climbed as high as he could and poked the nest with a stick and that's when he knew—they were gone.

The sun baked the dirt yard. Jasper got up from a ribbon of shade at the equipment shed and padded toward him. Jim ran his fingers over the dog's head. He thought of going inside, but it would be hot in there this time of day. Jasper followed him to the steps and they sat down.

A truck slowed on the road and turned. It was Will with Rory and McKenna riding in back. Will leaned out the window.

"Where's your mother?"

"Out in the hayfields."

"Do you want to come with us?"

"Where are you going?"

"From where I'm sitting, it seems like that shouldn't make a difference to you."

"Can Jasper come, too?"

"As long as he sits in the back—or on the floor."

"We'll ride in the back."

Jim opened the tailgate. "C'mon Jasper!" Jasper studied the tailgate, measuring the height, and sprang on. Jim jumped on behind him. "OK!"

"We'll go out to the hayfields and tell your mother you're going with us."

What the hell was this idiot, Mather, doing now, Will thought as he approached the hay ground. It had rained last night and it was too soggy to put up hay, but there was Meg raking and Mather stacking. How did this fat slob survive year after year doing everything wrong? You'd think he'd kill the livestock feeding them that rotten hay. Or it would ignite in the stack and set the whole place up in flames.

But somehow it seemed the Almighty watched over Mather. He never went off the road, though he was drunk more than half the time. He'd kept this place afloat and still had money to pay a hired hand. Will was struggling just to keep his head above water. He took good care of the cattle and the land and by the time he'd made his payment to Nick at the end of the year, he had nothing left. All that work—just to try and keep a hold of his place. This drunk S.O.B. got by. No sweat.

He drove past Mather. The neighborly thing would be to stop, but Will wasn't a diplomat, like his dad. He grimaced at Mather and waved. Mather nodded and spat over the side of the stacker.

Will stopped on the row that Meg was raking. With her cap and sunglasses, he couldn't see her face, but he saw her grin. She hopped off her tractor.

"Want some water?" Will asked.

"Sure."

Will handed her a canteen. As she swallowed, he wondered, was she seeing anyone now? Gwen hadn't told him anything.

"Where are you headed?" she asked as she handed back the canteen.

"I got a call that there's a washout up above that knocked the fence down. I thought we'd go fix it and take Jim along."

She glanced up and smiled at her son. "Thanks. I'm sure he'll enjoy it. Any cattle out?"

"I won't know until we get up there— may not know 'til the fall."

"I could ride up there and check for you."

"How could you get away from here?"

Meg glanced at Mather. "On a rainy day maybe."

"That won't be stopping you from haying." Will put his foot on the gas. "I'll bring him back."

"Have fun."

All three children giggled once Will accelerated on the county road and the wind rushed in their faces.

"Wooooooeeeee!" shouted Rory.

It didn't feel quite the same as running with the antelope. And though it swept the heat away, it wouldn't ever be as good as gliding high on the breezes as the hawks did.

The county road ended at a barbed wire gate. "Rory, get out and get the gate!"

"What about McKenna? Why can't she do it for once?"

"I'm not big enough."

"Life will be a lot easier for you, son, if you just stick to what you have to do and stop worrying about everyone else."

Beyond the gate, truck slowed, bumping over the rocks. This was the way they'd taken the cattle, thought Jim. Sun and wind had browned the prairie since then. They crossed the Crayden ditch, bone dry now. And to think of all the trouble they'd had pushing calves into the gurgling water.

Up and over a few more slopes and there was the valley below them, the willows and the creek where they'd left the cattle. The truck splashed through the creek and Jim looked at it longingly. He wanted to wiggle his toes on the slimy rocks beneath the surface.

Will followed the fence line up and down the gullies that split the mountainside. At last, they located the washout. The fence had ripped apart and one end had been pulled down the gully. Rocks and dead logs were heaped in the opening. Will shut off the truck and studied the scene. He got out and the children followed him.

"Dad, look!" Will followed Rory's outstretched finger to a mound of grey fur on top of the rocks.

"A badger," said Will. "He must have been caught in the flood."

Rory held his nose. "It stinks!"

"What's a badger?" asked McKenna.

"They're ill-tempered animals that dig holes in the ground that'll tear up a horse or a cow if they fall in one. We're better off without this one."

"His eyes are gone," McKenna observed.

"They've been pecked out," said Will.

"By what?"

"Some kind of bird. Look, we're going to have to move all this junk out of the way to fix the fence. Rory, get a shovel out of the truck and get rid of that badger."

Rory was still holding his nose. "I don't want to! It stinks!"

"I'll move the badger," Jim said.

Will looked at him. "It'll be too heavy for you."

"No. I can do it."

"All right. Rory, you can help me with these rocks here."

McKenna followed Jim to the pickup. "I'll help."

"How? Only one of us can use the shovel."

"We can take turns."

Jim carried his load down the gully followed by McKenna and Jasper. His arms began to ache, but he didn't want to admit it to McKenna. He dropped the carcass at the mouth of the gully in sight of the creek. In spite of the stench, he and McKenna studied it.

"Look at its teeth," said McKenna."They look sharp."

"I wonder what it eats."

Jasper pushed between them, dropped on his side and rolled on the dead animal. "Yuck!" the children shrieked. He got up and turned toward them, wagging his stub of tail.

The children shied away. "No, Jasper! You stink!"

Jasper stared at them, but forgave their rejection almost instantly. He waded into the creek and lay down in the water.

They followed the creek upstream past scattered aspen. "Look, a beaver dam!" said McKenna. "Let's stop and wait for them to come out."

Before they could spot any beaver, the horseflies nailed them. They scrambled up the steep bank to get away. Jasper sprang ahead of them and beat them to the top.

Jim pulled McKenna up the last few feet. Then they looked back down. Below was the heart-shaped beaver pond and the aspen murmuring to one another. Jim knew they were not far from Will and Rory, but here, alone with McKenna, he felt small. His gaze could not contain it all: the mountains shouldering up behind them and the valley tumbling away eastward and spreading on and on in the distance. From where the hawks cruise, he and McKenna would be specks.

"What's he doing now?" asked McKenna.

Jasper dug furiously among the rocks. "He must smell a

ground squirrel or something."

A stone fell aside and Jim picked it up. It had a discolored indentation all the way around the middle. Both ends were flattened.

"Look at this."

"What is it?"

"I don't know. It's a weird rock. It's weird how it has this stripe in the middle."

"Let's show Dad." McKenna ran down the hill holding the stone. "Daddy, look what we found!"

Will didn't look up until she shoved the stone into his hand. "Look, Daddy!" Will pushed his cap back from his forehead and turned the stone over and over.

"It's a hammer, an Indian hammer."

"How can you tell?"

Will ran his forefinger along the indentation. "This stripe here, there must have been a strap around it. That's why it's worn-in there. And the ends, see how worn they are? They've been used to hammer things. Poor guy must have felt bad when he lost this."

"Maybe a girl used it," said McKenna.

"She must have been a strong girl. Where did you find this?"

"Jasper found it," said Jim, "on top of that hill." He pointed to where they'd stood moments ago.

Will hefted the stone, gauging its weight. "Hard to believe that others lived here once."

"They lived here?" said Rory, quickly glancing at the hills above them.

"No self-respecting Indian would have lived here all year round," said Will. "They would have staked out some milder country for the winter. But this would have been a good place to camp and hunt in the summer. Plenty of view from here to see who or what was coming. Plenty of deer and elk. Buffalo, too, prob'ly in those days. And the creek below for water."

"Did they attack wagons from here?"

"Could have. They sure coulda seen them coming for a long ways. Why don't you kids go back up there and look for arrowheads?"

"Can I go, too?" asked Rory.

Will considered for a minute. "OK."

The children started back up the hill, but Jim turned. Already Will, working alone, looked puny among the pile of rocks and driftwood. The fence line seemed barely tacked to the land, flimsy as a kite. And whatever the Indian hammer had made—no sign of it now. This land was indifferent to them all, it shrugged them off.

He started back down the hill. "Wait for me," he yelled. "I'll help!"

17

"Thanks for the rock," Meg said.

Will shrugged. "He found it."

"On your land."

"A thing like that... it's something he should treasure all his life."

"I believe he will." She said it with a slight nod of her chin. She seemed happy, the happiest he'd ever seen her, although it would be hard to be unhappy on a day like this—the aspen waving their gold crowns, no wind and the sun melting that last tart chill in the air. With the whole glorious day ahead of them, it seemed hard to turn one's mind to the coming of winter. Better to jump the track of seasons and pretend the day would go on endlessly.

Still, the winter hair had grown in on the horses. Sissie, he noticed as Meg had saddled her, had gotten swaybacked. How old was that mare? She'd been on that place long before Meg. And Meg herself didn't look quite as girlish as when they'd first met. Fine lines were cropping up around her eyes. And God knew, time was scrawling all over him.

"How do you do it, Meg?"

"Do what?"

"Raise such a great kid on your own?"

Meg smiled. "You always act like you don't like the way I raise him."

"I don't mean to. What makes you think that?"

"The way you stare at me sometimes. You think I baby him."

Will looked away, not wanting her to see that she was right.

"I'm not one to judge, Meg. I'm not doing so well with Rory."

He waited for her response, but he knew she felt awkward at his confession.

"I take him with me after school and on weekends, but he never listens to what I tell him to do. By the time I've told him the right way to do something, he's already gone ahead and done it the wrong way. As soon as I start talking, a switch trips in his head. That's why I wonder, how do you do it?"

"Don't you just ever do anything with him for fun?"

Will looked at her. "Like what?"

"Horseback riding, for instance?"

"I didn't know he liked to ride."

"Why don't you ask him?"

Will nodded slowly. "OK. I will."

The conversation dropped and Will looked around. They were high above the valley now, but they hadn't come across any cattle. The frosty mornings must have pushed them down. Still, they had to ride up here and check. And it didn't seem like a waste of time. Meg was good company.

They followed a deer path into the woods. Shafts of light

filtering through the tree limbs skipped in front of them. The horses' hooves rustled in the new fallen leaves. Will rummaged for more conversation leads.

"Has Mather got his calves sold?"

"If he does, he hasn't told me."

"Think you'll stay on another year?"

"I don't have any other plans."

"Well, I'm... *we're* sure glad. We appreciate your help."

"Thanks."

Again, Will chafed at the silence between them. What was it about this woman that made him want to maintain a line of conversation?

Meg spoke up. "Where are we meeting Nick?"

Nick. He had come up with them and was riding the other side of the pasture.

"We're meeting him at the spring."

Meg caught the shift in Will's tone. "Gwen told me the two of you were getting along a lot better, now."

"He's with us today, isn't he?" Will spurred his horse to a trot as if he'd just ridden into a cloud of horseflies.

Nick traversed up and down the ravines. He spooked a few fat cows and calves and started them down. But there was not much up there. A good day just to suspend thought and enjoy the sun in your face.

He worked his way down the rocky slope to the spring. He could see Meg and Will before he heard them. They were sitting across from one another, but fairly close together. Meg's hat was off and wisps of her hair blew about her face. She looked happy, a little too happy, thought Nick.

"Fine day to sit by the spring," Nick said as he dismounted.

"Just waiting on you," Will answered.

Nick took a beer out of his saddlebags and put it in the spring.

He glimpsed his brother's disapproval and it tickled him.

"Find anything?" Will asked as he looked down at his lunch.

"Two dozen, maybe. I sent them on down the creek. We'll pick 'em up when we ride down. What about you?"

"There's nothing in the forest." Nick took out his baloney sandwich. "How's Jim?"

"Fine. He's doing real well. Thanks."

"Nice kid."

She glanced at Will. "I'm glad you think so. I'm real proud of him. What about your kids? What are their names again?"

"Laurie and Ryan. I don't know how they're doing. I haven't seen 'em in a couple of weeks."

Both Meg and Will stopped eating and stared at him. "Deborah left me for another man."

"When did that happen?" asked Will.

"A couple of weeks ago."

He seemed pretty calm about it, so Will pressed on. "Didn't she give you some kind of warning?"

"Yeah, when she stopped wanting to sleep with me I knew something was wrong. But I always thought I'd get around to dealing with it one day when we'd have some time alone. And when that day finally came, she was gone."

Nick looked over at Meg. She was uncomfortable.

"What will you do?" asked Will.

Nick shrugged. "What is there *to* do?"

"Are you going to try and get her back?"

"I don't know how to answer that. How do you go on from something like this? It's not like a spat where maybe you come home late after poker night and she won't fix you breakfast. Sooner or later you can fix that. But where she's gone and shared all of her life with someone else? How do you just kiss and make up from that? It'd be like keeping a bull in your living room. 'Yes, honey, I'll take out the garbage. Oops, let me just squeeze by this huge thing that you let in the house that weighs 'bout a ton. Honey, could you give me a hand? I'm stuck between his butt and the wall and I can't breathe. Could you get him to take a step or two?'"

Nick was pleased to hear Meg laugh.

"You love her, don't you?" asked Will.

Nick didn't respond, but asked Meg, "What would you do?"

Meg evaded him. "Funny that you'd ask me."

"Why?"

"I don't know anything about being married."

"You were married five years, weren't you?"

"That wasn't marriage. It was more like a rollercoaster ride."

"Well, see, you do know something about marriage! Let me ask you this…"

Will shot him a glare. He didn't like him hounding Meg.

"If your ex came here today, walked right into your yard and knocked on the door, would you take him back?"

Meg looked from one brother to the other, unsettled that both were hanging on her response. They were so comfortable in their lives. How could they know what it was like to be her?

"I'd want to," she said quietly.

Will jumped to his feet. "We'd better get on if we want to get out of here by dark."

A whistling noise passed just over Will's shoulder. It sounded a little like the rockets he set off with the kids on the Fourth of July. "What the hell?" he said. Another whistling noise on his other side.

"Get down Will!" Nick shouted. "We're being shot at!"

Will ducked down and they all looked up the slope to a pickup on top.

"Jesus Christ, Meg!" said Will. "It's your boss!"

Meg looked over her shoulder. A hundred yards to the east, a herd of antelope stampeded. None of them had been hit.

"God damn it!" shouted Will. He jumped on his horse, slapped it with the reins and bounded up the hillside. Meg and Nick followed at a slower pace, reluctant to push their horses so hard on the rocks.

Mather was in the truck. Three men were with him, one in the cab, another in front of the truck with a rifle and a third sitting on top of a cooler in the back. With the exception of Mather, they were all dressed in camouflage.

"Mather, what the hell are you doing on my land?"

"This ain't your land! It's government."

"The hell it is, you son of a bitch! What are you shooting at us for?"

Mather leaned out of the truck window and spat. "I'm guiding."

"Guiding!"

Mather gestured with his beer can toward Meg. "What ya so worked up 'bout when you're stealing my hand and my horse?"

"Get off my land now!"

"Fine. I ain't going to argue with you." He held out his hand. "Hand over the horse."

Meg spoke quickly, "I offered to help them out. I didn't think you'd mind. We borrow their scales every year."

"Well, if they're paying you anything, you'd better pay it over to me. I ain't paying a hand to go work for somebody else!"

"You don't pay her as it is," said Will.

Nick had dismounted and introduced himself to the other men. "Will, this is Stewart, Clark and Richard. They're lawyers from Michigan. You boys out here to get some antelope?"

"And deer," said the lawyer with the rifle. "He," pointing at Mather, "told us we'd be hunting on public land."

"Will," Nick offered, "I think they can hunt here today."

Will glowered at his brother. Nick continued, "We are borrowing Mr. Mather's labor and horse and we owe him something for that. And seeing as we are neighbors, we all oughtta help one another out. I think you should let them hunt here for today."

Will eyed the hunters and then turned back to Mather. "OK for today. But from now on you'd better call me before you 'guide' up here."

Mather spat just past Will. "Sure."

The hunter with the rifle got into the cab. Mather put the truck in first gear and it bumped along the ridge.

"Well, I can tell you one thing," said Nick, "four legged creatures are safe from Mather and that guy with the gun."

"Why did you do that, Nick? They might not hit an antelope, but they could hit a cow."

"Did you want him to take it out on her?"

They both looked back at Meg.

"I don't need you to stick up for me," Meg snapped.

"One of you, or both of you," said Nick, "ought to be workin' it out with him about when Meg can work here. 'Cause if you don't, he's gonna use the whole thing to take advantage of us."

"You just let him take advantage of us. He's charging those people."

"I let him take advantage of us so her pay wouldn't get docked. Maybe if they get their antelope and deer and Mather gets some money out of it and they have a few more rounds, he'll forget about taking money away from her."

"He's never shorted my pay."

"He'd be sorely tempted if this sideline business didn't go right today. Why give him an excuse?"

"What makes you think I need to be rescued? I didn't ask for your help and I don't need it. I can manage Mather just fine."

"If that's true, why didn't you tell him you were here today? You know Meg, the whole women's lib thing might be easier to buy if you weren't here just to hide out."

"The way I live is none of your damn business, Nick Swan!" She gestured toward the north. "I'll take the far northwestern corner," she said. She urged Sissie into a trot and was gone.

Will turned to Nick. "I hope you haven't cost me my hired hand."

"I hope to hell I have."

18

Snow swirled around the yard light, obscuring it every few moments. It was almost seven o'clock. Where was Gwen? Will thought about going to look for her.

McKenna walked up behind him. "Is she there yet, Daddy?"

"No, not yet."

"I'm hungry."

Will walked to the pantry and turned on the light. He reached for a box of animal crackers and passed it to the child.

"Can I get some chocolate milk, too?"

Will poured her a glass and set it on the kitchen table.

"Can you heat it up, Daddy?"

Will searched for a pot, poured the milk in and set it on the stove. Rory came in and spotted McKenna eating crackers.

"What's she got?"

Will had walked back to the door and was peering out at the yard light again. He was thinking that he ought to get going.

"Dad, can I have animal crackers?"

"Yeah, go get yourself some, son."

Rory grabbed a box of animal crackers from the pantry and tore open the top.

"I'm having chocolate milk, too," volunteered McKenna.

"Dad, can I have some chocolate milk?"

"Sure."

Rory reached for the milk carton. He poured it too fast and milk sloshed over the top of the tumbler.

"Daddy, Rory's making a mess and he's not cleaning it up."

Will whirled around and Rory took a step back from the table.

"I'm going to clean it," he said. He went to the sink and got a sponge. He put the sponge over the spilled milk and wiped. Milk dripped on the floor.

"Daddy, he's spilling it on the floor!"

Will whirled around again, shot over to the table and grabbed the dripping sponge from his son.

"Damn it, Rory! McKenna, go get some paper towels, please."

McKenna brought back a wad of paper towels and then shouted, "Daddy, the milk's boiling over."

Will turned in time to see the milk bubble over the pot and sizzle on the stove.

Then Gwen walked in.

"Where have you been?"

"Why is milk boiling over on the stove?"

Will jumped over to the stove and slid the pot off the burner.

"I had to get groceries. Then, you know what it's doing outside. Visibility's terrible. It was a slow drive home."

"You had to get groceries—tonight?"

"Did you get them?"

"Couldn't you have picked another night?"

"You're right, Will. I can wait until we're snowed in tomorrow and everyone's complaining that there's nothing to eat. Then I can take the snowmobile in thirty miles and pick up a few things."

"Rory, go unload the groceries."

Rory rushed out, relieved for the chance to exit.

"Mom, I'm hungry," said McKenna.

Gwen took a package of hamburger out of the refrigerator and set it in a frying pan. She dumped the boiled milk down the sink.

"Mom! That's my chocolate milk!"

"You don't need it right now. Clean up the table, please."

"But Rory was the one who made the mess."

"He's getting the groceries. C'mon, McKenna. Pitch in."

Will had fled the kitchen. Gwen started macaroni and threw in a can of stewed tomatoes on top of her hamburger.

"Will!" No answer. She called again, "Will!"

He leaned against the kitchen doorway.

"How'd it go today?"

"It went well. The calves are all in the weaning pen, bawling like hell. I just wish the weather would have held off a little longer."

"How do they look?"

"Real good. I think they should average seven-fifty. So if the prices stay up, Nick'll have plenty of money this year."

Gwen grimaced at this reference to Nick. It wasn't his fault he'd inherited half the ranch.

"Did Meg help?"

"Yeah. She was here."

"Did you work it out with Mather about her working here?"

"No."

"Great. You'll get her fired and then you'll be out there by yourself."

"You could give up your job."

"And then how will we pay Nick? I'd love to give up the job in town, but you didn't give me a vote in this deal."

"What would you have voted for?"

Gwen wheeled and faced him. "I would have sold the place, Will. You could have divided the proceeds and started off brand new somewhere else. And you wouldn't have been tied to your brother for the rest of your life."

Will blanched and backed out of the doorway.

"Yes, that's blasphemy," she muttered to herself. She drained the macaroni and poured it into the hamburger mixture.

"Supper's ready."

Everyone was silent at dinner. When the plates were nearly clean, Gwen asked, "Is homework done?"

"I did mine when I got home."

"Rory?"

"It's done," said Will.

"It's done—meaning you told him to do it? Or it's done—meaning he did it and you checked it?"

"Rory, bring me your homework, son."

Rory left the table to go to his room. Gwen and Will exchanged glances, but said nothing. Rory brought the homework back and set it on the table.

"Can I go watch TV?"

"No, sit here while I go through this."

Gwen cleared the dishes. Rory dropped heavily into the chair and kicked the legs.

"Now wait a minute, son, you made a mistake here. Nine times nine isn't eighteen. You know that. You got in too big a hurry. If you'd just take the time to think a little bit, you could get the right answers."

"Don't snap at him when you've waited until nine o'clock at night to go over it!"

Will startled at the magnitude of Gwen's outburst.

"Fine," said Will, "You don't like the way I'm doing it. You do it." He got up and left the table.

Gwen sat down and picked up the homework.

By the time Gwen finished her chores and went to their bedroom, Will was already in bed, reading. They glanced at each other. Gwen undressed and started a hot bath. She eased into it, leaned back and closed her eyes. She heard Will come in. He knelt by the bathtub, smoothed her hair off her forehead and kissed her. Part of her wanted to surrender, but the day's business had not been completed.

"Will, there's something I have to tell you."

Will leaned back. "What?"

"I enrolled Rory in school in town today."

"Why?"

"So I can pick him up every afternoon and take him to his tutor."

"His tutor?"

"Yes."

"Where are we getting the money for that?"

"I'll take care of it."

"Why does he need a tutor?"

"Because this isn't working."

"You're the one who wanted me to help him with his work. How can I do that if he's in town every day?"

"If he can't succeed in school, he'll never succeed anywhere."

"That's not true. He's got the ranch."

"And you can guarantee he's going to have the ranch?"

Will stood up. "Why didn't you talk to me before you made this decision?"

"Why didn't you talk to me before putting us in debt for the rest of our lives?"

Meg was playing checkers with Jim on Saturday afternoon when she heard a car in the yard. She went to the door. The sky was low and gray—ready to spit snow, but it didn't trouble her now. The yearlings had just been shipped out. Tomorrow morning, she could sleep late and not care how the wind howled outside.

It was Gwen and McKenna. Meg opened the door and waved. "C'mon in."

Gwen reached in the back seat and brought out a covered dish. "What did you bring?"

"Just something I thought you'd enjoy. I was baking pies today and I brought one over."

"Thanks," said Meg as she took it from her.

Meg looked good, thought Gwen. Her face was red and chapped, as always, but it made her look healthy. Her hair was glossy and hung to her waist.

"Sit down. I'll get some coffee. Do you want anything, McKenna?"

"Do you have milk?"

"Sure."

Meg poured a glass of milk and handed it to McKenna. "This tastes funny."

"It's powdered milk. Here, this'll help." Meg set some cocoa on the table.

"Is Mather still buying your groceries?" Gwen asked.

"No. I get an allowance. But sometimes it's not enough."

"What kind of pie is that?" asked Jim.

"Apple," Gwen replied.

"Mom, can I have a slice?"

"Can I have a slice, too?" asked McKenna.

"Sold your calves yet?" asked Meg as she sliced the pie.

"No. We're going to wait and go to the sale barn this year, unless we get a really good offer. Will's real encouraged about how they look. He thinks they're going to average seven hundred and fifty pounds!"

"That'll help!"

Gwen shook her head. "Not much. We're falling behind in payments to Nick."

"Has Nick said anything?"

"No. For as much as Will picks on him, Nick is really sweet to us. He cares about us a lot."

Gwen's voice started to crack and Meg looked up abruptly from her pie.

Gwen coughed, composed herself and went on. "I don't think he'd say anything unless we stopped paying altogether." She took a long slurp of her coffee.

"What's wrong?"

Gwen curled her hand into a fist and held it to her mouth. Tears trailed behind her glasses and down her cheeks. "Rory's not doing well at the new school."

"You didn't think he'd adjust overnight, did you?"

"He got into a fight, Meg. Someone called him stupid because he couldn't read as well as the others."

McKenna looked up from her plate. "Someone called Rory 'stupid'?"

"Yes."

"Then what happened?"

"Rory hit the boy and gave him a black eye."

"Does Dad know?" McKenna asked.

"Yes, honey."

"Why don't you guys go play in Jim's room awhile? Here…" Meg packed up the checker board and pieces. "McKenna, do you know how to play checkers?"

"No."

"OK. Jim, take this into your room and show her how."

McKenna lingered at the table. "Go on, honey," said Gwen.

"But you're crying."

Gwen wiped her eyes. "No, I'm not."

McKenna looked from one woman's face to the other. When she saw that they were not relenting, she followed Jim out of the room.

Meg waited until the door shut behind the children. "It's just the first week, Gwen. Things'll settle down. He'll make new friends."

"I thought I was doing the right thing. So he could have a tutor. I thought the change would be good for him. But he's miserable. And Will's mad at me. He doesn't think Rory should have been moved."

"But with you working in town, how else could he have gotten to a tutor?"

"That's just it. Will wouldn't have taken him. Will just wants to ignore his problems. He won't face up to it. You hand him report card after report card and he doesn't say anything other than, 'Try harder next time.' He doesn't see that things aren't getting any better and that to Rory, the failures are adding up."

Meg looked down at her coffee. She didn't know what to say.

"What am I doing wrong?"

"Nothing. You're not doing anything wrong."

"I must be, because this isn't the life I'm supposed to have." Gwen began to sob. "My children were supposed to be perfect. And my son is miserable and I don't know what to do about it. God, Meg, I rack my brain and wonder what I did to cause it. Am I too hard on him? Am I too lenient with him? You're raising a child on your own and he's fine! So tell me, what am I doing wrong?"

"You know I've had my bad days."

"Jim is doing better than Rory."

Meg leaned back, stunned at the jealousy in her friend's voice. How could Gwen be jealous of her?

"It's not my fault, Gwen," she said quietly.

Gwen reached across the table and squeezed her hand. "I know. I'm sorry. I didn't mean that—the way it sounded. You know you're like family to us. Forgive me, Meg."

"There's nothing to forgive."

19

Will was gathering baling twine on the feed ground when he heard an engine in the distance. He knew it was Meg. This January they not only had snow, but on top of it, two weeks of below zero weather. Meg hadn't been able to get Mather's feed truck started and had come for help every day, which Will found himself looking forward to. He squeezed back a grin and stooped to pick up more twine, rehearsing the bluster he would make over her feeble-minded boss and his rusty equipment.

Her face was more drawn than usual when she pulled alongside him. Before he could even grin at her, she said, "Sissie won't get up."

"Did you try to get her up?"

She nodded.

He knew better than to joke today. "Did you call Mather?"

"He won't do anything."

"What do you want me to do?"

"You need to shoot her because I can't do it."

Will heard the choke in her voice. "What are you about to cry for? The mare's tried to kill you 'bout every chance she's had."

Now Meg broke down completely. "That's what you think, but she's been with me five years now! I just used her to bring in sick calves three days ago!"

"Let me finish feeding."

She left the pickup idling and watched as he fed. She hadn't even tried to start the winch truck yet. She'd spent an hour trying to coax the horse up. She kept saying to herself that she could still call the vet, but she knew it was too late.

They drove back to the house and Will picked up his rifle. They were silent during the drive to Mather's. Will couldn't think of anything to say that would soften the event to come. Not something like, "Now you'll get a new horse," because she wouldn't. If anything, Mather would go to the sale barn and buy something off the dog food truck.

The horse lay flat in the pen. A die-er, no question. They should have done this days ago. "Why did you let this get so bad?"

"I kept hoping she'd turn around, hoping Mather'd call the vet, thinking about calling the vet myself.... anything. You're right, I shouldn't've let it get this bad."

"If we'd done this when she was still up, we could've walked her to where you want her. Where does Mather put the dead ones anyway?"

"Beyond the meadow on the range where he summers them."

"We can't get her that far alive. Have you been out that way with the Caterpillar?"

"No. I've been feeding around here so I could bring in sick ones on foot if I had to."

"So we could get stuck dragging her out there."

More tears brimmed in Meg's eyes as the cost of her irresponsibility sank down on her.

Will glanced away toward the gate opening. Could they even get a tractor in to drag the carcass out? Barely. He lifted the gun and shot the horse.

Meg began to sob. "I'm sorry, I'm sorry."

Will set the gun down and hugged her. She buried her head in his coat and hugged him back. He couldn't feel her body, just layers and layers of bulky clothing. He hugged her tighter.

"I'm sorry. I didn't mean to put you out. I know it sounds stupid, but I wanted to believe she'd turn around."

"It's all right," Will said, although he knew he'd spend the rest of the day moving a dead animal.

In the end, Meg ran the Caterpillar ahead to clear a path while Will went home and brought his tractor to drag the carcass. Mather's calves followed them, thinking they were getting fed at last, but when they saw the dead horse at the end of the chain, they spooked and ran for the willows.

It was early afternoon before they got Sissie to the dead animal pile.

"Do you want to come home with me and get something to eat?" asked Will.

"No. I've gotta go feed."

"Maybe tomorrow, then."

She didn't answer. He leaned over quickly and kissed her on the cheek.

She knew he didn't mean anything by it. It was a gesture out of pity, she knew that. But from that instant, she couldn't help looking at him in a new way. A gate had opened between them—every time they were alone, they were more respectful of one another and less awkward. Silences between them were no longer strained, but shared. And when the families were together, she'd catch his eye and they'd both smile. It was because he'd helped her on a bad day, that was all.

That fall, Will let Mather ship out from his corrals again. It had become a tradition since John had first allowed it, the first year that Meg had come. And Will allowed it for the same reason that John had—because of her.

When the cattle, the buyer and Mather were all gone, the dust swirled in the empty corral and the silence was eerie.

"Coffee?" asked Will.

"Sure."

They rode back to the house, but neither said a word. There was not even a breeze today. It felt like summer, except the leaves had already fallen and winter was poised to swoop down on them.

Meg sat at the dining table while Will made coffee. When he brought it in, she said abruptly, "I've been thinking."

"About what?"

"About leaving."

He snorted. "You say that every year. Every shipping time."

"It's different this time."

"Why?"

"I don't feel ashamed anymore. I made a mistake. I'm not proud of it. But it's done. It's over. And I've showed everyone—I've showed myself—that I could do it all on my own. I don't need to prove anything to anyone. So there's no more reason to stay."

"Are you talking about your parents? How would they know what you've done? You haven't spoken to them in years."

"But they've never left my head."

Will swirled the grounds in his cup. "Gwen'll be heartbroke."

"I'll miss her. I'll miss this place. I'll miss my place."

"And Mather?"

Meg laughed. "No, I won't miss him."

"I… *we*, we'll all miss you, Meg."

They sat silently for several moments before Will said, "When do you think you'll be leaving?"

"I need to go soon, before Mather gets another bunch of cattle. If he does, I won't feel like I can leave."

"Where will you go?"

"Back home. Not to stay. Just to try and make things right. Then, I'll see…"

She left and Will set the cups in the sink. The clinks against the porcelain reverberated in the empty kitchen.

He returned to his work for that day—replacing a culvert. As he drove through the meadow, his gaze skimmed the swath of green remaining in the grass. Bales were stacked half way to heaven. Above, the jet trails dissipated in the liquid blue, signs that the world just kept on passing them by. He got out of the truck and slammed the door. The silence swamped him.

He looked back across the meadows that he'd traversed in every season for most of his life, beyond them to the tree line, beyond there to the foothills, beyond to the mountains, the peaks capped with the first snow. Somebody driving through here would say, "A real pretty place you got here, Mr. Swan." And they'd be right. But they wouldn't feel the crush of it. And even if they could, they'd never understand why he went on and on and on, into the teeth of the next winter, the next spring. No one understood him that way. Except Meg, who always listened to him.

He mounted the backhoe and looked down. The culvert was already in place, just the dirt to fill in. Water trickled through the ditch. Fall water. Last water before the ditch would fill with snow.

He couldn't imagine the coming winter without her. He couldn't imagine not phoning and asking her to come and help wean, ship, vaccinate, calve. He couldn't imagine the phone silent morning after morning, instead of her call for help with that old winch truck.

And the house when he came in for coffee or lunch. The thump of his boots against the linoleum. The drop of the cup in the sink. It would be unbearable to sit there alone.

He got back into the truck.

Meg was stretching barbed wire around an extra stack of hay she'd put up when she heard an engine in the yard. She shaded her eyes, but it was too far away to see. Mather? He never came out twice in one day. A lone figure opened the gate. Will.

She watched the truck bounce across the meadow. She was pleased to see him. Maybe he needed help with his culvert. If he'd help her finish this stackyard, she'd go back with him.

He got out of the truck and walked toward her. She waited for him to speak, but he didn't say anything until he stood just inches in front of her.

"Meg, don't go." He took her hands in his. "Meg... I'm not a man who knows how to say things. All I know to say is that you can't go. I've always felt something for you. Always. But now. Now I don't know what I'd do if I didn't have you." He kissed the top of her forehead. Then he put his arms around her.

Meg felt as if a tornado had struck, knocking emotions from the cupboards where she'd locked them. Elation, confusion, shock, empathy, desire and—yes—love fighting to the surface for air. She reached up and traced the lines along his eyes and down his cheeks. Blue eyes—deep as the sky over their heads.

He kissed her lips. Then her cheekbones, her eyes. She kissed back, searching for his mouth. All the hard struggles of the past years, the bitter winds and loneliness, the disappointment in herself, these things were shedding off of her and at last, she was going home.

He stepped back from her. His hands were trembling. "I don't want to hurt you, Meg. I just want to see you." He unsnapped her Western shirt, pulled it out of her jeans, pulled the sleeves off one by one until it fell in the grass. He ran his hands up and down her sides and they both hesitated now, afraid of the next step.

She unhooked her bra and let it slide off her shoulders. Will inhaled sharply. Her skin was paper white in the fall sunlight. Behind her, the haystack smelled of lingering summer and around them, the meadows had blanched from successive frosts and the trees, branches upturned like empty arms, were mute.

"Your hair," he whispered. She took the elastic off her braids and unwound them until her hair spilled over her shoulders.

"You're beautiful, Meg. You're perfect."

He pulled her to him and she felt his rough hands gliding up and down her back. She stretched up and whispered in his ear, "Let's go to the house."

Making love with him felt like a soaking rain. As if she had been a red clay desert baking for years and years and now every pore of her received him and sucked him up until it was over and her mind drifted free.

Until she opened her eyes and looked at the clock. Three-thirty. Jim and McKenna would be home on the bus in just thirty minutes.

And Gwen. The thought of Gwen made her heart race. She sat bolt upright and looked at Will. He shifted to face her, surprised at her sudden movement.

"We can't ever do this again," she said.

20

"Jim's calf died," said Rory, almost happily as he shoved his fork into his mashed potatoes.

Gwen glanced at Jim. "What calf?"

"Will let me pull a calf last spring. It had a black mask, like a raccoon's. And it was dead this morning in the weaning pen."

Will shrugged. "I don't know what happened. He was fine— along with all the other calves. And this morning, all four legs in the air. It doesn't look like he had pneumonia. I don't know what got him."

"You don't feel badly about it, do you, Jim?" Gwen asked.

Rory interrupted, "It wasn't even his calf! It's ours!"

"Jim?" Gwen asked again.

"I just don't understand why he had to die."

"We don't understand why any of 'em have to die," Will said.

"It's the give and take of what we do. We work with God and at the same time, we're always struggling to get out from under His thumb."

"That's blasphemous!" Gwen snorted.

"But true."

"Why do people go to church, then, and pray?" asked Rory.

"Because they've never ranched. If you're on a ranch, you're always in church. It's just that God's sermons ain't always what everyone wants to hear.

"And besides, Jim, you shouldn't be disappointed. There's Number 43. Remember him? You got him nursing when his momma didn't want him and he must be the biggest calf out there. He must be close to nine hundred pounds."

"What about the ones I helped?"

Gwen caught the bitter edge in Rory's voice, but Will ignored it.

"They're all doing good, too."

Rory was doing better this year. For the first time ever, he'd made it to Thanksgiving without a phone call from the teacher and with report cards that were all "Cs." But Gwen felt that she couldn't relax. No telling when everything would blow up. And a blow-up was possible if he thought Will favored Jim.

Everyone turned as the porch door opened.

"Meg!" shouted Gwen, "come in and get something to eat!"

It seemed to Gwen that Meg had changed in the last few months. She had put on a little weight and her face was fuller. Her hair had dulled, the sheen was gone. And she always looked tired these days, although she didn't seem particularly troubled by anything. She seemed a bit shier. She had always been aloof, but she didn't meet Gwen's eyes anymore. She looked away. It was because she was too isolated, thought Gwen. She had been out here too long. She was turning into a wizened bachelorette ranch hand in front of their eyes.

"I'm not hungry," said Meg, her eyes bouncing off the table

and out toward the window.

"You want coffee, don't you?"

"Hmm… yes." Meg pulled out a chair and sat next to Will. She didn't look at him either.

"Did you get everything you needed in town?"

"Uh huh."

"What's new in town today?"

"They've put up the Christmas decorations."

"How are your new calves coming along?"

"They're too light, but at least they're not sick yet."

"Jim's calf died," Rory chimed in.

Meg turned to her son. "Are you OK?"

Jim felt embarrassed by all the female attention. "Yeah."

"After I clean up the dishes, come help me decorate the school for the Christmas supper," said Gwen.

"OK. I'll meet you over there."

"Why don't we ride together?"

"I've got to feed."

"That's fine. I'll come with you and help and then we'll go. I'd like to see what Mather brought you this time."

"You don't need to do that. I don't want you doing my work. You do enough."

"It's fine. I never get out anymore. It would be a nice change to pitch hay."

The wind was sharp when they stepped outside and iron grey clouds ripped across the sky.

"Snow tonight," Meg murmured.

"We need it. There's not much on the mountaintops."

"I thought you hated to drive in snow."

Gwen shrugged. "There're payments to make to Nick. And

without snow, there's no water, no hay, no cattle."

It was already spitting tiny hard flakes when they drove into Meg's yard. The new calves mobbed against the corral rails, bawling. They were a motley group: some barrel-bellied Angus, some pygmy reds and a few Brahmas.

"It looks like he went to the sale barn and bought the trash out of each group he could find. You'd think he would have made enough off the sale of those nice Charlais you raised last year to buy some quality cattle."

Meg jabbed her pitchfork into the hay. "That all went to Blake's Drive-In Liquor."

Gwen grabbed the other pitchfork. The mixed odors of hay, calves and manure were welcome after five days indoors. The calves shoved their muzzles into the hay and the noise subsided into contented munching sounds.

"How's work going?" asked Meg.

"Well, I haven't told anyone yet, but I got a promotion!" Gwen turned to Meg, her eyes sparkling with new-found pride. She'd been working at Teddy's Equipment and Feed, starting out as a secretary and then moving up to counter help. Gradually, she'd taken over for Teddy when he went on vacation. Now, he wanted to cut back his hours. Maybe come in from ten to three. He believed Gwen was ready to run the place.

"Are you getting a raise?"

"Yup. I'm not going to be hourly anymore. I'm getting fourteen thousand a year and health insurance."

"Congratulations, Gwen."

"It is going to be a lot more stressful. Running the whole store. I just hope Rory's OK so I won't have to worry about him so much."

"He'll be fine."

"Meg, there's something I have to ask you."

Gwen was surprised when Meg jolted straight up and nearly dropped her pitchfork.

"It's not a big thing. I just would like you to come with me and Will to Stockgrowers' this year." When she didn't respond, Gwen continued rapidly. "I know you haven't gone in a while. I know it's awkward for you. But I've found someone I'd like you to meet."

Meg sank her pitchfork back in the hay. "Last time I had a date at Stockgrowers', it didn't turn out very good. I know you mean well, Gwen, but no thanks."

"You can't go through life alone!"

The snow whirled between the two women, coating the hay, the corral rails, the calves' backs. Gwen couldn't read Meg's face. Was it really so blank, or was it the snow?

"I've got Jim," Meg answered.

"And when he leaves, what will you have?"

In the end, Meg gave in. It would give her a chance to dance with Will. A chance to be together with no one knowing they were really together. A chance to make him jealous of the other man Gwen had in mind. And she was tired, tired of the long nights listening to the wind howl and dreaming of Will beside her. It was December— the month when they plunged into night at four-thirty in the afternoon. She needed some kind of respite.

Meg met her new date in the entryway of the Plains Hotel, where she had felt such excitement all those years ago. Gwen introduced them. "Meg, this is Duncan Reid."

Meg held out her hand. "Hello." Duncan was shorter than she was. He was dressed in a Western suit with a grey felt cowboy hat. He held her hand firmly.

"Good to meet you."

"Duncan's family used to own a ranch in Green River. Now he's an accountant. He does the books for the store."

"Gwen tells me you're a ranch hand."

"Yes. I work next door to their ranch on the Mather place."

Duncan nodded appreciatively. "Tough life for a woman."

"Tough life for a man."

Duncan smiled. "So you're one of those women's libbers?"

"What do you mean by that?"

Duncan tried to difuse her defensive reaction with a chuckle. "You believe that women should be equal to men?"

"I don't know about that. I believe I should be judged for myself and not by somebody's expectations of who I should be."

Duncan smiled. "Sounds like an outlaw to me."

Meg grimaced. The evening was going to be tough.

She suffered through dinner with him and once dessert was done, she scurried to the Swans' table with Duncan trailing behind. Then she fidgeted through the dancing, waiting for her chance to be with Will. It came, after she'd worn Duncan out wth a fast number. When they returned to the table, Gwen had gone to the restroom.

"I'm bushed," Duncan admitted, mopping sweat from his forehead.

"I'm not," said Meg, looking at Will.

He led her out as the band struck up *Blue Eyes Crying in the Rain*. There were a lot of couples on the floor and he steered her toward the center near the Christmas tree. For a moment, he held her out by the shoulders.

His face was strained and she knew that he, too, felt pierced by the irony of this moment. Together, and yet not together. She breathed in the pine needles, the scent of beer, Will's cologne. There was nothing else to do or say, but lean into him. He put his arms around her and buried his face in her hair. As they rotated around the floor, she watched to see if anyone was looking, but other couples were talking or drinking or dancing with one another. She couldn't see beyond them back to the table.

But Duncan saw the two of them as he quietly sipped his beer.

Gwen didn't get a chance to question Duncan about the date until he came in the store around the end of January. She hadn't been able to get much out of Meg.

"Well, how did you like Meg?"

Duncan fiddled with his briefcase. "She seemed distracted."

21

Will down-shifted when the river headgate came into view. His gut sank—he knew what was there—but there was nothing to do but play it out. He pulled the truck into the borrow pit and climbed up the flume. The headgate had been padlocked. He jerked the padlock a few times. No water. Not a drop in his ditches. This morning, he'd heard that the water restriction had been ratcheted down to 1883 rights. His water rights were 1885, which were good, but in this drought year, not good enough.

He'd straddled the blessing and curse of a mild winter. Calving season had been easy, if there had ever been a time you could call twenty-four hour a day work easy. No blizzards—only a few skiffs of snow that had quickly melted. Hardly any scours at all. He'd only lost five calves—the best calving season of his memory. Now the year was about to unravel on him. Unless it began raining, or snowing, there'd be no grass on the range. No hay to put up in the meadow.

He drove on to Mather's place. Through the empty yard, through the hay meadow. Will glanced at Mather's ditches. There was water in them. Where was he getting it? He didn't have '83 rights. He'd find out from Meg. Sonofabitch had to be stealing it from somewhere.

Through the west gate and out onto the range. The dirt track wound up the hills, past Mather's bone pile, where Sissie's bones lay, on past the reservoir, where most of the calves were resting that afternoon. The dirt track disappeared and the rocky incline slowed his ascent. He crested the hill. Below him, Meg was stringing wire along some new posts with Jasper next to her. There was a tractor with a drilling bore on it and beyond, he saw the boys tamping dirt around a new post.

Will slammed the pickup door. The wind whipped through his shirt and he looked back inside where his jacket lay on the seat. To hell with it. He walked down to Meg.

"They've shut off the water."

She set the wire stretchers down. "Where?"

"They've shut it down to '83."

"I'm sorry."

"It's not your fault. Where's Mather getting his water?"

"I don't know. He handles it. He's been here a lot this week."

"He's stealing it. You know that."

"And what if I did know that, Will?"

He looked down at her. He could hardly see her face beneath her cap.

"Take off your cap."

She removed it. Wisps of hair whipped along the top of her head and she smoothed them back. Her forehead was as white as the drifts capping the mountains. He wanted to grab her right here.

"I need you."

Meg no longer knew how to respond when he said these things. She wanted to say: "I need you, too," or "I love you, too," as she had in the beginning. But lately, she'd wanted to say, "I'm the one sleeping alone night after night."

In the last few weeks, she'd had to remind herself of the pressures on him to keep from snapping at him. Yet he never acknowledged the pressures on her, or the frustrations that heaved inside of her.

When she didn't answer, Will looked over her head toward his son. Rory had stopped work and was watching him.

"How'd you get this big hole in the fence?"

"I don't know. Calves must have run through it, I guess. I'll have to go search for them tomorrow."

"Want some help?"

They searched one another's faces, allowing a subterranean conversation to flow between them. It was that conversation that she responded to.

"What about the boys?"

Will sighed. "They'll have to go with us, I guess. Damn it. I guess we're not going to be able to be together again until fall."

Again, Meg did not respond.

The sun had slipped beyond the mountains before they'd finished setting posts and stringing wire. Will and Rory rode home in Will's truck. Jim drove the tractor and Meg followed in her truck.

Rory was surprised when they stopped in the yard. "Why aren't we going on home, Dad?"

"Just need to say something to Meg."

"What?"

"That we'll bring the horses over here tomorrow to go search for those calves that got out."

Just as he stepped out of the pickup, Mather drove in the yard.

He spat out his window. "Evening, Will."

"Evening. What are you doing here so late in the day?"

"Just here to check up on things. I guess it'd be more to the point to ask why you're here."

Will nodded toward the truck. "I was picking up Rory. He helped Meg fix fence today. Did you hear that the water's been shut down to '83?"

Mather watched Jim and Meg drive into the yard.

"Yeah, I heard about that. What do ya 'spose we'll do now?"

"We? You've got water in your ditches."

Mather shrugged. "Must be a beaver dam or something."

"I'll let the water commissioner know. I'm sure he'll want you to pull it."

Mather's eyes narrowed, like a pig's. "You keep your god-damned nose out of my business and off my place! I don't want to see you here. I don't want to see your brats here."

"Well, the commissioner can always come out and talk to Meg."

"If he does, then she's worked for you for the last time. She ain't going to be at your place anymore."

"She's not your slave. She can go where she wants to. God knows you don't pay her enough to work here."

"Move her over to your place then. I'm sure you'll pay better wages. Then you can have her when you want her."

He may have had plenty to drink this evening, but he was still sharp enough to see Will's jaw lock. He glanced at Meg. By the way she jerked away from his gaze and looked toward Will, he realized that he'd split a log wide open to its softest, moldiest heart.

"Well, I'll be damned." He leered at the two of them.

Will spoke up. "I'm going to bash in your brains, you sonfabitch!"

Mather reached around for his rifle on the gun rack, but Will yanked the door open, grabbed him by the shoulder and tried to drag him out of the truck. Mather pushed him away with one arm while reaching for the gun with the other.

Car lights came over the bridge and the two men broke apart. It was Gwen.

She jumped out of the car. "What's going on?"

"We're going home. Rory, get in the car with your mother."

"Meg?"

"Gwen, get in the car. We're going home!"

Rory scrambled to the front seat of the car. Will, without looking at anyone, jumped in his truck. He slammed down the gas pedal, hoping his very motion would draw Gwen in its wake. He succeeded. He saw her lights in his rearview mirror. Only after he'd crossed the bridge and turned down the county road did he think of Meg.

The yard light snapped on, casting a cone of light over Jasper, Meg, Jim, Mather. The sounds of the night crescendoed around them, the river muttering over the rocks, the spring peepers singing.

Mather swaggered up to Meg. "If he's ever here again, you're fired. Understand?"

Meg nodded.

"That'll include the trailer." He jerked his head toward her bedroom. "I won't have you fornicating on my place. With all this trouble over water, that's all I need the neighbors to hear about. Is that clear?"

Meg nodded again.

"You say anything to the water commissioner, you're fired. You haven't seen any water in those ditches and you don't know how it got there. Is that clear?"

"Yes, sir."

Mather turned, got into his truck and drove away toward the meadow. Meg dropped on her knees and burst into sobs. Jim stepped back. Sobs wracked her until she collapsed head down in the dirt.

"Mom!"

She stopped and sat up.

"Mom!"

Slowly she stood, wiping her cheeks with her palms. He expected her embrace, but she crossed her arms over her chest and looked away.

"I'm sorry, Jim. I'm sorry you had to hear all that. I'm not a very good mom."

Jim felt the squeeze of the darkness closing around them. He was as alone as if she'd ridden off and left him behind to wait.

Gwen waited to confront Will until the children were in bed. "What's going on?"

"They shut down the river to '83."

"What does that have to do with Mather?"

"He's stealing water."

"How do you know?"

"I went to pick up Rory. There's water in his ditches."

"You were dragging him out of his truck because he was stealing water?"

"No. I told him I'd turn him into the water commissioner and he threatened to fire Meg."

"So then you tried to drag him out of the truck?"

"He was reaching for his gun."

"We'd better get back over there! What about Meg? There's no telling what he'll do when he's drunk."

"We're not going back over there."

"What?"

"She'll be fine. He's not going to do anything to her."

"He pulled a gun on you but he's not going to do anything to Meg?" Gwen walked to the closet and pulled out her jacket.

"Where are you going?"

"To see if Meg's OK."

"Gwen, don't leave this house!"

Gwen stared at him. "I thought you cared about her."

"I do. But it's me he's mad at. Not her. He'll leave her alone. And in the meantime, I don't want you going over there."

Gwen sat down next to Will and took his hand. "What's really bothering you?"

"There's no water."

"We've gone through droughts before."

"Not like this. Without rain, they're not going to open that headgate back up. And we'll get half a hay crop. Maybe less than half. We'll have to sell off cows this fall to get through the winter. That'll help with the payments to Nick, but then what happens next year when there's less calves, less income."

"We'll set the money aside from the sale of the cows. So we'll have money for Nick next year."

"That'll work, so long as we don't have to use that money to buy hay next winter."

"Will. . ." Gwen put her arm around his shoulder and leaned her forehead against his neck. His shoulders were as taut as stretched fence wire. "Wouldn't it be better if we sold this place, split the money with Nick and got a place of our own? So we didn't have to worry about this payment year after year?"

"No."

Meg rolled in her own sweat all night long. She wanted Will. She wanted his voice in her ear. But demons wriggled through her brain like snakes. Would Mather tell Gwen? If not, would he tell someone else who would tell Gwen? What had Gwen made of what was going on? Had she guessed? What were she and Will talking about right now? She would be demanding to know what was going on. What was Will saying? Would he confess? What would happen tomorrow? Would she lose him? And if she did, then what?

The minutes on her bedside clock flipped over and over. She watched Hercules glide across the sky.

She heard a truck in the yard and thought it was Will, but when she looked out the window, it was her father. Sunlight flared off the rim of his cowboy hat. She wondered how he'd found them as she lifted her hand to shade her eyes from the glare.

She embraced him, but he stood as unyielding as when he'd thrown Ronnie out.

"I'm here for Jim," he said.

"What do you mean?"

Jim came to the door, blinking in the sunlight.

"C'mon, son. You're going with me now."

"You can't do that."

"You can't take care of him."

"I've always taken care of him!"

Her father opened his hand and the boy took it.

"No!" She reached for Jim's other hand, but they were already two steps—then three—beyond her. As they drove away, Jim pressed his face against the rear view window.

There was a ringing noise. Incessant. Her eyelids flew open. The telephone. Will? Gwen?

"Meg. Are you all right?"

Gwen.

"Yeah, I'm fine."

"Tell me what happened last night."

Meg's thoughts scattered about like chicken feathers. What to tell her? What had Will told her?

"Will and Mather got into a fight."

"What about? What happened?"

"We were coming back from fixing fence. I was behind Will and when I drove into the yard, Mather was already there. They were arguing—about water."

"Did Will accuse Mather of stealing water?"

"Yes."

"Then what happened?"

"Will threatened to call the water commissioner and Mather turned around. Like he was reaching for his gun."

"Was he reaching for his gun?"

"I don't know, Gwen. It happened so fast. I can't be sure."

"What happened after we left?"

"Mather said Will couldn't come around here anymore. If he does, I'll get fired. Then he left."

"I'm so sorry, Meg. Did Mather try to do anything to you?"

"No."

"You don't sound right. Are you sure everything's all right?"

"Yeah, I'm fine. Just shook up, that's all. I had a bad dream about my father. I dreamed he came and took Jim."

"I'm really sorry, Meg. You just got caught in the middle of things. Will's so upset over this drought. We've been trying to build up the herd, after we gave Nick half the cows, and if we have to sell cows this winter, it's going to kill him."

Tears rolled out of Meg's eyes. "I know."

"And then he hates Mather. I'm just so sorry you got stuck in the middle."

Meg wiped her cheeks. "I gotta go. I've got to gather the yearlings that got out yesterday."

"OK. I'll come talk to you later."

It was dawn. There was just enough light to make out the dresser and mirror above it. The shadows ebbed in the room. Meg stood up and steadied herself against the fear that threatened to engulf her.

When Rory's eyes opened, his mother was standing over him. Light seeped under his window shade.

"Rory, I want to talk to you."

He sat up and rubbed his eyes.

"What happened last night?"

"What do you mean?"

"With your father and Mather and Meg."

Rory answered wearily, "We were fixing fence up in Mather's pasture. Part of the whole fence was down."

"Go on."

"Dad helped us finish. Then I rode with him, Meg took her truck and Jim was driving the tractor. Dad and I got to the house first and Mather was already there. Dad said Mather was stealing water and he was going to tell the water commissioner. He said the water commissioner would come talk to Meg. And Mather said he'd better not or he'd fire Meg. And Dad said Mather didn't pay her anything, anyway. And Mather said if she didn't like it, she could come over here and work for us all the time. And that's when Dad grabbed him and started to pull him out of the truck."

"That's when I came along?"

"Yeah."

"Did Meg say anything?"

"No."

Gwen went into the kitchen, poured coffee for Will and started to bring it to him. They almost collided in the kitchen doorway. He took the cup from her, but neither of them moved.

"How could you do that to her?"

"Do what to her?"

"I heard it all from Rory. Drag her into your fight with Mather?"

"I don't know what you're talking about."

"Rory said you threatened to call the water commissioner and have him come talk to Meg. What did you think would happen when you said that?"

Will turned his back on her and sat down heavily at the dining room table. "I don't know."

"All you think about is this ranch. And the rest of us are left out. It's one thing to turn your back on your family, but to jeopardize Meg's position, too? When she's helped us out, time and again. How could you do that to her?"

Will snarled, "I'm sorry. OK? I'll apologize to her later on."

Gwen's face froze in disgust and she left him sitting there. She dressed in her bedroom. If she hurried, she could catch Meg before she left. She couldn't bear to think of Meg out alone with this on her mind all day long.

Meg's truck was in the yard, but Jasper didn't trot up to greet her, so she suspected that Meg had already left. She knocked on the door. No answer. She turned the doorknob and stepped inside.

"Meg? Jim?" She wandered to the bedrooms, still hoping that they would be there, but the rooms were empty. Meg's bedclothes lay in a heap on the floor. Gwen stopped in the bathroom and turned on the overhead light.

She glanced at her face in the mirror. The hair at the top of her forehead was thinning. Lines were deepening into furrows around her eyes, the old rodeo queen's eyes. Looking back on all the days behind her, and ahead to all the days to come, she was only a ranch wife and mother, destined to play out her role to no one's notice, much less applause. She gazed out the window to the dusty yard. The meadowlarks were out. Her eyes dropped to the toilet. A package of condoms lay on the tank.

So Meg was seeing someone. Why hadn't she told her? And who could it be? Where would she have met someone? Gwen wondered whether she should press her about it. No, maybe when all this trouble had passed, she'd tell Gwen. Now was not the right time.

22

Maybe Mather was stealing water, or maybe it was just a beaver dam, but it hadn't made a lot of difference. There was not enough hay for Mather to run two hundred calves next winter. After all the threats that had flown back and forth that night, Meg could lose her job because there'd be no cattle to feed.

She didn't mention her worries to Mather. She was afraid to talk to him for fear he would bring up Will. Day after day, she imagined—and awaited—accusations, threats, taunts. She skulked around him and she was ashamed of herself for it.

If Mather thought about the drought, Will, or Meg, he didn't say anything. Every day he drove out without a word, climbed in his tractor and mowed. Meg raked, her spirits sinking at the raggedy windrows in front of her.

This haying season, Mather had brought his teenage son,

Sarge. Sarge was a miniature version of his father, the same broad chest, broad face and tiny eyes. Unlike his father, he still had hair, blond and curly, that he pulled back in a ponytail. When his father yelled, he winced as if he expected a blow.

Days of hot wind and sun followed. In the drone of machinery, Meg thought about Will. She hadn't seen him since that night, nor had he called her. And he stayed away, as Mather had ordered. She longed for him. And she could feel his longing, in return. She was waiting for him. But what was he waiting for? And how much longer could they go on? How much longer could she force her son to live this way?

"One good thing about it," said Mather, as he wolfed his lunch in the shade of the pickup. "Without any rain, we're going to have this haying done in another week."

Neither Meg nor Sarge responded. Jasper lay under Meg's pickup, panting. Meg stared at the grass at her feet. At noon, with the haying machinery parked, the silence was deafening. It muffled the voices around her.

Sarge turned on a transistor radio and the tinny music buzzed mosquito-like while Sarge crushed his pop can and Mather stuffed another wad of chew in his lip. He took a rag out of his overall pocket and mopped his face and head.

"Turn off that thing and let's go back to work."

They split up wordlessly toward their machines. Meg switched the ignition on. The noise felt like a refuge, dulling her anxiety.

She was raking around a stack they hadn't needed last winter. The outer layer of hay was blackening, but at least if there were calves here next winter, they'd have something to eat. A wisp of smoke rose off the top; it seemed to start, then stop, then start again. By the time she'd finished the windrow and turned around, there was no doubt—the stack was smoldering.

Meg looked down at her water jug, the only water she carried.

She couldn't hope to put out a fire with that and besides, it would be too dangerous to get near the stack. Best thing to do would be to get the hay machinery out of the way and call for help. Jasper peeped out from underneath her truck as she drove up. He was not used to her returning this early in the afternoon.

"Get in!" she shouted. The dog scooted inside the truck and looked at her, bewildered by the sudden activity. She mashed the gas pedal and drove toward Mather. She passed Sarge, who, like Jasper, looked after her, uncomprehending.

She pulled up alongside Mather and gestured for him to stop. He shoved the throttle down.

"What's the problem?"

She pointed. "The stack's on fire!"

Now the whole top of the stack was smoking.

Mather leaned back in his seat, slack as a sack of potatoes. "Well, damn it."

Meg's voice in her own ears sounded as if she was screeching. "Aren't we going to do something?"

"What's to do? Every member of the volunteer fire department is out in the hayfields. By the time any one of 'em show up, that stack'll be long gone."

"What about the meadow? What about the hay on the ground, the hay machinery?"

He looked at her as if she'd gone daft. "There's no wind. The stack'll burn and that'll be all."

Sarge had seen the fire and had joined them. "What are you standing around here for?" Mather barked. "Get back to work."

The boy shrugged and got back on his tractor.

Meg bit her lip and jumped in the truck. She called the fire department from the house. By the time she stepped back outside, the stack was in flames, spewing rolls of black smoke high in the air. Others would see it and they would come.

She grabbed all the shovels she could see, plus the used gunny sacks from the shed which she soaked down until they were sopping. Then she drove back out to the stack. The heat from the fire forced her to stop over fifty yards away. The wind it generated suffocated her as she stepped out of the truck. And now, she noticed, the west wind had picked up. She looked anxiously at the cut hay and grass for any sign of sparks. A puff of smoke spiraled out of a windrow in front of her.

Sarge drove up. "What do you want me to do?" he yelled over the roar of the fire.

"Get that tractor out of the way before it catches on fire!"

"What about Dad?"

They looked to where Mather was continuing to mow.

"Leave him. He's all right."

Meg moved her truck farther away. Jasper cowered on the floor, terrified of the noise and smoke.

A pickup pulled up and the driver nodded to her—Kurt Jarrell from the ranch next to the school.

"How'd it start?" he shouted.

"Don't know. I just looked over and it was blazing."

Meg looked over her shoulder. Other pickups now were weaving through the yard and fanning out across the meadow.

Will crossed the bridge. Jim and Rory looked through the windshield at the spectacle in front of them.

"Wow!" said Rory. This was better than anything on TV. The fire was higher than the buildings in town and the noise it made was louder than Fourth of July fireworks.

"Now listen to me," said Will. "You boys are going to stay here at the house. You are not to go out there."

"Can we watch from the corral?"

"Yes, but you're not to go any farther than the gate."

Jim peered anxiously. "Where's Mom?"

The words pricked at Will because he had been thinking the

same thing. "She's out there. Don't worry. I'll find her."

Men and women from the surrounding ranches, who had always regarded Meg as an oddity, now picked up shovels and gunny sacks and beat the flames alongside her. They spoke to her as if they'd known her for years.

"Good thing you got the hay machinery out of the way."

"Hell of a time for something like this to happen with the country as dry as it is."

"Glad you spotted it when you did or it'd be halfway to my place by now."

Or the more common question, "Where's Mather?"

The smoke was so thick Meg could not see Mather, but she heard him working the crowd.

"Kurt, glad to see ya! You left Linda at home to put up hay while you came out here to watch a stack burn, didn't ya? No, I haven't been doing any funny business. The damn thing just caught flame!"

"Meg!"

She turned just as Will touched her shoulder. Both of them were conscious of the people around them. But no one regarded his gesture as anything more than neighborly. They all knew she worked for the Swans part time. And what with Will having to pay off his brother, Swans needed the help. So it was not a surprise that Will would show some concern for the woman. Especially as her boss was chugging liquor right now behind the trucks.

Will sensed all this and did not remove his hand from her shoulder. "Are you all right?"

Her face was smeared with soot and the wisps of hair that always worked loose from her braids were singed. She knew the question was broader than stated.

"I'm fine."

Will's hand dropped. "You need to go back to the house."

Meg glanced at the others who pretended not to be listening. "No, I'm staying here with everyone else."

But Will was ready for this answer. "Jim's worried about you. He and Rory are at the corral. They can't see you, Meg."

She looked up into his face. He was serious.

"OK."

The boys were perched on top of the gate. Jim jumped off when he saw her truck and ran to her. She was surprised when he threw his arms around her. Maybe she wasn't as poor a parent as she thought. Or maybe he saw more in her than she saw in herself.

Rory called out. "Where's Dad?"

Before Meg could answer, the fire truck from Laramie arrived. As it rumbled out to the meadow, thunderclouds nosed over the mountaintops.

"I want to be with my dad!"

"He wants you to stay here."

Rory backed towrd the gate, defiant, and then Meg relented.

"I'll drive you out there, but you've got to stay in the truck."

Smoke billowing in the passenger window made the boys cough. "Shut the window, Rory," Meg said sharply.

He leaned out. "I want to find Dad."

"Stay in here with us."

Rory ignored her and opened the door.

"Rory!" He was gone, running around the line of pickups.

The fire truck soaked the ground in a wide radius around the fire. Will watched it sweep round and round. Abruptly, it slowed almost to a stop as a boy ran in front of it. His boy.

"Dad!"

Will jerked Rory's arm. "I thought I told you to stay at the corral!"

"Meg brought me out. She said I could come find you."

"She didn't tell you to run in front of moving trucks!"

"I wanted to see where you were."

"You're twelve years old, son. Can't you, for once, use your head?" Will turned away from his son in disgust. He couldn't even say why he was so angry. It was the heat—the drought—the fire—the nearness and unavailability of Meg.

Rory turned and watched the fire devour the stack. The charred poles collapsed with a crash.

It started to rain, just drops at first, then a downpour, then hail the size of golf balls. Will ran for his truck. He and Rory stared at each other through the windshield. The hail bounced over the blackened meadow, drumming on the pickup roofs.

Mather shoved his thick hands in his overall pockets. One by one, trucks were pulling away. He shook a few hands and thanked his neighbors for coming. He glanced up, saw Will's truck and stopped him.

"Will."

"Mather."

Mather peered into the cab and saw Rory, drenched and slumped against the passenger door.

"Will Swan, I'll be damned. The cut hay's blown away or burned, the hay saved from last year is burned and this hail has knocked the standing hay flat. God damn this business!"

Will silently thanked God it hadn't been him.

Mather looked off toward the smoldering blackened ground. "Thanks for coming."

Will nodded.

"But don't come back."

Will looked around for Meg. Her truck was still parked in the meadow and Mather was walking toward it, the hail bouncing off his head and shoulders.

23

John Swan's front porch hadn't changed much since Meg had last seen it. The roof sagged a little more and Nick must have cleaned up the machinery parts and broken furniture. She rolled down her window and listened. Yellowing cottonwood leaves fluttered down on the roof. And behind the trees, she could hear the river receding to the quiet fall mutter that winter would silence.

She had not been there since she had helped Gwen clean after John's death, but looking at the house now brought him back. She could see him sitting out front in an old leather chair held together with duct tape. She longed for him to be there. Not because he would understand or approve, because he wouldn't. But had he lived, his presence would have insured that the fences that both divided and enclosed them all would not have collapsed. When John had been around, she had understood her life better.

He would not like it that she was here, now.

In the moments after Will arrived, they let the sounds of leaves and river fill the silence between them. They had anticipated this moment for months and now, neither could think of anything to say.

"I'm glad you're here," said Will.

Meg nodded and took his hand. Will unlocked the front door and it swung open, but before he entered, he hugged her.

"Oh, Meg," he whispered. He pressed his hands down the length of her back and hips, down over her buttocks and back up again. "How wonderful you feel!" he said.

He began kissing her face, moving toward her mouth, when she stopped him.

"I want to talk, Will."

He stepped back. "OK."

The room smelled musty. Nick hadn't been there all summer long. There were dead flies on the windowsills and the breeze from the open door rolled dust balls across the floor. Anna Swan beamed down on the room, young and undaunted forever.

They dropped down on the couch and without looking at him, Meg said, "What's going to happen to us?"

Will took her hand in both of his. "We've been going on about a year now, haven't we?"

Meg nodded.

"You want to give it up?"

"I can't keep going on like this. I can't keep lying to Gwen. I can't keep sleeping alone night after night thinking of you. I can't keep worrying about Mather saying something. I can't do this to Jim."

"What's the answer then?"

"I want to go back to where I was, where I wasn't ashamed of anything. I want you. Every day. I want to get up in the morning with you and go to work and not have to be ashamed again. Aren't we right for each other?"

"I've never fit with anyone like I do you. But Meg, you know better than anyone what this ranch means to me. It's my life. There's so much of me in this place that I don't know where it ends and I begin. And I just can't do something that would put it more at risk than it already is.

"What would happen if we got together? We'd have to leave here. I couldn't ask Gwen to leave, could I? What would we do? Where would we go? I don't know, Meg. I'm not going to end up being the man that you want me to be.

"And then, what about Rory and McKenna?"

Meg's heart sank as she listened to him. She had already known everything that he was going to say, but hearing the words spoken was like listening to a jail door clank shut. She jerked her hand away to wipe the tears spilling out under her glasses.

He pulled her against his chest. "Oh, Meg. Please don't cry. I don't mean to hurt you. God knows I want you as much as you want me.

"We can give this up, you know. I'll let you go. And you'd be free to find someone new, someone better than me. You deserve that. It'd hurt me, but I've got it coming because the last thing I wanted is to hurt you."

Meg pulled away. "You say that, but you know I won't do it! I can't do it!"

Will didn't answer because it was the truth. He knew she wouldn't turn him down. They'd go on just like this. He licked the tears off her cheeks, rolling the salt on his tongue. Pop, pop, pop went the snaps on their Western shirts and as he settled down on top of her, she sighed, almost against her will. This, after all, was the only comfort. The springs in the couch creaked and outside the dirty windows, the fall unraveled.

24

Rory turned to Gwen when she pulled up at the school. "Mom, can Casey and James spend the night on Friday?"

Gwen smiled. "Sure."

He joined the other boys waiting for him in the playground. What pleasure it gave her—that other children were waiting for *him*. Rory finally belonged. He had friends. He had good grades. He and his father were still in a tug of war, but that could straighten out over time, if she could get Will to be a little less critical and Rory to hold his temper.

She drove back through downtown and up over the viaduct. Below, the railroad yard was quiet and she glanced down at the tracks running south out of Wyoming. Laramie looked sleepy on this late fall day as the calendar drifted toward Thanksgiving. From the viaduct, she could see new snow icing the peaks. Today, with the sun streaming over the town, you could almost forget that the snow was coming.

The "Ag" student she'd hired to wait on the counter was in, but the store was chilly. She turned on the heat and started the coffee. The cowbell jangled above the door and ranchers began to drift into her office.

"How's Will?"

"Sold your calves yet?"

She looked forward to the ranchers and their wives who came in and shared their news. She liked to think that she sold them more because she made them feel at home. She always kept the coffee fresh.

But midmorning, Ms. Hart called her from the country school.

"Gwen, McKenna threw up at recess. I have her lying down in the teacher's lounge now."

"Is it all right if she stays there till noon? Then I can get a hold of Will to pick her up."

"Yes. That'd be fine."

This was the one disadvantage of working in town. She couldn't be near McKenna and she missed volunteering at the country school. The guilt that she suppressed at leaving her daughter out there bubbled to the surface again, especially because McKenna would have to wait until noon to go home.

At noon, she called home. The telephone rang and rang. No answer. Well, Meg'd help her out. She called Meg's number. There was no answer there either. She must be helping Will with something. But what? What was so important that neither of them was coming in for lunch?

And what to do about McKenna? The "Ag" student was leaving for class. Who would watch the store? And who would get Rory?

There was nothing else to be done. With a grimace, she flipped the "Closed" sign outward. She hated to do this. Customers who were running other errands in town would stop here on their way home. It was that time of year—what with pregnancy testing, weaning and shipping—for the cattlemen to pick up their fall supplies. These people didn't go to town every day. Maybe this was their one day in town this month.

In desperation, Gwen tried Will and Meg again. No answer at either place.

She could get McKenna home, find Will to stay with her, then come back and open up the store again. She'd pick up Rory at Casey's house, as she always did after closing. She calculated the time it would take to make this circuit. Two hours, if she could find Will quickly. She put up another sign on the door: "Back at two" and jumped in her car.

She drove as fast as she could and got to the school in twenty minutes. She found McKenna dozing under a blanket in the teacher's lounge. Her forehead was hot. "McKenna."

McKenna's eyes flew open. "Mommy."

"How are you feeling, honey?"

"OK."

"What happened?"

"We were playing 'tag' and I was It and I just started throwing up." McKenna started to cry. "Everyone ran away from me."

Gwen shifted her to a sitting position. "It's all right. When you come back, they'll have forgotten all about it."

Gwen put on McKenna's shoes and coat and loaded her in the car. McKenna blinked in the glare of the afternoon sun.

Gwen floored the gas again, dodging the pot holes in the dirt road. As they turned toward Mather's, Gwen saw Will pull out ahead of them.

"There's Dad," McKenna murmured.

Gwen didn't answer. He wasn't supposed to be over there. Maybe he'd taken Meg back? Why hadn't she taken her own truck?

She followed her husband back to their yard. He got out of his truck and turned toward her.

"You're home," he said. His tone was flat, as if he meant to punt the burden of conversation to her.

"McKenna's sick. I tried and tried to get you. Where have you been?"

"I was getting the corrals ready for preg-testing next week."

"And Meg was with you?"

Will nodded.

"Why didn't she take her own truck?"

Will shrugged. He wasn't looking at her. "Just thought it'd be easier to pick her up. That's all."

"And you didn't come in for lunch?"

"I'm here now."

The condoms she'd seen on Meg's toilet—it couldn't be. Even if Will had the inclination, Meg would never do something like that. She and Meg were too close. But Will's manner was so distant... so guilty.

"I've got to get back. I need you to take McKenna."

Without saying another word, Will rushed to the passenger door and scooped up McKenna.

He spoke over his shoulder as he hurried away. "See ya tonight."

Gwen drove slowly back to Meg's and got out of her car. Now that she was no longer on the ranch full time, she had forgotten how silent these November days were. Once the sun tipped over the median, it seemed to plummet out of the sky and dusk came early. It already seemed late to her. It already seemed like the end of the day.

She heard a rumble from the corral, a tractor. She followed the sound. Meg was scooping manure with a backhoe and dumping it in a spreader. Mather's calves were home from their summer range. They pressed against the fence, curious at the noise.

Jasper came toward her wagging his tail. She stroked his head over and over until she heard the tractor shut off. Then she opened the gate and met Meg half away across the pen.

Meg looked anxious. "Is everything all right?"

"McKenna's sick. I had to bring her home."

"Do you need me to go over?"

"No. Meg. Where were you this morning?"

"I was with Mather. He was here to look at the calves. We're shipping next week."

"Will says you were with him."

Now Meg looked confused. She didn't know what to say.

A perverse impulse drove Gwen on, like stomping on the gas even as the cliff approaches.

"You're sleeping with Will."

Meg started to shake her head, but Gwen cut her off.

"Tell me the truth."

Meg's face blanched.

"I want to hear it, Meg. Say it!"

"Gwen, I don't want to. . ."

"Say it!"

Her hesitation—guilty, or was it smug?—infuriated Gwen. She reached up and slapped her as hard as she could.

Meg held her hand to her cheek. "Now you know. I love him."

Gwen reached for a shovel resting in the spreader and flung manure in Meg's face.

"How could you?" she cried. She stumbled to the corral rails and fell against them, sobbing, "How could you? How could you?"

Meg followed and put her hand on Gwen's shoulder.

Gwen jerked away and screamed, "Don't touch me!"

25

Jim peeked around the curtain. A few parents lingered over the casserole dishes, but most were clearing away their paper plates or standing in the coffee line. He had the lead role in the play this year: Sheriff Will B. Allright, the sheriff who would round up Santa's reindeer after they'd been scattered over the globe by the wicked elf, Slew O'Trouble. There had been confusion in the weeks before the play because his leading lady, McKenna—as Mistletoe—had left school.

The abrupt shift of his personal landscape made him feel as if he was being punished without knowing why. One day McKenna was gone and Ms. Hart told the class that she didn't know when she would be coming back. Jim didn't worry about that. Gwen probably moved her to town school with Rory.

When he got home, his mother was tense and silent so he

didn't tell her. On Saturday morning, she was standing in his doorway when he woke up.

"You can't play with the Swans today."

"Why not?"

"Gwen's taken them away."

"Why?"

"It's nothing you've done. It's me."

"What happened?"

Meg slumped against the doorway. "I hurt Gwen. I hurt her very badly."

"How?"

"She thought I was her friend, but I'm not."

"I thought you were friends."

Meg nodded and bit her lip. Tears welled in her eyes. She cried so often now, ever since Will's fight with Mather.

"Can't you just tell her that you're sorry?"

"No, son."

The new calves had not come in yet, so there wasn't much to do. They drove to the summer pasture, shut down the windmill and picked up the remaining salt blocks. Even though Jim pointed out a coyote, Meg hardly responded. She could feel the coming snow in the hush around them, and in the thickening clouds above. By the time she let Jim drive home, sure enough, fat snowflakes splatted against the windshield.

"Turn the wipers on," was all she said.

He had the truck in second gear, easing over the rocks in the road. With a sidelong glance at his mother, he accelerated and hit a rock so hard that the salt blocks nearly bounced out the back.

"Jim, take it easy or I'm not going to let you drive anymore!"

"I just wanted to see if we could go a little faster."

"You've been over these rocks a million times. You know you can't go fast here."

"This is my first time driving!"

"You're not getting any more times if you don't slow down."

Once he pulled into the yard, Meg stomped to the house without looking back. She seemed to have forgotten all about him. Jasper butted his hand and he knelt and hugged the dog. The snow dropped in sheets, so thick it was hard to see. He threw back his head and let the flakes land on his tongue. There was the briefest tickling softness before they dissolved.

Jim and Jasper struck out in the snow. The edge of the river was frozen now, but water still ran down the middle, occasionally lapping over the ice. Snowflakes piled at his feet, their individual designs coalescing into a white blanket. Snow lined the cottonwood limbs, turning the trees into ghosts.

They zigzagged through the willows, jumping over old cow turds. They found weasel tracks and followed them for as far as they could until the tracks crossed the ice and disappeared.

As they turned for home, the yard light came on. Jim went into the house, hoping for his mother's greeting, but the silence was even deeper there. Meg was staring out the kitchen window into the whitening oblivion beyond.

Tonight, Will had picked them up. When Jim asked if Rory and McKenna were coming, Will and Meg looked at each other. He tried to interpret the unspoken current between them, but couldn't make anything of it.

"No, they won't be coming," Will said. There was something in his tone that cut off the "why" question, so Jim skirted it.

Inside the cafeteria, they sat by themselves. People said hello, or nodded at them, or asked how they were doing, but everyone moved on and sat at other tables. Once they had filled their plates, they didn't get up for seconds. As Jim peeped out from the curtain, Meg and Will were still alone with their styrofoam cups, avoiding the stares of everyone.

    The oddness of walking out the front door and seeing cars and houses and pavement made Rory dizzy. Open space was gone. And instead of cows to milk, water holes to chop, cattle and horses to feed, there was nothing to do.

    He and McKenna leaned against a paintless board fence. Slats were missing here and there and Rory kicked at a loose one.

    "Let's play tag," said McKenna.

    "Don't want to."

    "Let's go inside then."

    "Why don't you go?"

    "C'mon," McKenna whined, "let's do something."

    Rory walked to the front gate and unlatched it.

    "Mom said, don't go outside the fence."

    Rory looked back over his shoulder. "Go tell her, then."

    Instead, she followed him out into the street.

    They walked for blocks past more houses, more cars, dogs in fenced yards and cats scurrying away along the sidewalks. They didn't see anyone they knew.

    "Where are we going?" asked McKenna.

    "I don't know," said Rory, but he did know. He was following the sun west toward home. He knew he couldn't get there, but his feet were carrying him that direction.

    They passed the library, the fire station. The Christmas decorations were already up along Fourth Street. The wind rattled them, whipping the tinsel loose. They found the bakery. They stared in the window at the iced donuts and cookies and cakes. Rory opened the door.

    "What are we doing here?" said McKenna.

Rory didn't answer. He faced the tall man with the stringy pony tail standing behind the counter.

"It's Rory, isn't it?" the man asked.

Rory nodded.

"And McKenna," said McKenna. "How do you know us?"

"Don't you live next door to Meg?"

Both Rory and McKenna were silent at the mention of her name. They'd heard it dunked in a stew of tears, accusations and denials in the last several weeks. It was not a good name anymore and a name they had become afraid to hear.

"What are you doing in town?"

"We live here now," said McKenna.

"You do? Do you like it?"

"It's just for a little while," Rory interjected. "We're going home soon."

"Oh. Do you guys want something?"

Their eyes were drawn to the display cases.

"We don't have any money," said McKenna mournfully.

"It's all right. What do you want?"

They sat at a table and nibbled their frosted sugar cookies. McKenna got a turkey and Rory got a pilgrim. McKenna fingered her cookie, choosing the best way to eat it. At last, she nibbled off the head, then the feet and then bit into the tail. Rory had already wolfed his and was standing up.

"Wait for me."

"Hurry up, then."

Rory walked around the corner and again headed west. The railroad tracks were in front of them. They walked alongside until they came to the iron stairway leading up and over the tracks. They both stopped.

"We've never been up here before," said McKenna.

"Let's go."

"What if we fall off and get run over by a train?"

"We can't. It's caged in."

They ran up the stairs and along the walkway until they were in the center overlooking the tracks.

"Wow!" said McKenna. Far to the south, a steady light gleamed, coming closer and closer. Then as it approached the station, the horn sounded: WA-WA-WAOUGHUUUU. The engine shot past the station and under the bridge. The children jumped to the other side to watch it go, the cars clanking underneath them and then, the roof of the little yellow caboose—going, going, gone.

Rory followed the train until it was out of sight. Where was it headed? The shadow of a world beyond Laramie intruded on him. He'd thought other places were just names he had to memorize from a textbook. But the idea that that train was hurrying Somewhere Else intrigued and frightened him. The only other place he'd ever been was Cheyenne during Frontier Days. What was out there?

"Where do you think it's going?" asked McKenna.

Rory shrugged. "Don't know. Alaska, maybe." And he thought of Eskimos and reindeer.

The sun slipped down, and long shadows scooted across the tracks as the children watched other trains come and go, some going north, some south.

"I'm getting cold, Rory," said McKenna.

From the bridge, Rory could see the mountains. The sun was sinking behind Sheep Mountain now. After seeing the trains, he didn't want to go home anymore. He wanted to jump down on top of the cars below and be whooshed off to somewhere else where his parents weren't fighting and there was no ranch to miss. He shivered.

"C'mon." They walked eastward into the lengthening shadows. Streetlights snapped on and the little neon cowboys and horses blinked over the bars.

A police car pulled alongside them. The officer rolled down

his window. "Hey, is your name Rory?"

"Yes."

"Get in the car. Your mother's looking for you."

They slid in the front seat next to the officer. "Your mother's been very worried about you."

"I know," said McKenna. "We weren't supposed to go outside the yard."

"Then why did you?"

"Rory went and I had to see where he was going."

"Next time, you really shouldn't go anywhere without telling your mother."

"Can you put the siren on?" asked McKenna.

"No. That's only for emergencies."

In the houses they'd passed earlier in the afternoon, the lights were on. They saw silhouettes of people watching TV or sitting at their dinner tables, people who had a place to be.

The officer slowed, turned the corner and pulled down their street. At their house, the outdoor light was on and the fence seemed to have sagged a little more in the hours they'd been gone. They waited while he rang the doorbell. They could feel their mother's anxiety in the way she yanked open the door.

"Evening, Mrs. Swan. I found your children."

"Thank God. Thank you so much." Gwen reached out an arm for each child and hugged them in. "Where were they?"

"On Third Street. They looked as if they were starting for home."

"Thank you, Officer."

He nodded and turned away. Gwen closed the door.

In the overhead light, Rory was surprised by how gaunt his mother looked. There were dark hollows underneath her eyes and cheekbones. She knelt down in front of him.

"Why, Rory?"

He shrugged. "I don't know."

"Didn't you think I'd be worried?"

"No. Well, yeah. I didn't really think about it."

"This isn't the ranch. You can't just go wandering off without telling anyone."

"When are we going home?"

Gwen started to cry. She reached out and gripped her son's shoulders. "Rory—your daddy doesn't love me anymore. He loves someone else. I don't know if we're ever going back. You're going to have to be patient and this will all get worked out somehow."

The children stared at her dubiously. How would it get worked out? They were living here in a drafty old house and the life they used to live had been severed from them—as completely gone as a cancer-eye cow shot dead.

The doorbell rang and the three of them jumped. When Gwen didn't immediately respond, there was pounding on the door.

"Gwen, Gwen!"

Rory opened the door. It was Uncle Nick.

"Hey, Mister Rory! How are you?"

Rory grinned. "I'm fine, Uncle Nick."

"What are you doing here?"

"We live here now."

"Are you going to let me in and show me?"

"I guess."

McKenna ran to him and he swept her up.

"Uncle Nick, have you seen our daddy?"

"No, but I expect I will."

26

Nick waited until the snow drifted four feet deep before he went out to help his brother. If he'd gone any earlier, Will would just send him back to the house—his pride, as usual, slamming the gate on all practical alternatives. But with the snow drifting, some kind of trouble would be afoot now and Will would be too desperate to turn him down.

He could only see Will's tracks for a few feet ahead. Everything else was a white haze. The radio intoned the list of highway closures: I-80 west to Rawlins, closed, I-80 east to Cheyenne, closed, Highway 287 south to Fort Collins, closed, Highway 230 to Fox Park, closed, Highway 130 to Centennial, closed.

Then the damn idiots put on beach music: *Surfing USA!*

Well, at least the drought was over. If the winter didn't kill off the remaining livestock, maybe Will'd pay him some money next year.

Will's figure appeared out of the haze. Or something human-like, anyway. Between the coat, overalls, goggles, hood and scarf over the mouth, there were no recognizable features. Nick slammed on his brakes.

Will slogged around to Nick's window.

"The tractor's stuck."

"Good to see you, too."

Will ignored him. "Can you take me back to the house to get the Caterpillar?"

"I was coming out here to help you."

Will walked back around the truck and plopped in the passenger seat with a sigh. He pushed his hood back, took off his scarf and wiped his forehead.

"Drought's gone," he said.

"Hm."

"How'd your cattle do this year?"

"Good."

"What'd the calves weigh?"

"Nine hundred," Nick lied.

"Nine hundred? You're lying."

Nick shrugged. "Think what you like."

"How'd you get that weight?"

"I've told you before, brother. Three-way crossbreeding."

"You musta made a lot of money."

"After I paid their board, I pocketed a little. But I don't have enough yet to buy a ranch." Nick resisted the urge to eyeball his brother.

"We had a hay shortage." Will paused. "I only kept fifteen replacement heifers. I had five open cows. And I figured I'd better cut some to make it through the winter. So I sold thirty cows in all."

"You'll be able to pay me this year then?"

"Yeah, Nick, but I don't know what next year's going to look like."

Nick let the windshield wipers keep time between them.

"I don't have Gwen's income anymore. I guess you know she left."

"Did she have a choice?"

"Of course she did. I didn't tell her to leave."

"So you were going to give up Meg?"

Will worked his scarf over and over through his big hands. "Meg's got no one. You know that. I just couldn't say no to her."

"Didn't know you were so charitable. So you're carrying on with her out of pity?"

"Yes—and no."

"Well, have you moved her in the house?"

"No."

"Why?"

"Because we're still talking about what the right thing is to do! There's the children in all this!"

"Hm... What about calving?"

"I'll manage like I've managed the last few years with Meg part time."

"You're going to pay her?"

"I have all along!"

"When does Gwen get her cut?"

"What the hell are you talking about?"

"The cattle are part hers, aren't they?"

"You're talking like we're getting divorced? Who said that?"

Will got out of the truck and slammed the door. Nick watched him tramp to the Quonset hut and heave himself up into the Caterpillar seat. Nick backed up to let him out and then followed. His tire tracks from just a few minutes ago were already half drifted in. Will's figure ahead of him faded in and out in the sheets of snow. Even with all his clothes, he had to be freezing on that thing.

The tractor was half sunk in a ditch that Will must have

missed in the blizzard. The cows crowded in around the feed wagon.

Nick chained the rear axle of the wagon to his truck and pulled it free. While Will worked on the tractor, Nick chopped a few bales and threw them over the sides to shut up some of the cows. The wind sliced through him as if he were purely naked. A wind like this would glaciate your bones while they were still in your flesh. Why in hell had he decided to come out here anyway? These weren't his cows.

Without a word, Will hitched the tractor back up to the wagon and drove into the wind. I guess that means he wants me to feed, thought Nick. He moved to the back of the wagon, chopped the bales and dropped them off. The cows pounced on them.

Once they finished feeding and moved all the equipment back to the barnyard, Nick followed Will into the house. Will didn't stop him.

It was hard for Nick to suppress his reaction. The kitchen looked like their father's after their mother had died: dirty dishes on the kitchen table, dirty pots piled on the stove. The dining room table was cluttered with weeks of old *Boomerangs* and *Fence Posts*. Muddy tracks and grime all over the floors. You'd think he'd have moved Meg in here just to clean up. Or had she even been in here since Gwen left?

Will rummaged in a cupboard. "Soup all right?"

"Yeah."

"Split pea is all that's left."

"That'd be fine."

Will turned and caught his brother's survey. "It's not like it was when Gwen was here."

Nick nodded in mock sympathy.

"I can't ask Meg. She's got Jim. It wouldn't be right."

"Hmm."

They slurped their soup in the dining room while the wind heaved snow against the house.

"Are you still alone?" asked Will.

"Yup."

"Are you seeing anyone?"

"Not steadily."

"What about your kids?"

"I see them once, twice a month maybe."

"How are they?"

"They're doing fine. They're in junior high now."

"Aren't you…" Will stared into space for a second, "lonely?"

Nick smirked. "When I get 'lonely,' I just go to the bars."

"Don't you want to have someone around again?"

"Not 'specially."

Will's spoon clattered in his bowl. "I want her back, Nick."

"Who?"

Will grimaced. "You know, Gwen—and the kids. I want them back."

"They ain't dead. They're only twenty-five miles away. Why don't you go get them?"

"What'll I do about Meg?"

"Do you want them both here? You're going to have to make a choice, brother. And you'd better get it done before calving."

"It's easy for you to say, but what would you do if you were me?"

So many responses stampeded through Nick's skull that he knew it was time to leave. He stood up.

"You're a damn fool, Will."

With his hand on the door handle, he turned around for one last look. His brother still sat at the table. What was left of his hair was flattened to his head and his cheekbones had been rubbed raw by the wind. White stubble peppered his cheeks and chin.

"I'll see you around hay season." And he shut the door on the mess behind him.

27

Meg looked at the clock as she came in the door. 4:30. She had been up the last two hours helping Will pull a calf. No point going to bed because she'd have to be up in another hour to take care of Mather's cattle.

Nothing had been resolved in the four months since Gwen had left. She had waited patiently through Will's shock the first two months and by the time she was ready to ask him what would become of them, calving had started. They were sleeping sometimes at Nick's house, sometimes in her house, but never in his.

"I just can't do that," he said and the words stung because they meant he still thought of her as a mistress, not a partner. She had wanted to ask, "when," but held back because she knew she had to give him time to decide. It would never last between them if she pushed it.

Still, if she hung on and he chose her, she'd finally have a place here. She wouldn't be Meg, the runaway ranch hand from Hayden, Colorado. She'd be Mrs. William Swan, a ranch wife with her own family and cattle. And Jim would have a father and a home.

But what would happen if he chose Gwen? That thought was like peeking over a cliff. She wouldn't be able to bear the humiliation and the hurt—she'd have to go. But where?

She raked through those thoughts as she drank her coffee, occasionally glancing at her reflection in the kitchen window. She put her coveralls back on and went out. Light spilled over the horizon, suffusing last night's snow with a rosy tinge. Once the sun was up, it felt warm on her back and billions of snow crystals refracted the light. The landscape was blinding. As she drove out to feed, she saw a fox, far out in the meadow, leading four kits. She stopped to watch them.

Will hadn't asked her to help with calving this spring. Without any discussion, she drove over every day after she fed Mather's cattle. But it annoyed her that he didn't care about her problems here. They weren't her cattle after all, but they were still her livelihood. It was a herd of animals sharing the same winter with all of them. Only difference was these cattle didn't have enough to eat.

Mather ignored his hay shortage and brought in another two hundred calves. He told her that he'd buy hay if the winter got too bad. She'd nodded, knowing he was lying—if the winter got bad, the price of hay would go up and he wouldn't buy a bale.

Again, he'd bought calves from the back end of the sale barn and they'd run the gamut of sicknesses this winter: pneumonia, pinkeye, hoof-rot. Four of the steers had died of water belly. A month ago, she'd told him if he didn't buy hay, she would have to cut back on the amount she fed.

He'd wiped the tobacco juice off his chin and nodded at her. "It'll be all right, Meg."

"What do you mean?"

He walked toward his truck. "You'll figure it out. You always do."

"I thought you were going to buy hay if the winter got bad!"
He started the truck. "Not at these prices!" he yelled back.

And that was the last time she'd seen him.

She began rationing the hay. She fed a long thin line that the stronger ones gobbled up. The weaker ones stared at her. They followed the tractor back to the gate and bawled. Soon they stopped following. It wouldn't be much longer before she started losing them.

One night in bed, she'd said to Will: "I'm running out of hay."

"Did you tell Mather?"

"Yes."

"It's his livestock, Meg. I wouldn't worry about it if I were you."

She paused. "Can I have some bales?"

"Hell, Meg, Mather can buy it like everyone else!" He sighed and turned over.

Would John have helped if he'd lived? He'd hated Mather, too, but he wouldn't have been this indifferent to starving animals. He'd have found some way to get her some hay. Unlike John, she realized, Will never understood anyone's troubles but his own.

After she fed, she drove to the river and checked the willows for any sick ones. Sure enough, a calf had died. He lay in the river and the water rippled over his muzzle and sunken ribs.

Jim helped her haul it to the dead animal pile and then they met the Swans at the calving shed. Rory and McKenna were standing outside one of the pens.

"Hi," said Meg.

The children didn't respond to her or Jim. The only sound was the snow melting and dripping off the tin roof.

Will was in the pen. He was bent over a scrawny calf, holding it up to its mother's udder.

"What's wrong?" said Jim.

"Burned bag," Will muttered, "Cow's tits get sun-burned and she kicks the calf. This calf's been kicked so many times he's given up. Half the herd is like this and the other half has scours. It's a god-damned mess."

"What do you need us to do?" asked Meg.

"I need you here to help me doctor bags and get calves sucking again. Rory, you take Jim and the two of you go check calves."

"What about me?" asked McKenna.

"I want you here with us."

McKenna looked at Meg. "I don't want to be with her."

"Then you go back and sit at the house."

"I'll stay here."

Rory and Jim stepped back out. The glare was so intense that Jim couldn't see without squinting. It was warm enough to take off his cap but the brim was shielding his eyes from the sun. If he took it off, he wouldn't be able to see at all.

"How are you?" he asked Rory.

Rory shrugged. "OK."

They spent half an hour chasing the cantankerous horses around the horse lot. None of them wanted to venture away from the hay feeder and the warm sun by the barn wall. Two surrendered out of pure laziness and they haltered them. Jim sank his fingers in the shaggy belly hair of the horse he'd caught. It was as good as putting on a glove.

They saddled up and loaded their pockets with scours pills.

"You want a rope?" asked Rory.

"No, I don't know how to rope."

"How are you going to catch calves then?"

"Just sneak up behind 'em and grab 'em."

The sun was high now and the cows were breaking from the feeding ground, some heading for water and others searching for their calves. Rory and Jim rode up to their first group of calves, a small, unattended bunch. One flicked its tail and Jim glanced at its hind end. Diarrhea spurted out like water.

"Here's one," said Jim.

"Are you going to get it?"

"Yeah."

The calf scrambled to its feet and tottered away as Jim jumped off. He quickly snatched the back leg, reached over, grabbed the front leg and flipped it. It wasn't like his early days anymore—when Rory had poked fun at him for being so useless. He knelt down behind the calf's shoulder and curled the top leg tight.

Rory knelt by the calf's head, put his finger in the corner of its mouth and slipped the pill in over the hump of tongue. He held the calf's jaws shut until it swallowed. The calf struggled and with every move, diarrhea squirted out.

"This calf's too weak," said Rory. "He'll have to come in."

"We don't have the cow."

Rory looked around for an approaching cow, but even the other calves had run away.

"We'll check the others and come back for him." Rory looked at the ear tag. "Number 29, can you remember that?"

They found the next one on the feeding ground. Rory followed him, untying his rope. He tossed his loop, dallied and the calf was down on the ground.

All the calves and cows stampeded at the commotion, except the mother of the downed calf. She charged over to them and roared.

Rory kept the rope taut while Jim rode up. "Let her calm down a minute," he said.

The cow pawed while the boys approached. She sniffed at the calf, raised her head and sniffed at the boys. She backed as they came closer.

"Easy," said Rory. He knelt down on the calf and loosened the loop. Jim slipped the pill down the calf's throat.

"I'm afraid to get up. She might charge us," Rory said.

"Let's both get up slowly and back away."

They pulled the rope off the calf's head and stepped back. The calf kicked and the mother rushed forward, sniffing every inch of its hide. Then the calf jumped to its feet and they walked away.

"Whew!" said Rory. "That was fun!"

Jim didn't say anything. He thought of the cow's eyes on him, how wide they were, how manic and furious. It hadn't felt like fun.

The next calf set off at a dead run. Just as Rory tossed his loop, the calf stopped and turned. He tried to rein the horse to follow, but something went wrong and they went down. Rory hit the snow, rolled over and looked up at the sky overhead.

Jim blocked his view. "Are you all right?"

"Yeah. What happened?"

"Your horse slipped. Your saddle's all packed with snow. Maybe you shouldn't be roping out here today. It's too slick and look, the horse's feet are balling up."

Rory looked over at the balls of snow on his horse's hooves.

"They've got scours, don't they?"

"You're not going to catch that calf anyway. He's too big."

Rory stood up. "We'll see." He climbed back into the saddle and looked over at Jim. "Damn. My butt's wet."

The boys laughed.

They rode farther out, following the cow-calf pairs. Jim veered to the corner of the meadow while Rory rode through the center. At the fence line, Jim stopped to watch a calf nurse. The cow wasn't kicking at him; still, something was wrong. His tail didn't wag like other calves when the milk filled their bellies. And his ribs were showing.

Jim eased up against the fence and pushed the cow away. He looked around for Rory. Rory was checking other calves. The calving barn was over a mile away—a long distance for a cow and tiny calf.

The cow obliged and trudged patiently back through the snow. The calf ran alongside, alert and frisky. Rory caught up with them.

"What are you doing?"

"Taking this pair in."

"Why? What's wrong?"

"This calf's not getting any milk."

Rory eased over to the cow's side. "She's got plenty of milk. Did she kick him off?"

"No."

"Well, then, what are we doing?"

"There's something wrong."

"It's going to take us an hour to get them to the barn. And you don't know what's wrong. Maybe nothing's wrong."

"No, I think something's wrong."

"We got a whole herd to check out here! And we still have to go back for that sick calf and his mother."

"I'm taking them in."

"You stupid retard! You don't know anything about what you're doing!"

"I know just as much as you!"

"I'm going to jerk you off that saddle!"

Jim tried to ignore him, but Rory took his rope out and twirled the loop.

He snickered, "I'm going to do it, I'm going to do it" over and over again.

Jim shouted, "All right. Do it, asshole!"

Rory roped Jim and pulled the rope snug. Jim let go of his reins, grabbed the rope and pulled back, but Rory was stronger. He turned his horse to the side and yanked Jim to the ground. Snow filled Jim's nose and ears.

"Ha, ha, ha—look at that little retard now!"

Jim jerked the rope in frustration, but Rory didn't give him any slack.

"They're getting away," Jim said, as the cow and calf

wandered off.

"Who cares? There wasn't nothing wrong to begin with."

"What if that calf dies? Then your dad's going to be mad."

"He'll blame me anyway, retard, 'cause he loves you and your whore mama."

"I hate you, Rory!"

"I hate you, too."

Rory wanted to boot his horse and drag Jim through the snow, but then the little mama's boy would tell. And if he let Jim go, he'd walk back home and Will or Meg would see him.

"I'm going to let you go. And I'll help you with that pair. But you gotta promise not to tell."

"You better go get my horse, too."

Rory brought back the horse. He got off his own horse and helped Jim dust off the wet snow. They followed the pair's tracks until they found them and turned them back to the calving shed.

Rory threw open the door while Jim waited outside. "Dad!"

Will emerged into the light with Meg behind him.

"We brought in a pair. Jim thinks something's wrong with them."

Will walked around the pair. Jim was nervous. Would Will vindicate him or not?

"Let's get 'em inside."

Jim nudged his horse and they pushed the pair into the barn. Meg rushed the cow through the pen and into the stanchion. The boys stood at the fence.

Will bent down and squeezed each of the tits. They were hard and tight. "Her tits are crusted shut. This calf's not getting anything."

He scraped the crud off and then milked the tits until good streams of milk flowed. He stepped away. The calf rushed up to the bag and nursed hungrily.

Will stepped to the railing. "How did you find this calf, Jim?"

"I watched him nurse and it just didn't look right."

"That's good work, son. Rory, you could really learn something from him."

Without a word, Rory headed for the door.

"Rory!" Will called.

The door clanged shut behind him.

"What's wrong with him?" Will muttered.

Meg looked at Will. "I'll go get him," she said.

Was this the way it would be if she moved in with him? Would she be intervening between Will and Rory, just as Gwen had always done? Jim would have a father, yes, but Rory would have none.

The snow was turning to slush underfoot. With the balmy weather, cows and calves had scattered across the meadow. Patches of ground poked through here and there. Meg walked back toward the house, calling Rory. She checked the Quonset, the barn, the house. She remembered the big tree that the children used to play in across the river. She waded in and surprised a group of mallards at the far bank. They circled once overhead and flew upriver.

Meg pushed through the brush. The sun dangled low in the afternoon sky and the snowbanks on the mountainsides glistened. She stopped and listened. Rory's sobs reverberated through the empty trees. The last time she had heard that sound was at John's grave.

She turned back and met Will, McKenna and Jim in the barnyard. Jim was leading the two horses.

"Did you find Rory?"

"He's in the tree across the river."

"Did you talk to him?"

"I think you ought to."

Will grimaced and left her standing there. McKenna trailed behind him.

"Mom," said Jim, "there's still a sick calf out there, Number 29. He has scours. We were going to bring him in, but his mother wasn't around."

"You go on with the others. I'll get him."

She took one of the horses and nudged it into a trot. After circling the meadow, she found them by the river. The calf hadn't nursed all day. As she drove them in, the lingering snow turned the same rosy hue that she'd noticed at dawn.

She shut the pair in a pen and snapped on the overhead light. Other cows pressed against their pens to watch her. She gave the calf a dose of penicillin. Then she warmed consommé on a hot plate, poured it in a bag with a tube and eased the tube down the calf's throat. She listened to make sure it lodged in his stomach and then let the consommé drip down the tube. After she washed the tube, she looked in the pen again. The calf still wasn't nursing, but at least he was standing. She would never know if she'd saved him or not because she wouldn't be back. She would never be back.

The moon was out by the time she put up the horse. Lights blazed in the house.

"Where've you been?" asked Will.

"Found a calf pretty sick with scours. I brought him in and dosed him."

"I'll check him later."

"Where are the kids?"

"All asleep in front of the TV."

"Did you talk to Rory?"

"Yeah, he's fine. Meg, Gwen's going to be here any minute."

"I know. I'm going." She shook Jim awake and put on his coat. Will followed them outside.

"Jim did such a great job today. You ought to be proud."

"Rory did a great job. Did you tell him?"

"Yeah. Sure. He's just a little jealous of Jim, that's all. But Jim's got skills that'll take Rory a while to learn."

Meg helped Jim into her truck. "Rory has no chance here

unless Jim and I leave."

Will stood still for a moment as the words sank in. "What do you mean?"

"I mean if we leave, you and the kids and Gwen can be a family again. Rory wants that."

"I never meant to put you in a position like this, Meg."

Tears started to clog Meg's throat. "I know you didn't."

He pulled her close and laid his cheek against her hair.

"I've always loved you, Meg. And I don't want you to go."

She pulled away. "But you don't want me to stay."

Jim woke up to the sound of Jasper panting in his room. He reached out with the back of his hand and rubbed it against the dog. Jasper jumped up and licked his face. Cold air wafted through the room. He peeked out the doorway. The front door was wide open and he could hear pots and pans banging in the kitchen.

He stumbled out to the living room. Boxes were strewn around the floor.

"Mom, what are you doing?"

"We're leaving."

"Why?"

She was crying again. "Because it's time to go."

"Can't we stay with Will?"

She shook her head.

"Why not?"

She shrugged. "He's not our family."

Jim dropped on the couch. The Swans were the only family he'd ever known. "Who is our family?"

"I'm going to take you to them."

"Where are they?"

"In Colorado."

"Can I stay here?"

"You've got a grandfather and a grandmother that you've never seen. Don't you want to see them?"

"No."

Meg sat next to him. "I promise you this is going to be OK."

If it was going to be OK, then why wouldn't she stop crying?

A truck and trailer pulled into the yard. Mather. Meg quickly wiped her face and met him as he stomped up the front steps.

"I brought you some hay," he said, as if he'd brought her a bouquet. She looked past him. The trailer was loaded with a week's worth of bales.

"What's a matter? Cat got your tongue? You didn't think I was ever going to bring any, did you?"

"No, I didn't. But... I've got to go."

"What do you mean?"

"We're leaving tomorrow."

"God damn it! This is all about the Swans, isn't it?"

"No, it's not."

"Yes, it is. I shoulda fired you when I first found out about it. What the hell made you think that man was going to risk his ranch for you? I thought you were a pretty good hand, but in the end you're just a stupid woman. And how am I s'posed to care for these cattle if you leave?"

"Same way I've been caring for them all this time."

"Are you going to feed today at least?"

"Yes. And in the morning, too."

"And who's going to unload all these bales?"

"Jim and I'll do it."

"Well, get at it, so I can go back to town and find some help." Mather pushed past her toward the kitchen. "You got any coffee in here?" He didn't wait for her to respond. He found the pot and a cup, filled it halfway and topped it off from the bottle in his pocket.

Meg stepped out into the muddy yard. She expected to feel sad at doing her chores for the last time. She knew every inch of this strip of land, every ditch and wind-beaten fence post. But as she walked to the winch truck, the place felt unfamiliar. The equipment shed with its leaky roof, the stacks of rotting lumber and rusted barbed wire, the scrawny yearlings who struggled through the winters, the smelly box where they lived—she saw it all through a stranger's eyes and wondered how she had ever ended up there. When she found the place that very first night, why hadn't she glanced at it and kept on going, as all strangers did?

"Can't we stop by the school and say goodbye?" Jim asked as they were loading the truck the next morning.

"No. I've got a stop in town to make."

Jasper watched in confusion as they hauled suitcases and cartons out of the house. He scurried underneath it to the safety of the soft dirt.

"Jasper!" Jim called.

With a grunt of relief the dog leaped in the truck, knowing now that no matter what has happening, he was going with them. Jim rested his hand on the dog's head and wiped away tears with the other. The truck rumbled over the river bridge, turned on to the county road and they were gone.

In the parking lot of Teddy's Equipment and Feed, they sat and listened to the wind pelt grit against the passenger window. Jim didn't ask what they were doing there.

Meg sat for five, then ten minutes before she said, "I have to go in."

She opened the front door. There were some customers in line at the cash register. Gwen raised her eyes, spotted Meg and turned away again. Meg hung back and watched as the customers paid for their purchases and left.

When the door closed behind the last one, Gwen said, "What

are you doing here?"

"I wanted to talk to you."

"There's nothing to talk about, Meg."

"I'm leaving." She gestured outside. "The truck's packed up. I want to talk."

Gwen looked outside at the pale little boy sitting alone in the truck.

"Not here. Let's go outside."

It was too windy to stand outside. They got into the truck. Gwen looked down at the tear tracks on the boy's cheeks. Well, she had nothing to feel sorry about. She hadn't hurt this child.

Jasper looked anxiously between her and the boy.

Meg turned to face her. "I used to think if I could do it, get through the day, get the work done, handle Mather and the cattle, I'd matter to everyone. And it would all make up for—the mess with Ronnie. But I know now, we don't control what happens out there. And doing it alone—well, in the end, I couldn't."

"I told you that. John told you that. Yet you didn't know it until you slept with my husband?"

"I listened, but I didn't understand... until it was too late."

Gwen squirmed. "Is this some kind of apology?"

"Would you listen to me if it was?"

"I hear you. You've grown up at the cost of my family!"

"I never stopped looking up to you, Gwen. And I'm asking you to go home."

"While you and Will have been into each other, I've learned some lessons, too. I don't miss it out there. I don't miss the house, the cooking, the wind, the cattle, any of it!" She jumped out of the truck and slammed the door.

Meg started the truck, but didn't put it in gear. Instead, she leaned her head against her hand.

"We have to leave because of you and Will?"

"Yes, son."

"Why can't Gwen just go home without us having to leave?"

"Because she wouldn't."

"She says she's not going, anyway."

"She'll change her mind."

Meg pulled out of the parking lot.

"Will we ever come back?" He watched her shift—first gear—second—third—fourth. The houses were dwindling as they flew past and the highway stretched ahead toward Jelm Mountain. Meg turned up the radio and the cab filled with a soft mournful voice.

> *"We'll set down the blanket*
> *on the green and grassy ground,*
> *with the horses and the cattle*
> *a grazin' all around."*

Jim pressed his nose against the window.

> *"Paint's a good pony and he paces when he can,*
> *Goodbye Ol' Paint, I'm a leavin' Cheyenne."*

The music soothed away the grind of miles beneath them. They weren't leaving a home. They were soaring above it all, like eagles, up over the Swans, up over Mather and the mobile home and the cows and calves and the river and mountainsides and meadows and all the wild birds and animals that had shared their lives with them. In a beat they flew by the sign, "Leaving Wonderful Wyoming," and then "Entering Colorful Colorado."

28

Long tables outside the Prairie Star Church of Christ were heaped with food: ham, roast beef, jello salads, macaroni and cheese casseroles, rolls, meringue pies and cakes of every description. The gathering following Mather's funeral was too large to hold inside the church recreation room and had been moved outdoors, in spite of the weather. Though it was late May, it had snowed the day before and chilly gusts blew the paper plates yards away. Everyone wore coats and hats. The only reminder of spring was the dandelions in little glass jars on each of the tables.

Mather's country neighbors had complained about him for as long as Gwen could recall, yet the ranching community was well represented. They'd never bypass a free meal.

Mrs. Mather sat stiffly in a folding chair. Her face was ashen, her eyes dry. Had she cried at all, wondered Gwen. Knots of people clustered around her. She nodded politely and her lips moved, but she seemed to regard the gathering as an ordeal.

Mather's children, all sullen teens now, stood behind their mother. The gusts whipped their hair in their faces. Sarge, who had been with his father when he died, sat at one of the tables and retold the story to as many people as were willing to rehear it. Everyone knew it by now, but not everyone had heard Sarge tell it. He spoke solemnly, drawing out every detail so people would listen to him longer.

The whole thing had begun when a new water commissioner, Mayall Fletcher, had been hired. Word soon spread that Fletcher believed in a fair irrigation system and the only way for it to be fair was if cheating was eliminated. That meant, he explained as he spread his gospel from ranch to ranch, that ranchers had to clean up their ditches, fix any leaks and remove any beaver dams or blockages that would enlarge their water right and impair someone else's.

Gwen was there when he said it to Will: "Snowpack is forty percent of normal this year and everyone's got to do their part. If everyone pitches in, those of you who've got the rights to the water will get it. I'm gonna be checking and we'll all get along as long as we cooperate."

The message was clear, but was it to be believed? Everyone stole a little water in years like this.

So the telephones in all the ranch houses rang when word spread of a confrontation between the new water commissioner and Mather. Fletcher had discovered a beaver dam on Mather's portion of the river and demanded that he remove it. Mather said that Fletcher had no business being on his property. Fletcher said he had every right to be there to enforce the water laws of the state of Wyoming. Mather said even if he had a right to be there, he had no right to make him remove an obstruction that he hadn't put there, but that God, acting through His Creation, had seen fit to put there. Fletcher replied that he had every right to make him remove it because water was backing up and flowing on Mather's property, water that Mather had no right to since there was no way in Hell that there'd be enough water in the river to fill Mather's right this year. Mather replied that if Fletcher cared more about those farmers over in Wheatland than he did about the suffering ranchers in his own community then he ought to remove the beaver dam himself. Fletcher gave him five days to remove it.

At the end of five days, the sheriff arrested Mather and he spent a couple days in jail. The worst deprivation for him there was the absence of liquor. Sarge paid his bail and he emerged pale and shaky and told Sarge that it wasn't worth the fight.

"Let's go get some dynamite," he said.

Sarge paused here for dramatic effect. "It was a real big dam, 'bout three foot high and blockin' off the whole river. We planted charges up and down it, set 'em off and not a damn thing happened. So Dad packed a bunch more charges in it and I said, 'Dad, I think it's too many' and he told me to shut up. Like he always did.

"He packed 'em in and we stood on the bank and he set off the charges and there was an explosion like I've never seen. Well, I've never been in an explosion ever, but rocks and sticks and dirt and shit were flying everywhere and I pushed my face against the ground and covered my head with my hands and prayed, 'God, please don't kill us.' And finally, I heard just little things falling out of the trees, little twigs and stuff falling like rain and I thought it was over and I got up and I said, 'Dad' and there he was. A rock had busted him in the head."

Will and Nick had stood nearby, listening.

"Funny how acts of nature killed both Dad and Mather," Nick said.

"What do you mean?"

"Well, a blizzard killed Dad and a drought killed Mather."

"Just goes to show if we ranch long enough, it'll kill us all. You ready to go?"

Nick scanned the tables in case there was some edible item that he had missed.

"Yeah. I guess I won't be needing any supper tonight, Gwen. They've fed us pretty well here."

Gwen smiled, relieved to be free of the evening meal. She hadn't wanted to start cooking for an extra person again, but Nick seemed happy here. He belonged here.

In the months following Meg's departure, Gwen had kept her distance from Will, but in spite of herself, her indignation languished. She knew from the children that the house was a mess. She heard from Nick that he hadn't been paid for the last year. When Will had asked her to dinner just before haying, she'd consented, though she'd cursed herself for doing so.

She was surprised when she opened the door and saw him dressed as if he was going on a date—showered, shaved and cologned with pressed jeans and shirt. For an instant, she saw past the man to the awkward kid she'd married. Now with his weathered face and graying sideburns, he looked seasoned.

"Who pressed your clothes?"

"Well, hello to you, too, Mrs. Swan."

"No. Who did that for you?"

"I took 'em to the cleaners."

"And picked them up?"

Will's jaw clenched. "Yeah, and you know damn well that meant an extra trip to town. Now are we going to supper?"

They sat in a booth at the back of the Diamond Horseshoe, but people spotted them and approached out of friendliness—or curiosity. Will stood up every time, shook the men's hands and made the usual small talk about water and cattle.

He sat down again once they left. "This'll be all over the county before midnight."

Gwen smiled with him. "That a married couple went to dinner."

Will gestured at her steak. "Isn't it any good?"

"It's fine. I'm not that hungry."

"Don't waste it. Get a doggy bag."

"I'll take it home and Rory will eat it."

"He's really growing now. His head's at my collar bone."

"He'll be tall, like you and Nick."

Their conversation stalled and Gwen looked away. She wasn't going to do his driving for him.

"Gwen, I don't know how to do this. I want you to come home. And not just because it's haying. The kids need you. I need you."

"What about Meg?"

"I thought you knew she'd gone."

Gwen shrugged. She was surprised to find herself crying again. "You have feelings for her."

"No, I don't. She started it after her horse—Mather's horse—died and I felt sorry for her. She was a lonely girl and I let myself get took by that. I thought I was helping her. I know now I wasn't doing anything but hurting everyone, including myself."

"Which one of you broke it off?"

"I did. I came to my senses."

"She must have been very hurt."

Will choked a little on his baked potato. "She was, but I told her it was all for the best, that she was still a young woman and that she'd meet somebody else. But I didn't tell her to leave. That was her decision."

Gwen remembered her last conversation with Meg and wondered whether Will was lying.

"She's gone now and we have to go on. Please, Gwen."

Gwen wiped her eyes with her napkin. "Things are going to have to change, Will."

"I won't be hiring any more female ranch hands, if that's what you mean."

"No. That's not what I mean. I mean, driving back and forth to town day in and day out so you can keep Nick off the ranch is not the way I want to live. I want to have things like they used to be—when we were a family out there together. If I'd have been out there, none of this would have happened. Nick inherited the ranch same as you. Let him be there."

"Even if I could stand him, which I can't, giving up the buy-out means his kids inherit the ranch. And then what happens to our kids? What about them?"

"Nick's children will have a share anyway because you can't afford to buy him out. You're behind now. With the interest, you'll never make it up."

"He might forgive the interest."

"Would you?"

"No."

"You do as you want, Will, but the only way I'm coming back is if my life is there, not half there and half in town. And the only way we can do that is if you make peace with your brother."

When she'd said it, she hadn't believed it would happen. Will's pride, after all, was dearer to him than anything else and to have to call his brother and ask him home... Will would sooner chew on nails. But living alone must have made him more desperate than she'd realized because two weeks later he called her and said he needed a good cook for the hay crew.

"What hay crew?"

"Me, Nick, Rory and McKenna. Nick's already moved down here. He's been working for a week."

Gwen glanced over the dismal church grounds, the gusts whipping the tablecloths and the clumps of weeds pushing up on the beaten ground.

"You two go on to the truck," she said to her husband and Nick, "I want to say goodbye to Mrs. Mather."

"You spoke to her before," said Will.

"Will, the woman's husband is dead."

"It's prob'ly her first day of rest since the day she was married."

Gwen ignored him and walked back to the widow. She leaned over and took the woman's hand. "If I can do anything…"

Mrs. Mather looked up at her wordlessly. Frizzy shocks of white hair fell from underneath her hat and blew into her face. She squeezed Gwen's hand.

All of them were silent in the truck going home. Gwen gazed out over the prairie. It had turned to light sage—there'd been enough moisture to get the grass started. In the distance, a long ribbon of antelope drifted.

"What do you 'spose they'll do with it?" Nick said over the whine of the truck.

"You mean the ranch?" asked Will.

"Yeah, what else?"

"Sarge could take it over."

Nick snorted. "He don't look like ranch material."

"Then I guess they'll sell it."

"How much will they want for it, d'ya think?"

"Why, you got ideas?"

"Why not? The place is right next to us. We could run another hundred head on it at least."

"It'd be another headache, that's all. And one we'd be paying interest on."

By the time they pulled into the barnyard, Gwen felt like she could nap. All the food, plus the stuffiness of the cab, had made her sleepy.

"Sure you don't want supper tonight, Nick?"

"Naw. I believe I'll go irrigate till dark."

She and Will walked to the house. She stopped in the kitchen, pulled out a pot and filled it with water.

"Thought you weren't going to fix supper tonight."

"Kids still need to eat." She peeled half a dozen potatoes and dropped them in the water. Then she tugged the wet clothes out of the washing machine and went out to hang them on the line.

The spring peepers were singing. The cacophony sounded lunatic, hysterical and above it, at least a dozen snipes were swooping and trilling whoo—whoo—whoo—whoo… It was life around her clamoring to continue. She held up the corner of a sheet and snapped the clothespin over the top, picked up the next length, snapped on the clothespin, picked up the next length and tears spilled down her cheeks. How was it that this place could fill her heart even as it weighed her down and crushed her? All other paths had closed to her now. She would be here forever.

29

Meg met Edie and Gabe at the Elks Café in Walden. The drifts were four feet high along the sidewalk and the night cold stung her cheeks. Inside the restaurant, the couple sat side by side expectantly. Meg was surprised at how old they appeared; they looked as brittle as toothpicks. Either one of them could blow away in the wind. It was amazing to think a couple this old could still be ranching up here. They had no children, they'd told her on the phone.

Gabe tried to stand up to shake her hand, but the table blocked his path and he sank back down.

"You must be Meg. I'm Gabe and this is Edie."

Edie nodded. Her eyes were searing, like a hawk's, and her long white hair was pulled back in a pony tail.

"What'll you have to eat?"

Meg shrugged. "I don't need anything."

"You drove all the way up here from Hayden, didn't ya? You must be hungry. Go on. Order yourself a steak. Scrawny thing like you's got to have something between herself and the cold."

Who is he calling scrawny, Meg wondered. The waitress brought her a cup of coffee and the couple watched her slurp it.

"We're glad you answered our ad," said Gabe, "but why would a young woman like yourself want to work for two old die-rs in this godforsaken place?"

"You don't look like die-rs," Meg lied.

"If we were cattle, we'd a been canned years ago."

"Why stay here? Why not retire?"

"Retire," Gabe answered, "that'd kill us for sure. I can't go as long as I got cattle to feed every morning and she can't go as long as she's got me to feed every morning. So I guess we've reached a stalemate."

"Ranching's what I want to do—I don't want any other job—and if I take this one, I'm close enough to see my son on the weekends."

Edie spoke for the first time. "He's not coming with you?"

"For now, he's going to stay with my parents. Just 'til I'm settled down somewhere."

"Got to be hard for a mother to leave her child behind. How old is he?"

It was hard, but Meg didn't want to show it. "Eleven."

"And you won't miss him?"

She did already. "I'll see him on the weekends."

"We had a boy," Gabe interjected, "but he hung himself in the barn."

Both faces deflected Meg's pity. "We had him for twenty years," mused Edie. "Sounds like a stretch when you're starting out, but when it's passed you see it's a space no bigger than a puddle. Sure you wouldn't rather have that boy with you?"

"He's better off where he is right now."

UNBROKEN

Did she really believe that?

It took them a quarter hour to leave the restaurant: to scoot out of the booth, wrap each other in hats, scarves and coats, thoughtfully count out the bills, hobble inch by inch down the icy sidewalk, struggle through the drifts and climb into the cab. Meg followed them out of town onto a dirt road that wound through fat clumps of sage. The sky sagged with stars while the land around her was black beyond her headlights. Finally, one lone yard light, like a fallen star, glowed a mile off.

They showed her upstairs to a chilly room that smelled of moth balls, the son's room, she thought. She opened the closet and found it full of men's clothes in plastic cleaning bags: clothes waiting to be unwrapped, snapped or zipped, waiting to soak up sweat—or cologne. His high school picture was on the bureau, handsome and smiling in his FFA jacket.

She turned off the light and slipped under the thin sheets in her long underwear. She ached for her own son.

The first night at her parents' house, she'd felt like driftwood going over a waterfall. Here they were—family and not family—passing the mashed potatoes, the pot roast and gravy, the peas. She couldn't face how much her parents had aged. The skin underneath her mother's chin sagged. Her father's hair had turned white. When she'd imagined them over the years, they were unchanged. What made her think that time had stopped for them?

She cleared her throat, "We've been on a ranch the last five years."

Both of them stared at her, battling back words they wanted to say. Meg expected torrents of anger and hurt, but instead Mamie looked down at her plate.

"We know."

"You know?"

"A woman called us—Gwen Swan. She told us that you had taken a job with a rancher in Laramie and that you were all right."

"When did she call you?"

"Years ago."

Meg looked down and the food began to blur. "Why didn't you come…?"

Her mother cut her off. "Well, Meg, why didn't you?"

"I tried."

"Then why now?" said Ben.

"I thought I'd made a home for Jim and me there, but it wasn't enough."

Ben sat back a little, weighing the acknowledgment in his daughter's voice. "We're glad you came. We're just sorry that it took you so long.

"What do you think, son, would you like to stay here with us?"

Jim looked blankly from one anxious grandparent to the other.

The next morning, Meg overheard her father and Jim in the kitchen. They sat at the table with cereal boxes and a plate of toast between them. The sun poured in the window over the sink. They were already pals. Within the week, Jim was her father's new helper and the proud owner of a bay quarter horse with a diamond on its forehead. On weekends, Ben and Jim rode off together with Jasper between the horses.

But Meg rejected the job offer her father made her and moved into a mobile home in town. She took a job as a cashier at Safeway and most days, the prices of groceries crowded out thoughts of Mather, of Will, of Gwen.

On slow afternoons, as she gazed out at the parking lot, those images would come flooding back. Sissie. Her heart jumping when she'd hear Will's truck in the yard. The bittersweet blend of loss and pride she felt every fall as the calves clamored up into the semis. But most of all, the land itself moving through season after season: the meadows dotted with violet shooting stars in the spring, the breezes combing through the long grasses in the summer, the fluttery gold aspen leaves and the sparkly mornings in the fall, the wind driving the snow against their trailer home in winter. It seemed a hard trade-off: all that for this view of an asphalt parking lot day in and day out.

She searched the newspaper for another ranching job and broke the news to Jim one night at supper.

"I don't want to leave," he said. "I want to stay here with Ben and Mamie."

Her father interceded for him the next day. "Don't do this, Meg. The boy's happy here. Leave him with us. Just till you're settled."

"Till I'm settled?"

"Until you have a place permanently. You know, you might get married again."

Meg bit her lip. She knew he was happy here, but how could she give him up now? For more than a decade, caring for him and anticipating his company throughout her long days had fueled her will to persevere.

"Meg, I know how much it must have hurt when you learned it wasn't going to work out with Ronnie. You believed in him. I was wrong not to see that. And I know Jim made up for it. If you can tell me that what's best for him is to go off with you again, then you do it. I trust you to know what's best."

She hadn't always done what was best—that's what he meant, but she was grateful to him for not saying it. When Jim came home from school, she asked, "What about Jasper?"

"He should stay with me, Mom."

She left for Walden at dusk. In the rearview mirror, Jim waved and Jasper sat next to him, whining.

30

The cafeteria was crammed with buyers and sellers and every time someone opened the door, animal odors and cigarette smoke blew in from the breezeway. Meg's cup of hot chocolate steamed in her hands and she looked around anxiously, hoping not to see anyone she knew from Laramie.

Edie and Gabe seemed too drained to pick up the coffee cups in front of them. All of them had been up since three a.m. They'd stepped out into a blizzard and they'd fought the mounting drifts to load the calves on the semis. The storm dogged them as they inched down Cameron Pass, navigating from one reflector pole to the next. It was noon before they arrived at the sale barn. Then they'd tramped through the muddy lots, searching for their calves. Now, as they rested here, Meg wondered how the two of them were going to sit through the sale and then through the long journey home, especially if the storm didn't quit.

She jumped at the pressure of a hand on her shoulder and looked up to see Nick Swan standing over her. Damn! What if Will was here, too? Or Gwen? What would she say? How would she explain this to her new employers?

"It's good to see you, Meg."

She'd aged quite a bit, thought Nick. Real lines now around her mouth and eyes and her hair, a dull ash color. He held out his hand.

Meg looked at it, unsure. Finally, she took it.

"This is Edie and Gabe Hardy from Walden. I work for them now." She gestured to Nick, "This is Nick Swan."

He shook their hands. "Pleased to meet you. You're lucky to have Meg. She's a hell of a hand."

"We love her," said Edie. "We don't know what we'd do without her."

"How long have you been with them?"

"Almost a year."

"Mind if I sit down?"

Before Meg could object, he'd squeezed beside her in the booth. "What are you all here for today?"

Gabe answered, "We've brought our calves down."

"Hell of a day for it."

"Yeah. It's been rough. What are you here for?"

"I brought down our gummers and our open cows. I was getting ready to have some lunch and leave."

"You drove all the way from Casper in this?" Meg asked.

"No. I'm not in Casper anymore. I'm back on the ranch with Will and Gwen."

Their names stung Meg, but after a pause she asked, "How are they doing?"

"Good. The ranch is doing well. Rory and McKenna are OK, except Rory's been in some fights in school."

"What school is he in now?"

"He's in junior high. They all get in trouble there. He'll be all right."

"It's been nice talking to you, Mr. Swan, but we'd better be getting on to the sale," said Gabe as he stood up. "You stay here if you want, Meg, and talk to your friend."

Meg wanted to get up and leave, but Nick had her trapped in the booth. He didn't move.

"I've always wondered where you went."

She didn't look at him. "I've got to be going, Nick."

"How's Jim?"

"He's good. He's living with my parents."

"Why?"

"He's happy there. It's OK for the time being. I'll move him up with me this summer."

"So you went home?"

"Yes."

"You should have done that a long time ago."

"I've got to be going."

"It was brave—what you did, Meg. I admired you for it. One day, Gwen will, too."

"What are you talking about?"

"Breaking it off with Will—I know what that took out of you."

"He told you?"

"He didn't tell me a damn thing. And I haven't talked about it with Gwen, either."

"How's Mather?"

"He's dead. He packed too much dynamite in a beaver dam and when it exploded, a rock fell on him and killed him."

"Who's got his place?"

"No one. I think they're going to sell it. And I want to buy it."

"I've got to go," Meg started to push him out of the booth, but when he didn't budge, she stopped.

"Can I come see you?" he asked.

"No."

"Why not? Do you have someone else?"

"No, it's just that. . ."

"It's just that years ago you slept with my brother. What does that have to do with now?"

She pushed against him and this time he stood up.

"I just about kicked myself when I found out, because I wanted you all along. All along."

She left without looking back. The door swung shut behind her. The chill enveloped her and the auctioneer's voice blared over the loudspeaker.

Mather was dead. She didn't feel any loss. She missed his ranch more than him. The rest of Nick's words bounced around her head like loose ping pong balls. She'd allowed thoughts of Gwen and Will to sink beneath the flow of ranch days. There was no point worrying anymore about troubles she could no longer solve. But seeing Nick and hearing of them rekindled the pain of losing the man she'd loved and the guilt at betraying the woman who had befriended her. That man was a fool to think she'd want to be reminded of those feelings.

Nine months after the sale, she was out baling late in the afternoon when she saw the flash of a truck pull into the meadow. At first, she thought it was someone Gabe knew because it pulled up to his mower. Then it crossed the meadow toward her. The hay windrows were gold in the falling light and she watched the tires swish over one after another.

Nick stepped out of the truck. His stride was confident, as if he had just seen her five minutes ago.

She knocked down the throttle and took out her ear plugs.

"I got you a night off."

"What?"

"I talked to Gabe and he says you can have the night off."

"Why are you here? Why aren't you haying?"

"We got rained out."

"Do Will and Gwen know you're here?"

"It didn't occur to me to tell them. Do you want me to?"

"This isn't going to work."

"It's not about anything working. It's about a dinner and dance at Woods Landing. There's a live band tonight."

"No, thanks."

"What else did you have planned?"

Meg looked around. "This."

"You're going to stay on that tractor till you fossilize?"

She looked down on him, wavering.

"It's just a dance, Meg."

"I've got to clean up."

"C'mon then. Shut that thing down and let's go."

An hour later they were flying past the "Welcome to Wyoming" billboard. Meg wore a white Western shirt and jeans. She'd washed her hair—apple shampoo as far as Nick could tell—and let it loose on her shoulders.

Before she'd left, Edie had knocked on her door. "Can I come in? I've brought you a little something." Edie's eyes twinkled. She pressed a tiny bottle of eau de toilette into her hand. "I thought you could use this."

"I don't need this. Nick and I are just friends."

"He'd like to be more than a friend. You ought to let him. He seems like a nice man."

Meg pulled off the stopper and smelled it.

"You can't stay with us forever. We know that."

"Maybe, but I'm not going with him."

"Why not?"

"Because I can't."

"What are you punishing yourself for, Meg?" She took Meg by the shoulders and turned her to the dusty mirror over the bureau. "That young woman in there. Let her out before she's gone."

Down at Woods Landing, the music was so loud it shook the walls.

"You want something to eat first?" Nick yelled in her ear.

"Yes, I'm starved."

They sat down and ordered hamburgers and fries. The fiddler, in a bowler hat, beat his bow against the strings and sang:

I am the bravest cowboy, that's ever roamed the West,
I been all o'er the Rockies, got bullets in my breast.

The wooden dance floor was packed with sun-burned couples. It was hot, even though all the windows were open, but no one seemed to care. Meg smiled. It had been a long time since she'd seen anyone have fun.

Nick watched her over the rim of his beer mug.

"Ready to dance?"

I wore a wide brim high hat, my saddle too was fine
And when I court that pretty gal, you bet I'll call her mine.

Meg had forgotten how good it could feel to move, to sway and twirl, to pull and be pulled back. Nick's arms loosely encircled her and she could smell cologne mingled with sweat in his shirt.

The band galloped through *I'll Go Stepping Too,* which left the couples panting and stumbling off the floor for more food and beer. Then the fiddler played the opening chords of a waltz:

I wish my heart was made of glass, wherein you might behold…

Nick held her at arm's length.

"Do you want to dance to this one?"

She nodded and they waltzed slowly over the floor. The fiddler crooned over his strings: *Oh how your name is written here, in letters made of gold.* In spite of herself, she let her head sink to his shoulder. It felt good to rest it there. She closed her eyes.

> *In letters made of gold my love,*
> *Believe me when I say,*
> *You are the only one for me—*
> *Until my dying day.*

It was midnight when they left. The air had turned cold. The Milky Way streamed across the sky. The music played on, diffusing throughout the expanse above.

"There's a meteor shower tonight," said Nick. "Do you want to watch?"

"Where would we go?"

"The top of Jelm Mountain. That oughta be a good spot."

"I don't have a coat."

"Guess you'll have to share mine."

It took nearly an hour to lurch up the narrow washed-out road to the top. Others were already there, quietly waiting in the backs of trucks or sitting on blankets.

Nick spread a tarp in the pickup bed and they sat down and

leaned against the cab.

"You can have the coat," Nick said, holding it out to her, "I don't need it."

"You sure?"

"Yeah. It's OK. Is the truck bed too hard?"

"No. I'm fine. How are your kids?"

"They're about grown up. It's funny—looking at them and remembering how I was at their age. I'm hoping they aren't as stupid as I was."

"Why do you say that?"

"I was always a hothead. My friends could get me to do any stupid thing just by telling me that I couldn't do it. And then I'd do it and get in trouble and it just built up the fence between me and Dad a little higher.

"One year they bet me that I couldn't ride a green-broke colt in the Jubilee Parade. We had just broke some, so I took one and entered the parade. Things were a little hairy, but basically OK until a cannon went off and the horse took off running like hell. All the baton girls and bands split in front of us, flying to the curbs as fast as they could. I thought the floats would stop him, but he'd just jump to one side or the other and keep on running."

"Weren't you scared?"

Nick shrugged. "They've all gotta stop running sometime. It was just a matter of what was going to stop us. I saw the railyard fence dead ahead and I thought that would stop him, but he tried to jump it, caught on the top and flipped over. Nothing happened to me, but the horse had to have dozens of stitches, which Dad made me pay for. He was a good horse after that."

"And how did John take that?"

"Just more evidence that I didn't amount to much. Look— they're starting up!"

Two parallel fireballs streaked across the sky. Then another three followed. Oohs and aahs and squeals of pleasure rose up around them. Then five more. It was like a fireworks show—only better. Oranges, reds and deep violets trailed across the heavens. Some of them burned out overhead. Others streamed colors to the far horizon. Sometimes there was a pause between barrages and sometimes they followed one after the other for twenty minutes or more. Meg understood that the show wasn't for her, or for any of them, but wasn't their wonder part of the splendor?

"Are you happy?" Nick whispered in her ear.

"Right now, I feel like a little kid."

"What about before right now?"

"I don't know what happiness is." She paused to watch more meteors. "But I got to live the life I chose."

"Working on ranches for other people?"

"Working under this sky."

"Do you still love Will?"

She turned to him, annoyed. He didn't back down. He continued to stare into her face, his eyes deep pools of darkness in contrast to the flaming stars overhead.

"Do you think you could love anyone else?"

Meg snorted and turned back to the sky. "This is a lot of questions for a dinner and dance."

"You win, Meg Braeburn."

At the first pale light unfolding over the eastern mountains, they drove back down and by 8:00 a.m., Nick had her back at the tractor where he'd found her.

31

When had her mother gotten so ugly? McKenna watched the reflection in the mirror. Her hair was thinning to where McKenna could see her skull. Get away, she thought. Get away from me.

Gwen lifted her daughter's hair to braid it and McKenna pulled away.

"Don't you want me to braid your hair today?"

"No thanks, Mom."

"The wind's blowing. It'll get tangled."

"I'm only walking from the truck to the bus."

Gwen's hands dropped to her daughter's shoulders and McKenna shrugged them off.

"What is it?" asked Gwen.

"Nothing."

"Why won't you let me touch you?"

"I'm just trying to get ready. That's all."

Her mother left the bathroom. McKenna finished brushing her hair and reached for the lipstick and mascara that she'd hidden to take to school with her.

When she stepped out in the hall, she saw her father and Rory sitting under the dining room light. Rory looked up and tried to catch her eye, but she ignored him.

"McKenna! Your breakfast is ready!"

She rushed past her father and brother into the kitchen.

"I'm not hungry. Let's go."

"What do you mean you're not hungry? Are you sick?"

"No. I just don't want anything."

"Well, at least take a piece of toast."

"Mom. It's ten after six. Let's go."

Without another word, Gwen went out to the porch, grabbed her overcoat and sat down to pull on her boots. McKenna shifted impatiently and then they both stepped out into the January wind. It caught McKenna's hair and blew it into her face.

Will had started the truck for them and McKenna welcomed the hot air blasting from the vents.

"I know things are lousy right now, McKenna, but you don't have to treat us all like pariahs."

McKenna was silent.

"We're your family. Rory's made some mistakes, but he loves you very much. We all do. Your behavior is just making things worse."

"You know what the boys say to me on the bus, 'How's your hoodlum brother?' What am I supposed to say? They're wrong? All this stuff has happened and nobody's thought about how it hurts me."

"So the answer is to ignore the three of us? To treat us like we don't exist?"

"Here's the bus."

McKenna slammed the truck door. As Gwen watched the

children wave to her daughter and she envied McKenna's opportunity for escape, as she always had. Despite what talk McKenna might hear, her hours would not be full of pain.

Gwen put the truck in reverse.

Back in the kitchen, Rory was washing the dishes. He avoided her eyes. They'd hardly spoken in the week since she and Will had picked him up at the jail. And what was there to say? Their failure as a family lay stinking before them.

"This morning you'll help your mother feed while I'm in town and this afternoon, you'll help Nick with his calving shed at Mather's."

"OK," said Rory. He dried his hands and went out to the porch.

Will and Gwen looked at each other and she saw in his eyes what she felt in her own heart, helplessness. They'd raised generations of cattle, but one boy was beyond them.

They'd let him spend the weekend with a friend in town— Lucas. Gwen hadn't liked Lucas, or his mother. Lucas' father wasn't around. The mother worked as a waitress at The Lariat and spoiled the boy, Gwen thought. He was sullen and rude, but the friendship made Rory happy so she'd let her objections slide. Then, in the middle of the night, the phone call had come. The boys were missing.

Rory's voice interrupted her thoughts.

"Dad," said Rory, "the river's way down. I had to chop clear to the bottom before I could find water."

"If it's like that tomorrow, you'll have to move the water hole. Are you two all right together?" He said it to Rory, but neither Rory nor Gwen answered. He pushed past them and left.

They faced each other for the first time that morning. It felt so odd to have her son—almost a grown man—at home, like a little child. It was shaming.

"Is the wagon loaded?" she asked.

"I loaded it last night."

The sky was swept clear, but the wind howled through the cottonwoods. With every gust, it grew stronger, louder. They'd never stay warm out today. A section of tin had broken loose on the barn roof and banged up and down.

Rory went to start the tractor while she fed the horses. They shuffled to the feeder, waiting for her to push hay through the bunks. Uh-uh-uh-uh-uh-uh—the starter whined over and over. The horses bit at one another, squabbling over who would eat first.

Will and Gwen had driven to Lucas' house right after the telephone call. His mother had already called the police and for the next hour, they waited and listened to her say over and over that she'd left them in Lucas' room and had gone out with some friends to have a drink—just for a few minutes—and that she'd told them to call her if they needed anything. She didn't know what time she'd gotten back, so she couldn't say how long they'd been gone. Will had paced back and forth across her kitchen floor and at one point, jerked the refrigerator door open. Every shelf was packed with beer.

"Did you check to see if any of this beer is missing?"

Her eyes had narrowed and she'd snapped, "What do you mean by that? Lucas wouldn't take any beer. He's a good boy. Does your boy drink beer?"

Gwen couldn't listen to that starter anymore. She dropped the pitchfork and stomped into the Quonset.

"Rory! You're going to wreck that tractor and then we'll never get them fed. Go get the Caterpillar and we'll pull-start it."

The Caterpillar whined, whined, whined without turning over. Gwen cursed and wondered what to do next. Nick had taken the other tractor over to the Mather place. They'd have to drive over and find him and in the meantime, the cattle would come bawling up around the barnyard.

At last, the Cat engine caught, thank God. She marveled at how a whole day could revolve around an engine turning over.

Rory backed the Caterpillar in front of the tractor and chained them together. He shouted over the engine's rumble, "You want to drive the Cat or the tractor?"

"I'll sit in the tractor."

Rory inched forward. Gwen watched the chain tighten and felt the tractor start to roll. She let the clutch out and the engine roared to life. Exhaust sputtered from the stovepipe and now she could no longer hear the wind.

Good, the cattle would be fed on time.

The deputy had rung the door bell around three a.m. He was pale and grim and Gwen was terrified of the words forming in his skull. He looked from one face to the next.

"Which one of you is Mrs. Shipmon?"

"I am." The woman stepped forward, elbowing past Gwen.

"Your boy's in the hospital, ma'am."

"Is he alive?"

"Yes. He's been in a car accident."

"What happened?"

"Are you Mr. and Mrs. Swan?"

They nodded.

"Well, it looks like they stole a car. The car belongs to Mrs. Shipmon's neighbor behind her, in the alley. He'd left the keys in it.

They went joyriding around town until we spotted them. We tried to get them to stop, but they headed out of town, on up the Summit. They were going too fast and they missed a curve, lost control and rolled."

Gwen's voice squeaked out of her throat. "What about Rory?"

"He's fine. We have him in custody."

"Who was driving?" Will asked.

Lucas, thought Gwen.

"The Swan boy. We found a lot of empty beer cans in the car."

Lucas' mother snarled, "You thought your boy was too good for mine. And now he's nearly killed him."

"Mrs. Shipmon, your boy's not dead."

"How badly is he hurt?"

"I don't know."

Lucas' mother ran from the house and jumped into her car.

"You folks want to come to the station and post bail?"

"Post bail?" Gwen whispered.

After he left, they sat in the truck. It was bitter cold, but Will's hands lay inert in his lap, as if he had no strength to reach for the ignition.

"What should we do?" he asked. It wasn't as if he was talking to her. He was staring out over the steering wheel toward the lights on the street.

Tears ran down Gwen's cheeks. Part of her wanted to get him right now before he was beaten, or worse, by another inmate and part of her wanted him to stay there and rot because she was so angry. After she'd tried so hard… Had he done this just to spite them?

"I think we should go home," Will said as he picked up the key.

Even though she wanted to say "No, don't, don't leave my baby," she said nothing.

"Mom! Do you want to drive or feed?"

"Will you get too cold sitting in the tractor seat?"

"It's all right. I'll be fine. You can feed."

It didn't really matter. The wind stabbed through her anyway. It was blowing so hard that she couldn't even hear the cattle, although she saw them running from the riverbank. Her hands were frozen before she could begin chopping the bales. She jumped off the wagon and stopped Rory.

"You're going to have to feed. My hands are frozen."

"Do you want to go home?"

"No. I'll be all right."

She climbed in the tractor seat and turned into the wind. It seared her face so hard her eyes watered. She looked back and there was Rory, chopping the bales and tossing them to the hungry cattle behind. He looked exactly like Will now and she could almost forget about everything that had happened.

Five days later, they'd driven into town to pick him up. The ground was bare, just skiffs of dirty snow tapered around the sagebrush. The sky was a bright blue, not the ice blue she was accustomed to in January, and there was no wind. Rory had been born on a day like that. Will had driven, just like now. She remembered the sun peeping over the horizon and the snow crystals twinkling like tiny prisms. How buoyed she'd been by possibilities!

The deputy seated them in a bare conference room and when they brought him in, she'd said, "All I want to know is, why?"

His hair was matted down and stubble peppered his face. He stared at her angrily and said, "I don't know."

The sunlight poured in the dining room while, outside, the gusts broke against the house, rattling a lamp chain on an end table. As she worked in the kitchen, she glanced at him. He sat staring out the window. She turned down the potatoes, wiped her hands on the dishtowel and sat down facing him.

"We're going to have to pay that boy's hospital bills."

Rory didn't look at her. "I didn't mean for him to get hurt."

"I know you didn't, but Rory, we're lucky he's alive."

"Do you think I can go see him?"

"I don't know. His mother's angry. I'd be angry, too, if I were her. Maybe in a few months."

"We always made fun of that old guy behind them in the alley. He'd drive two blocks to pick up his snoose and whiskey and we'd watch him drive back and he always left his keys in the car. We thought it would be funny to take the car for a while."

"Who took the beer?"

"We both did. I drove because Lucas doesn't know how to drive yet. We drove around town for a couple of hours. We'd stop and have some beer and then drive around some more. We raced a few kids on Grand. That's when the cops saw us."

"Why didn't you stop, Rory?"

"I didn't want to get caught. And then the car rolled and Lucas was screaming and the cops were yelling. It all happened too fast."

Gwen couldn't think of anything to say. It seemed she'd spent so many years trying to sand down her son's rough edges, while shielding him from the judgments of teachers, other parents and his father and now, there was no role left to play.

"Do you think I'll have to go to jail?"

"The lawyer is going to try and keep you out."

He looked at her. "Will I ever have friends again?"

32

Gabe decided to keep the calves through the winter. They'd put up enough hay and he was hoping for better prices, maybe in the spring, or clear to the next fall, if he had to keep them that long. But it meant that Meg spent the entire day feeding. They were deep into January now and it snowed every day. Every morning, Meg plowed trails for the cattle, first the cows, then the calves. If she was lucky, she'd have the calves fed by noon. But if cattle needed doctoring and she had to bring them in, it would be dark before she finished feeding.

She couldn't remember when she'd ever felt so tired. She climbed the stairs around eight o'clock every evening and fell asleep before she could spare a thought for Jim or Nick. Jim was in junior high now and on the honor roll. She hadn't seen Nick since Christmas when he'd joined them in Hayden. He told her he'd bought Mather's place and was trying to fix it up.

After the year turned, Gabe weakened. He fed the bulls and checked the water tanks. Then he parked his truck in the garage and shuffled the fifty yards to the house. Meg suggested that he park in front of the house and she'd put the truck away, but he shook his head.

"An old man's gotta have a little bit of pride left, don't ya think? It's bad enough I have to watch you do all the work without you babying me as well."

If the weather didn't let up, Meg didn't know how she'd manage through calving. They all pretended that Edie and Gabe would work the calving shed, but Meg knew it was impossible. She knew she had to tell Gabe to sell the calves, but day after day, she postponed it. It would be another blow to the old man's pride.

On Groundhog Day, the temperature was ten below, but at least it wasn't snowing. The peaks jutted out of the cloud mantle and as the sun rose, the clouds burned away, leaving the snow sparkling through the valley.

It's going to warm up today, she thought.

Her trails were still in good shape, so she could start feeding right away. That would leave her time in the afternoon to ride through the cows and look for early heavies. She saw Gabe leave the yard and head for the water tanks while she started for the feeding ground.

Gabe and Edie fed with a winch truck, like Mather had. When she set the hooks for her first load, she looked over to the tanks and saw Gabe parked there. When she came back for a second load, his truck was still there. What could he be doing? She fed a third load and still his truck hadn't budged. She shook the forks free of hay and drove to the tanks. He seemed to be sitting in the truck.

She called, "Gabe!"

She opened the door. His eyes had turned to glass and the skin on his wrists was blue and cold. Shards of ice slowly twirled in the water tank, melting moment by moment. Cows ambled from one hay pile to another while the calves bawled for their food. The snow crunched underfoot. Gabe's ranch was leaving him behind.

Nick came up for the funeral and afterward, they drove to the Elks' Café, which was packed with its regular lunchtime customers and some of the funeral party. The hostess found them a booth and they ordered coffee.

"It looks like you're going to be out of a job."

"I don't know that. Edie hasn't said anything."

"Why the hell would she want to stay there anymore?"

"Why the hell does anyone stay on a ranch?"

"Don't get out the buckshot here. All I meant was, that's her retirement. She's gonna sell it and get gone."

"She hasn't said that."

"So you're going to stay on?"

"As long as she needs me."

"What about if I need you?"

"Will and Gwen aren't going to let me come back. And even if they did, how is this going to work?"

"First of all, it's not up to them and second, you wouldn't be living with them. You'd move on to the Mather place with me. They've forgotten all about you, Meg. They've got their own problems with Rory now."

"How naïve can you be? And who said I wanted to live on the Mather place again? I don't want to be reminded of him, or Will."

"It's not the dump you remember anymore and you wouldn't be working for Mather, or anyone else. You'd be working for yourself."

"No. I'd be working for the Swans. Have you told Will and Gwen that you're seeing me?"

"No."

"Nick."

"What do you want me to do? Announce it, like I need their permission?"

"It's their ranch."

"It's mine, too. Look—just come down and see what I've done with Mather's place. Just give me that much of a chance."

"I can't do that before calving."

"Why not?"

"Because Gabe never sold last year's calves. I've got them, too."

"How are you going to manage all that?"

"I'm hoping Edie'll go ahead and sell the calves."

"When are you supposed to start calving?"

"Two weeks."

"Two weeks. And you've got yearling calves, too? I don't know why I ask you how you'll manage because I know you will, but again, this is somebody's else's place. If you're going to work yourself to death, don't you want to do it on your own place?"

"I'm not leaving Edie."

It was June before she took Nick up on his offer. Through the long calving months, she seesawed between missing him and pecking at herself for being such a fool as to dream this could work. How could she think of returning? But interwoven through all these thoughts was the vision of Gabe dead in his truck and the world moving on, moving on.

Still, she wasn't prepared for the memories that rushed at her as she drove back down the pass and across the Hollow. She reflected bitterly on how hard she had tried to make it on Mather's ramshackle ranch, only to stoke her pride, which, in the end, had been so flawed.

After she turned by the mailbox, she stopped on the old wooden bridge. It wasn't the same place after all. The piles of used posts and rusting equipment were gone. There was a new mobile home with a pine deck and a new barn. The Mather place, the place where she had worked, had vanished.

Nick rose from a chair on the deck to meet her. "Well, what do you think?"

"It's amazing—what you've done here. It's… all changed."

"You sound like you regret it. Did you want it to be the same place?"

She smiled. "Yes. And no."

"Let me show you around."

He showed her a row of Russian willows he'd planted behind the house. When they grew, they'd make a good windbreak and they'd provide shade over the house in the summer. He showed her the new corrals he was building. He'd leveled half the meadow and put in new irrigation ditches. He planned to level the other half in the fall.

They leaned against the corral. With the tour over, a moment of awkwardness ballooned between them. Already the hay was tall—it undulated in waves.

"You don't like it?"

"It's just hard to come back, that's all," she blurted. "There's nothing here of Mather anymore." Or of me, she thought. "It looks like you've got a good hay crop."

"Just have to decide what we'll be feeding it to."

"What do you mean?"

"Meg, I thought about what you said—how you didn't want to come back and work for the Swans. You're right. So, if you want to be here, we'll raise what you want. I guess you've just about earned the right to do that here, with what you put into the place. So what will it be?"

"Nick… "

"C'mon. What'll it be?"

Meg's eyes followed the billowing grass. "Well, if I had my own place, I'd want horses."

"Horses it is."

"Nick…"

"What?"

"I can't. It's just another damn mistake."

"The wall's in your head, Meg. Look around, nothing but open country out here. It just about goes on forever, doesn't it? We'd have it to share for the rest of our lives."

"What about Gwen?" she whispered.

He turned and took her face in his hands. "The two of you were best friends once, weren't you?"

Meg nodded.

"One morning, she'll forget to put on that anger and that friendship will be there again, like it was never gone in the first place."

She laid her hand over his. "You're so sure."

He kissed her. "I know I'm right, Meg. And, I found a hand for Edie."

"You did? Is he any good?"

"He's very good."

"Does he drink?"

"He's given it up."

"Who is he?"

"No point in telling you that yet. I haven't asked him if he's interested."

They decided that Meg would tell Jim on her own. She drove straight through to Hayden, picked him up and took him to the Burger King. Once they'd sat down with their hamburgers and Cokes, she studied her son. He wasn't a boy anymore. His face was still solemn, as it always had been, but the plumpness was gone from his cheeks. His jaw had grown longer and his brows were thick. With his red hair and blue eyes, he was a handsome boy, a boy that awkward girls, as she once had been, would dream about.

"Remember how we'd said you'd come live with me when I got settled?" He looked at her skeptically, so she plowed on. "I'm going to be settled. We're going to be settled. I'm marrying Nick.

We'll live at the Mather place. He's totally changed it. It's real nice now. You'll like it."

To her surprise, he glared at her.

"They *hate* us."

"Who?"

"Will, Gwen, Rory… all of them."

"Son, they don't hate you. It's me…"

"Mom, Rory and I got into a fight one day. He roped me and yanked me off my horse."

"What were you fighting about?"

"You."

"Why didn't you tell me?"

He shrugged. "It didn't matter. We left."

They sat silently for a moment. Meg began again.

"We'll finally have a place of our own. We won't be the help anymore. We'll be a real family. All your life, I've wanted that for you."

"I've got that here! I'm not going back. There's nothing there for me."

"What about me? We were together, you and me."

"You're the one who left."

Where was the son she'd meant to raise, the one who would understand—and forgive her—always? In her mind, she heard a door slam. How fleeting that smug vindication had been when she'd slammed it on her parents and how hard it hit her now.

33

Gwen surveyed the miles of sagebrush around them. "How far is this place from the highway, Nick?"

"About the same as ours."

She glanced at Rory. He hadn't taken his eyes away from the window since they had gotten in the car. She could read his thoughts. He was being exiled, even though he had agreed to it and they'd told him that he could come home whenever he wanted.

The road dipped down a sharp incline and ran along a hayfield. Gwen could see the two story house in the distance.

"Nick, who put up all this hay?"

"The neighbors did. She paid them with a portion of it. I think that's one of the first things she'll want Rory to do—haul hay."

Will, too, was staring out the window and hadn't said a word during the trip.

They pulled up in front of the house and a frail woman with a cane pushed the screen door open and tottered down the steps.

"I've been waiting for you." She held out her hand. "You must be Rory."

"Rory," said Nick, "this is Ms. Hardy."

Rory looked afraid to take her hand, then shook it quickly. She looked lively, thought Gwen, but how was she strong enough to care for herself, much less a ranch?

"I know you'll want a drink after such a long trip."

"No, Edie, we've got to be getting on," said Nick as he unloaded Rory's suitcases.

"Don't you want to see where he'll be staying?"

Gwen started to speak, but Will interjected, "Nick's right, Ms. Hardy. We've got our own ranch to run."

"I haven't gotten to meet any of you."

"This is Gwen Swan, Rory's mother," said Nick, "and this is Will, my brother and Rory's dad."

Everyone shook hands and then the men shoved their hands back in their pockets.

Nick patted Rory's shoulder. "You take care, son. We'll see you soon."

Will grabbed his son's shoulders, pulled him in and then pushed him away.

"I'd like to stay and have something to drink," said Gwen.

The men stared at her, displeased.

"I can bring you something out here."

"No, don't trouble yourself. We can get something back along the way."

Gwen reached out to hug her son. As she did, she choked back a sob. Rory lifted his arms, but didn't return the hug.

"You can visit any time," said Edie.

Everyone but Rory started to get back in the car.

"Nick, give my love…"

Nick cut her off. "I will, Edie. So long. You take care." He gunned the engine and drove away.

"Nick, who was she sending love to?"

"A mutual friend of ours, another woman rancher. We met her down at the sale barn."

"And you're going to see this woman?"

"Prob'ly—before Edie will."

Nick had proposed the whole scheme to them late one night after a day haying. "There's a woman near Walden," he'd said, "she just lost her husband. She wants to stay on her ranch and she needs a hand."

"She doesn't have any children?" asked Gwen.

"They had one son who killed himself."

"How did you meet this woman?"

"I met her and her husband at the sale barn 'bout a year and a half ago. They're good people."

"What are you asking?" said Will.

"I'm suggesting that Rory go live with this woman and help her out."

"Live with an old woman on a ranch? He's only sixteen."

"What can't Rory do on a ranch?"

"What if something happens to this woman?"

"He'll call for help, the same as if he was here and something happened to one of us."

"What about school?"

"Why do you want to send him back to school? He's lost a year and it'll be hard for him to go back. He struggled with it anyway. Leave him alone and he can always go get his G-E-D."

"Why can't I go live with you?" Rory interjected.

"Because, son, it might be better for you to get away."

Nick was speaking of himself, Gwen thought. But Rory

wasn't Nick. He was so much more—irresponsible—and Nick had been older when he'd left.

"Have you talked to this woman about Rory?"

"Yes, I have."

"She knows he's been in trouble?"

"She knows he's been in trouble, but that he's a good boy."

"What do you think, Rory?"

It's a way out, he thought. He dreaded going back to school and facing his classmates' taunts about having to repeat a grade. If he refused to go to school, he had another winter ahead listening to his father tell him every moment of every day that he couldn't do anything right.

"I'll do it."

"What kind of outfit does this woman have?" asked Will.

"Cow-calf, although she's going to cut back this fall to a hundred and fifty head."

"That's manageable, but it's going to be a tough haul, Rory. You're not going to have me and Nick to fall back on like you do here."

Rory stared back at Will. "I know."

"How are you going to cope when you've got your tractor stuck, you've got a hundred and fifty to feed and twenty of those need to come into the calving shed?"

"Why don't you think I can do it?"

Nick heard the defiance in Rory's voice.

"He can do it—as long as he wants to."

"What if he wants to quit just when things get rough? Is he going to leave this woman high and dry?"

"Well, in that he's no different than any other ranch hand. She can pull someone outta a Walden bar and take the same chance. But I think her chances are better with Rory."

Rory hauled his belongings up the stairs. He'd be sleeping in the dead boy's room, she'd told him. He opened the closet. There were the boy's clothes hanging in plastic and his FFA pictures on the bureau. Creepy.

Outside the narrow bedroom window, the house cast a long shadow over the dirt yard. Beyond, in the meadow, haystacks were rounded like bread loaves. A plateau surrounded the ranch on all sides, cutting off his view of the highway.

He went back downstairs and she fed him Salisbury steak and gravy, mashed potatoes, homemade bread, fat sliced tomatoes and milk. He wolfed the food and watched her gnarled hand slowly lift a fork to her lips.

"Why do you keep all of his things up there?"

Her eyes speared him. "You must never have lost someone that you loved. 'Else, you'd know that their things are precious."

"I lost my grandpa, when I was little."

"Didn't you keep his things?"

He remembered the wallet his mother had given him and how he'd thrown it against the wall.

"No."

Again, those sparkly eyes watched him. "Then you didn't hold on to him. You let him slip away."

"I remember him! You don't go and look at all those things, do you?"

"No, I can't get up those stairs anymore. But I know they're there. So I can think about how he lived and not about how he died. How did your grandpa live?"

All that came to mind was hazy images. She was right. He had let Grandpa slip away.

"I don't remember."

"When you go home, find something of his, so it'll put you in mind of how he lived."

Outwardly, he nodded. But what did she mean?

His first job was hauling hay to the neighbor's. He got up at dawn, ate the breakfast that Edie fixed for him and began loading the hay wagon. It grew hot quickly and he peeled off his shirt. He sat down on the stack for a moment. From here, he could see the whole wide country—the baked plains and bare peaks beyond. There was a steady murmur of grasshoppers, but no other sounds. The earth teetered on the verge of slipping back toward winter. He smiled, satisfied.

He jumped down to the wagon and grabbed a pitchfork to even out his corners. A truck pulled up and a tall man, skinny and weathered as a cedar post, approached him. A hand-made cigarette dangled from his lips.

"You must be Edie's new boy," he said and he held out his hand. "I'm Wynn Criyton."

Rory shook his hand. "Rory Swan."

Wynn drew on his cigarette as he looked him over. "Haven't you heard of wearing a hat?"

Rory brushed the top of his head. His parents had always made him wear hats. "I didn't think I needed one today."

"If you don't wear a hat, you'll get skin cancer and lose your ears." The man slowly removed his hat. His ears were bandaged. "Now would you like a hat?"

"Yes, sir."

Wynn walked back to his cab and pulled out a straw cowboy hat. He handed it to Rory, but Rory hesitated.

"You don't like it."

Rory struggled to find words that wouldn't offend the man. "I don't like straw hats."

"Who are you trying to impress?"

Rory shrugged. "I don't know."

"Then it doesn't matter how the hell you look."

Rory put on the hat.

"Do you rope?"

"Yeah."

"My sons and their friends rope every night. You're welcome to join 'em."

"Where do you live?"

"You're about to find out because I'm the one you're hauling hay for."

Wynn had two sons who were Rory's age, Greg and Matt. Rory fidgeted as Wynn introduced him, but no one asked any questions. They shook his hand.

They found him a horse and the older boy, Greg, said, "Have you ever heeled before?"

"I'm lucky if I can catch the head."

"We're not great either. We just fool around."

They had a small arena and as the dusk settled, the lights snapped on. In the shadows beyond the rails, Rory imagined bleachers lined with people. He could hear the announcer, "Number 23, Rory Swan." Dust sifted under the lights.

"Ready?"

Rory pressed the horse back in the box and nodded. The chute opened and a yearling steer broke away. Rory squeezed the horse and they sprang up along the steer's side. Rory tossed his loop, caught the head and turned off. Matt came up behind him and caught the heels on his first try. A thrill gripped him. They'd done it!

Wynn sat on the rails with a stop watch. His cigarette glowed. "Too slow," was all he said.

34

Nick must have a new girlfriend—he'd stopped eating with them months ago—but Gwen didn't understand why he didn't bring her by. Now it was Thanksgiving, Rory was coming home and Nick had said he wouldn't be there. If he wasn't serious about her, why would he have Thanksgiving with her?

Gwen rolled out a third piecrust and looked at the clock. 11:30. She could get the pies in the oven and go for a quick walk before starting her stuffing. Will and McKenna had gone to get Rory and wouldn't be back until midafternoon.

Ms. Hardy had said she was happy to have Rory. He spoke of the Hardy place as if it was his own operation. He seemed proud of it. And he'd made some friends that he roped with. She was relieved that he was doing well, but anxious to see him. She hadn't seen him since he'd left.

She shivered as she stepped out on the porch. She looked forward to the holidays, but the chill was a reminder of the long winter about to begin. Over twenty years on this ranch. The work—calving, branding, hay season, roundup, shipping and the plunge back into January had anchored her against the ebb and flow of good times, bad times. You didn't set down roots on a ranch. A ranch sank roots into you.

Outside, swatches of snow from the last storm were melting in the sunlight. She walked along the river, happy at the absence of wind. Ice was forming along the banks. She thought about how the children used to play there, McKenna, Rory—and Jim. Those voices would always be there. She sat down on a log, turned her face toward the sun and closed her eyes.

When she returned and opened the door, the smell of warm pie washed over her. She stood still and breathed it in. She had been right to stay, after all. Her family was safe and she and Will had gone on.

She had just started a fresh pot of coffee when she heard a truck in the yard. It was Nick.

He left his boots and coat on the porch and came in and hugged her.

"Happy Thanksgiving, Gwen!"

"You, too, I thought you weren't going to be here."

"I'm not. Is that coffee and pie I smell?"

"The pies are for dinner, but you're welcome to some. What do you want?"

"Pumpkin. And some coffee." He went to the refrigerator. "Any whipped cream?"

"Cool Whip in the freezer."

She set him up at the kitchen table. He spooned Cool Whip over the pie and into his coffee.

"I swear, Nick, aren't you going to be eating today?"

"Yes, I am." His tone made Gwen realize he'd come to tell her something important. She poured her own coffee and sat down, waiting for him to go on, but he hesitated.

She nudged, "You've been seeing someone."

"For a long time. And I married her."

"I don't understand this. Why haven't we gotten to meet her?"

"It's Meg."

Coffee sloshed out of Gwen's mug, burning her wrist. She grabbed a napkin and pressed it against her skin. "How?"

"That time I first met the Hardys I saw Meg, too. I've always felt something for her, Gwen. Always."

"I don't believe this! How could you do this?"

"I understand you don't want to see her and you don't have to. She's over there."

"Across the road?"

"Across the road."

"After all I've done for you, all the times I've stood up for you, first with John, then with Will."

"I didn't do this to hurt you, Gwen."

"No. You did it to get back at Will! That's what it's always about. You and Will. Still vying for the attention of a dead man!"

"It didn't have anything to do with it."

"With dozens of single women around here that you could have chosen from? Oh, Nick, it has everything to do with it."

"I'm not going to say I'm sorry. She's who I want to be with. I'm not ashamed of that."

"You should be ashamed of lying to us! That whole thing with Ms. Hardy and Rory. You knew her because of Meg. Ms. Hardy needed someone because you were marrying Meg."

"Meg wouldn't leave unless I found someone else."

Gwen jumped out of her chair. "You're a piece of work, Nick Swan! A damn piece of work! What about Will? What's he supposed to do?"

"He has a wife. He's always had a wife."

"You didn't think about his feelings?"

"Damn it, Gwen! He didn't love her! If he had, we all wouldn't be here right now. Why should I square my life with my brother's choices?"

"How are we supposed to go on?"

"Like we always have. Meg won't be here. You won't see her. Will won't see her. All I ask," he said as he scooped up his last mouthful of pie, "is that you leave her alone."

"Oh, I will! But I don't want you back in my house either."

Nick put his plate in the sink. "I'm sorry you feel that way," he said as he went out.

Gwen watched him leave and then leaned her forehead against the chilled glass on the door. The whole thing had been a ruse so Meg and Nick could get married! Rory was just a pawn in it! She couldn't confront Meg, but she could say something to Ms. Hardy. She hurried toward the phone.

But… she'd seen Ms. Hardy for herself. There was nothing devious about her. She wouldn't have known about Meg and Will.

To let Rory remain with Ms. Hardy would reward Meg and Nick's fraud. But to take him away? Then Ms. Hardy would have no one. Well, Meg could go back if she loved Ms. Hardy so much and Nick could drive back and forth to Walden!

Gwen decided she wouldn't say anything to her family today. She'd wait until tomorrow.

When they pulled in the yard, she rushed to the kitchen door. She watched as they got out, her heart pounding in anticipation of seeing her son again. How tall he'd gotten! And he'd grown in sideburns. He walked behind his father, his head a little bowed as if he'd become shy, as if he was meeting strangers for the first time.

McKenna came in first.

"Hi, Mom. We're home. Kitchen smells good."

"Smells good in here," said Will, stopping in the doorway. Gwen peered around him.

"Hi, Mom!"

She wanted to hug him, but he wasn't a little boy anymore. She touched his arm. "How are you, son?"

Rory looked as if he wanted to hug her, but didn't know how. Tears brimmed in his eyes.

"I'm good, Mom."

"Hurry and bring your things in because we'll be eating soon. Have you eaten today?"

"I had breakfast."

"You've gotta be hungry now, then."

"Yeah. I've been waiting for this all day."

The last minute scramble of carving the turkey and spooning food into serving dishes dissipated the awkwardness until at last, they were all sitting down and the food steamed on the table. Gwen could tell Rory was pleased to be home, but he was also apprehensive.

"I'm glad you're home, son," Will said finally.

Rory nodded—a man's nod, sharp, abrupt.

"It's good to be home."

"Will, Rory says Ms. Hardy's steers averaged eight hundred pounds. That's better than what we did."

"You ought to be proud, Rory."

"It wasn't all me. Ms. Hardy's got some Simmental bulls and they put a pretty tall frame on those calves."

"When will calving start?" asked Gwen.

"First of March."

"How many are there?"

"Twenty-five heifers. A hundred and fifty cows."

"She didn't breed the heifers to the Simmentals, did she?" asked Will.

"Oh, no. She's got two longhorn bulls for them. They were both bottle calves and they're tame as dogs. Even with those horns you can walk right up to them and feed them out of your hand."

"You be careful, Rory," said Will, "Bulls like that will as soon pin you against the fence as they will eat out of your hand. It's all the same to them. Dogs want you to love them. But a bull, one second he could eat out of your hand and the next, you're in his way."

"How are you going to calve out that many by yourself?" asked Gwen.

"Greg and Matt are going to help me after school. Their dad said I could call him during the day if I get into trouble. I'll have to do night watch by myself."

Will spoke up. "Those are the boys you rope with?"

"Yeah, we rope most nights. They've got a lit arena. Me and Matt are going to enter the team roping next spring."

"Where will you get a horse?"

"They're letting me use one now. Wynn—that's Greg and Matt's dad—says if I help break their colts next spring, I can have one of them."

"You don't know anything about breaking horses."

Rory shrugged. "Wynn'll show me. I'll learn."

"The man must be doing pretty well to have horses to give away."

"He's not giving me nothing. I'm working for it."

"How's Ms. Hardy doing?" Gwen said quickly.

"OK. She cooks real good, although not as good as you, Mom. She doesn't let me watch TV. If we're not roping, she makes me read to her at night."

Gwen and Will exchanged glances, thinking of the battles they'd had to get him to read.

"Dad," Rory started, "is there anything of Grandpa's left?"

Will seemed surprised. "I don't think so." Again, he looked toward Gwen.

"His saddle," she said. "It's in the hayloft."

"Can I have it?"

"You haven't spoken of your granddad since the day he died," said Will.

"Ms. Hardy says if you have something of someone that's died, you can hold on to how they lived."

"Dad used to set you right in front of him in that saddle when you were little."

"What about it, Will?" asked Gwen. "Can he have the saddle?"

Will's focus dropped to his plate. "Next spring, maybe."

It was after ten when Gwen finished in the kitchen. Her mind was too tangled from all she'd heard today to make any more decisions. She poured a cup of coffee and sat down at the table. Bring Rory home now? It would seem like a punishment to him. But to have to live side by side next to Meg the rest of her life, she couldn't abide it.

Will came in. "What're you drinking coffee for? We don't have night watch yet, do we?"

"No. You want some?"

Will sat down across from her and shook his head. "No." He paused. "Seems like Rory's doing real good."

"Hmm."

"I was hoping he'd want to come home."

Gwen's voice trembled. "Me, too."

Will reached for her hand and squeezed it.

"Will, Nick was here today." She paused. "He and Meg got married."

Gwen scrutinized his face, looking for the slightest twitch that would give away his emotions. He dodged her, bowed his head, took both of her hands in his and kissed them.

"Did you know?"

Will didn't raise his head. "No. I didn't know."

"What are we going to do? What are *you* going to do?"

He met her gaze at last. His eyes were the color of the January sky, icy blue. That's what had attracted her to him so many years ago.

"I'm going to get up tomorrow and feed cows."

Gwen was tense over the next several weeks over Meg's return to the neighborhood, but their lives reshuffled to skirt her presence. Nick didn't come to the house anymore. He and Will spoke by phone.

She caught glimpses of Meg from time to time on the county road. Meg waved, but Gwen stared straight ahead. If the woman wanted friends and neighbors, then she shouldn't have come back. Gwen saw her again briefly at the Stockgrowers' dance out on the dance floor with Nick. She was dressed just as Gwen remembered her—in a Western shirt and jeans. Against her will, Gwen found herself following her, wanting to see her face. But the couples swirled around them and they were gone.

Nick took the first-calf heifers to calve over at the Mather place and left the cows to Will and Gwen. As calving intensified, Gwen forgot about Meg during the day. But on night watch, walking to the sheds with the Milky Way wheeling above her, she remembered the relief she'd felt all those years ago at having someone near to hear her groans about John, or her anxieties over Rory. She hadn't lived the kind of life that others would applaud, or remark on in any way. Yet Meg's presence as a witness to how hard she'd tried had been such a comfort after all.

On a warm day in April, Gwen and Will decided to run errands in town. They went to a diner for lunch and when they came out, the sky had turned hazy and the wind had come up. They rushed to get their groceries, but by the time they'd loaded up, the squall had already begun.

They crept out to the airport. West, beyond the airport lights, the blizzard had settled in, blotting out the prairie, the highway, the mountains, the sky.

A highway patrolman stopped them.

"Highway's closed," he said.

"I live out there and I've got cattle to feed," Will answered as snow blew in the window.

"Suit yourself."

Will drove as slowly as he could, following the reflector poles and the white line on the side of the highway. "So far, we're lucky. It's blowing, but it's not drifting."

"But look how deep it is already. Close to a foot." Then Gwen spotted tracks that veered between the reflector poles. "Will, stop. There's somebody off the road." They looked and saw a truck in the borrow pit, Nick's truck. And the slim figure shoveling snow could only be Meg.

Will stopped.

She smacked his arm. "No! Go on!"

Will peered out of Gwen's window.

"We can't leave her here, Gwen."

"She can get out herself. She's dressed for it."

"Gwen!"

"Will, you are not to stop! Keep driving!"

They drove home in silence. Snow swirled under the yard light. Will ran for the house. McKenna looked up from her homework, startled as he burst through the door.

"McKenna, go help your mother unload the truck."

"What's going on?"

"Just do it."

"I don't know why you're yelling at me," she pouted as she reached for her parka.

Will yanked the phone off the hook and dialed. Gwen came in with a load of groceries, set them on the table and watched him. She left the door open and the wind blew in. She listened as Will told Nick where they'd seen Meg and when.

Will hung up the phone and bowed his head.

"Well, it's taken care of, isn't it?"

"She's pregnant, Gwen."

35

The plains, golden beneath the rising sun, rushed by outside the window. Rory's head seemed foggy despite the light in his eyes. Last night's ride in the arena—the spectators cheering at the rail, the holler that rose from his chest when he realized that he and Matt had won their first team-roping contest, the beer that Wynn had let them drink and finally, the taste of his girl's, Sarah's, mouth—all these images whirled before his eyes just as the landscape flew by outside. He struggled to hang on them, but the light was burning them away.

"So, you won last night," Nick said.

"Yeah. First place."

"How much money?"

"Fifty dollars, twenty-five each."

"Where do you go from here?"

"We both gotta hay this summer. But over the winter, we'll keep practicing and we'll go full-time next spring."

"Have you told Ms. Hardy yet?"

"How'd I have time to tell her anything? I got in after midnight and you got me up at five this morning."

"What were you doing until after midnight?"

"Talking—with Greg and Matt."

Nick looked at him out of the corner of his eye.

"It wouldn't seem that you'd have all that much to talk about."

Rory ignored him as he remembered Sarah's lips and their tongues in each other's mouths. But he thought he could distract his uncle.

"How's Meg?"

"She's good. I think she'll get through haying, but then she'll have to stop for a while."

"And Mom?"

"Well, she still doesn't speak to Meg, if that's what you're asking."

Rory leaned his head back against the seat. He was going home for the weekend, the last weekend he'd be home until haying was done. He closed his eyes and the night came rushing back. The thrill they'd felt when they'd learned they made the finals. How his hands shook as he gathered his reins in one hand and felt for the rope with the other. How his blood pounded in his ears as they waited for the steer to hit the trip string. How he swung once, twice and turned off. How Matt got the heels before he'd even finished dallying and they watched amazed, as the steer fell over. They weren't even half way across the arena. They looked to the referee. Had they started too soon? No, it was good. They'd won.

They found Wynn. Rory was too excited to speak.
Matt said, "What do you think, Dad?"
Wynn looked off into the night and shrugged.
"It wasn't bad. The two of you have come a ways."

"We're going to go professional, Dad."

"Then you've got a long ways to go."

They went with Wynn to watch the rest of the rodeo. The bulls were on now. Rory looked through the crowd and saw Sarah's face as she came up the stands, searching for him.

Rory looked to Wynn. "Can I go with her?"

"If she's better company."

He caught her hand and they rushed back down, out under the stands where it was dark.

"Wake up, boy! You're home!" Nick slapped his knee and Rory sat up. He turned to his uncle. "Aren't you coming in?"

"Your mother doesn't want me. Go along now."

In the yard, long skeins of cotton drifted from the upper limbs of the cottonwoods. The year was turning—shifting into high summer when the days would be hot and dry, heat lightning would flash along the horizons at night and the nights would be chilly, reminding them, it won't last, it won't last.

His mother was cooking the noon meal. "Rory! You look like you just woke up!"

"Mom, we won the team roping at Cowdrey last night!"

Gwen wiped her hands and hugged him. In the circles beneath her eyes, he saw the ghost of the rodeo queen. She understood what glory was, so she would understand his desire to go on.

"We're going to go professional, Mom, next year."

"You don't even have your high school degree yet."

"I can get a G-E-D. I'll do it this winter."

"What about Ms. Hardy?"

"I'll find her someone else. I promise."

"You'll only be seventeen. Not old enough for that way of life."

"I'm ready. Where's Dad?"

"In the shop. Getting the hay machinery ready."

Beyond the shade of the cottonwoods, it was already hot and the barnyard was dry and dusty. He found his father sliding a sickle into the mower. Will had taken off his shirt and his hands were covered in grease. He jumped when Rory spoke up.

"Can I help you with that, Dad?"

"Rory!" Will had last seen his son around branding. Since then, there had been a change. His face was wider, his arms were more muscular.

Rory held out his hand and Will looked down and shook it. The grip was firm and warm.

"Dad, I've got something to tell you. The team roping in Cowdrey last night? Me and Matt won it."

"Won?"

"Yeah, we did it."

"Your grandfather would be proud. I wish he was here."

Rory watched the beads of sweat trickle down his father's forehead.

"Look, tomorrow, I'm going to start mowing. Can you take your sister and go up to the mountains and check on the cattle?"

"Yeah."

"And Rory, take your granddad's saddle."

Rory nodded. "When I go back, can I take it?"

"You're not going to be riding the rest of the summer, are you?"

"We'll keep practicing after work."

Will stared at him for a moment. "John would want you to have it. I wish you could have known, son, how much you meant to him."

Rory swallowed. "Thanks, Dad." He was surprised to see, for the first time, that his father was struggling.

Will wanted to say more, but felt that he'd already said too much.

At supper, Gwen said she wanted to ride, too. "But let's not take the trailer," she added.

"Why not?" asked Will.

"Because it's just a hot bumpy ride up there. It would be so much more pleasant just to ride. We can start out early when it's cool."

Will shrugged. "If that's what you want to do."

"That's going to take forever," McKenna whined.

"Do you have somewhere you have to be?" her father asked.

"No. It'll just make the day long. That's all."

"You like to ride, don't you?"

"Yeah."

"Well then, you should be happy to ride all day long."

"McKenna," Gwen interrupted, "it's just this one day. Just for me."

They rose when the stars were still out and saddled under the naked lightbulb in the barn. By the time a sliver of sun topped the horizon, they had galloped three miles from home. The meadowlarks sang along the barbed wire fences and the country stretched before them, sparkling and fresh.

They slowed to a walk. Gwen looked on either side of her. McKenna was a good horsewoman, tall and pretty in the saddle. She'd be old enough to try out for Jubilee Queen next spring, if she wanted. And Rory was in John's saddle, a solid young man, after all.

She wanted to say these things to her children. She wanted to say how handsome they looked in this early morning, how lucky she felt to be here with them in this blessed country under this immense sky, but the words died in her throat. They would only stare at her, embarrassed.

They topped the last rise and the land dropped down to the barbed wire fence below. Willows marked the creek that zig-zagged up the mountainside, and there was the timberline five miles above.

"We'd better split up here," said Rory.

"Split up? Can't we ride all of it together?"

"It would take too long, Mom, especially if we're going to ride down. McKenna can take the southern side here, you can go up Middle Fork Creek to the timberline and I'll do the bluff to the north. We can meet at the spring and have lunch."

"I'm going," said McKenna. She nudged her horse and they trotted off southwest.

Rory rode north with his mother until they reached Middle Fork, then she turned west and he continued on. There were no cattle down this low. By now, they'd all be as far up the mountain as they could get.

The bluff was so steep and rocky that it took him a half an hour to zigzag his way to the top. A sharp wind blew and he stopped to put on his windbreaker. The bluff was tufted in Indian paintbrush—corals, oranges and scarlets waving in the stiff breeze. Above, two eagles circled. He rode west with the wind in his face and the northern fence line to his right. Below the fence, the land fell away to the hay meadows of another ranch.

He didn't find any cattle until he'd almost reached the western fence line. The snow must have melted late at this elevation for the grass was still thick and green. A dozen cattle and their calves lay dozing in the sunshine. They rose and stretched at the horse's approach and he looked them over one by one.

One of the calves had an abscess in his jaw. It was a good thing he'd thought to bring some penicillin. He untied his rope. The calf trotted away from the rest of the group eastwards, back down the bluff. Rory followed, with the cow behind him. The calf broke into a sprint and Rory's loop shot out over him. The loop caught and he turned off and dallied.

He patted the horse and checked the tautness of the rope. The calf struggled on the ground. The cow had caught up to them now and bawled furiously over the calf. Rory took a piggin string and tied up the calf's feet. Then he released the head.

He took out his pocketknife and lanced the abscess. Now, a little penicillin and he'd be OK.

But the calf bawled long and hard. The cow looked at Rory, charged and knocked him to the ground. He tried to scramble away, but she knocked him down again. Then she dropped her knees down on his chest and rocked from side to side, knowing that what she wanted to hear was the cracking of bone. He was screaming, screaming in her ear, but it didn't scare her and after a while, he went limp. She rose to her feet and walked quietly back to her calf.

It was hot by the time Gwen and McKenna met at the spring. They dismounted, cupped their hands in the cool water and drank. Then they looked northwest for Rory.

36

The edge of the green canopy whipped in the breeze over the coffin heaped with yellow roses. No, thought Meg as she walked up from the car with Nick. No.

Two hundred people or more, all with reddened faces, had come in from the hayfields. There was Gwen, Will, McKenna. Jim had come with her parents. Wynn Criyton pushed Ms. Hardy's wheelchair up to the gravesite. Her lined face was bleak and empty. Wynn's boys were there, quietly gripping their hats in their hands. A girl, whose face was swollen from sobbing, had come with them. Mrs. Mather was there. All her children, grown now, crowded behind her.

The grave was next to John Swan's. Meg felt his presence. He could not grieve with them. He had passed beyond grief. He was here to witness.

Was that Jim, wondered Gwen, as she watched the slim,

red-haired young man silently take his place beside Meg and remove his hat. The last time she'd seen him had been in Meg's pickup the day she left for Hayden. She remembered, even as she raged at Meg, how those blue eyes had fixed on her face. The man standing next to him—must be his grandfather, the veterinarian. You could tell they were related. Jim would probably go on to college and vet school, too. How lucky Meg had been.

And there was the grandmother. She looked like an older version of Meg, with that same odd receding chin. She slipped her arm into her husband's and nodded at Gwen. She had sounded so grateful years ago when Gwen called to tell her where her daughter was. That's why she was here.

Jim stole a glance at McKenna. He hadn't thought of her in years, but how pretty she looked now: pale with waves of dark hair falling on her shoulders. He wished she'd stop crying for just a second and recognize him.

McKenna couldn't see anything but that day over and over again. They'd waited almost an hour, then they'd set out to look for him. They crossed Middle Fork and the deep bowl of prairie before climbing the bluff. It was slow, zigzagging up and up, scrambling over the boulders. They reached the top and there was nothing, only Indian paintbrush and wind and fluffy clouds catching on the mountaintop. They called, "Rory," but their voices shredded in the wind.

When they found his horse, McKenna's throat tightened. He whinnied as they approached. The reins were broken, the rope was missing, but Grandpa's saddle was fine.

"He must have gotten bucked off," Gwen said. It was midafternoon then and the sun was in their eyes.

They saw the cow and calf before they saw Rory. The calf struggled on the ground and the cow stood over it, nosing it every now and then. So strange, this cow-calf pair all alone with no trees or water in sight. Then they saw the wind billow the windbreaker on Rory's body.

Gwen shouted, "Oh, my God!" and kicked her horse hard. McKenna pulled back. She didn't want to see. She watched her mother drop to her knees, tip Rory's head back and breathe into his mouth. Then McKenna screamed. The cow looked up at her, startled.

"McKenna!" Gwen shouted, "Go home! Get your father and Nick!"

McKenna whirled the horse around and kicked him harder than she had ever kicked any horse, ever. They raced eastward along the bluff until they reached the slope. She pulled back a little, but not enough and the horse stumbled over stone after stone. Too slow, too slow, she thought and she drove the horse on. She watched the red clay road come closer and when his hooves touched down, she took up the reins and smacked him and they went pounding over the prairie. Every second, she could hear his lungs pump air, but time seemed to stretch beyond them. It was hours before she reached the last gate to the last dirt road toward home.

When she rode into the barnyard, her father was just pulling in from the first day of mowing.

He shut off the mower and said, "My God, McKenna, what did you do to that horse?"

Gwen gave up trying to resuscitate her son and sat up. She took his hand and looked into the eyes that stared blankly at the sky above. The calf struggled on the ground. She rose and saw the lanced abscess. The cow backed away a few steps.

"You did it," she said. "You took my boy's life."

She knelt down while watching the cow and undid the piggin string. The calf rose stiffly and went to nurse. The cow turned and walked away.

Gwen went back to Rory and sat and held his hand until the light grew too dim to see any longer and the stars poked out of the twilight. The Milky Way drifted above her for hours until she saw headlights approaching.

The pastor mumbled something about his wife singing. She stepped forward.

> *My latest sun is sinking fast,*
> *My race is nearly run.*
> *My longest trials now are passed,*
> *My triumph has begun.*
>
> *O come angel band.*
> *Come and around me stand.*
> *Bear me away on your snow white wings*
> *To my immortal home.*
> *O bear me away on your snow white wings*
> *To my immortal home."*

The last note dissipated in the wind. Cotton floated down from the tree crowns, coating the graves below. The crowd was silent. Angels with snow white wings? To them, death was as familiar as sunrise. The hogs, cows and sheep they'd all butchered. The calves, born dead, frozen dead, dead from scours, bloat, blackleg, or fallen in the river. Beloved dogs run over by accident in the barnyards. The old horses that couldn't be kept up anymore and were shot. And last, the family members slipping away in hospital beds, or killed in drunk driving accidents. No angels. Only the impassive sky above and sunrise the next morning.

There was a sound and they all turned their heads. Will Swan was sobbing.

The fringes of the crowd broke up and moved away, some to their cars, some to console the Swans. They hugged and kissed and cried, but soon let go and turned their backs on the grave until only the Swans and the Braeburns were left.

Ben Braeburn reached for Will Swan's hand. "I'm sorry for your loss," he said.

Will nodded, the tear streaks shiny in the stubble on his face.

Mamie Braeburn murmured to Gwen, "You helped us get our daughter back. I wish we could do more for you."

"You don't understand. I didn't help you at all."

Mamie squeezed her hand. "Oh, but you did."

They turned to leave and Jim called back to Meg, "Mom, walk with us to the car."

Meg started to speak, but then closed her mouth and followed.

37

Meg rocked the tractor back and forth, but it was no use. She flipped the switch off and the engine putted out. The stillness of bitter cold hung over the river and meadow and the foothills beyond. The Swans' first calf heifers crowded around the wagon, their ears pricked forward, waiting. The tractor meant food and warmth, but what did the silence mean? They shied away when Meg jumped off the seat, then whirled to face her, vapor rising from their nostrils, all with the same question in their eyes. Where was breakfast?

The first day of December and five feet of snow on the ground. Still, Meg didn't feel the weight of winter just yet. This was her first day out of the house since the twins were born and the cold that burned her cheekbones almost felt good. Nick had warned her that she might get stuck and since one of them had to be with the babies all of the time, she wasn't sure what to do. Could she pull the tractor out herself with their Caterpillar, or should she get Nick and have him call Will to come help. She'd decide on the walk home.

Sam, her new red heeler, bounded up to her, wriggling for attention. He didn't care about the cold. He jabbed his muzzle in the snow and tossed the crystals in the air, snapping at them as they fell.

She walked home in the tire tracks. The snow crackled underneath her paks and some warmth flowed back down her finger-tips. A figure on horseback rode toward her and Meg shaded her eyes to see who it was. It was Gwen.

Gwen pulled the horse to a stop. She gestured back toward Meg's house.

"I stopped there to see you and Nick said you were out here."

Meg didn't know what to say.

"Nick let me hold the girls. They're beautiful, Meg."

"Thank you."

"I'm going to get off. I'm getting cold." Gwen dismounted and they stood face to face.

"I saw your new mares at the barn. It looks like both of them took."

"We'll have foals in April. We bred 'em to a red roan stud that Dad found."

"Nick says you're going to be raising horses."

"I'm going to try."

They paused awkwardly until Meg spoke up.

"How's McKenna?"

"She didn't want to go back to school, but once she did, she picked up again. She's in 4-H and she's going to raise a steer next year. Boys have been calling and for a long time she wouldn't talk to them, but now she does. She doesn't hound me anymore about why she can't do this or that, though I know that'll fade the moment she wants to go out on a date. She's trying to be good. She's trying to—to make up…"

"Do you think that's the right thing?"

"No. Maybe it's not."

"And Will?"

The women exchanged a long look and finally, Gwen spoke.

"He cursed the weather this morning. It was the first time that he sounded like... before. I told him I was coming here and he said, 'it's time.'"

The women shifted from foot to foot as the chill burrowed beneath their clothing.

"I've got to be getting back," said Meg. "I got the tractor stuck."

"Can I help?"

Meg paused. "If you'd like. Then I wouldn't have to get Nick."

"Nick seems a little overwhelmed at the moment. But if the man can handle dozens of baby calves, surely he can handle two little girls for a while."

Nick looked out the kitchen window when he heard the Caterpillar fire up.

He called out to the napping babies in their cribs, "Your mother got the tractor stuck, just like I said she would." He saw Gwen driving and Meg riding in the rear back out to the meadow. "And Gwen's helping her."

He watched until the two women were twig figures far out in the blinding white.

Acknowledgments

I am grateful to the following people who provided needed criticism and encouragement: Lauren Sarraf, Letty Coykendall, Dorothy Lang, Janet Lane, Ruth Arthur, Judith Rozner, Mary Ann Harlow, Julee Fortune Marshall, Dee Jones, Rose Pratt, John Winkel, Beverly Swerling and Charlotte Cook.

Thank you to Bruce Roseland for the use of his lovely poem, *Prairie Prayer* from his volume of poetry, *A Prairie Prayer*, winner of the 2009 Will Rogers Medallion Award.

Thank you to Vance Barron, Jr. for all the work he put into the author photograph.

Thank you to Trish Nelson and Dee Jones for assistance with final editing.

Thank you to Annette Chaudet for her belief in my Wyoming tale.

Thank you to Leonard Johnson who always had time for more stories. Thank you to Joe Coykendall who taught me the value of listening. May their memories be for a blessing.

About the Author...

Jamie Lisa Forbes was raised on a family ranch in southeastern Wyoming. She obtained degrees in philosophy and English from the University of Colorado, Boulder, where she graduated with honors in 1977. She then spent a year in Israel studying and working on a kibbutz. She returned to Wyoming in 1979 where she ranched and raised a family over the next fifteen years. In 2001 she graduated from the University of North Carolina School of Law and now practices in Greensboro, North Carolina.

She enjoys spending time with her grandson and playing the old time Appalachian fiddle. With her Arabian horse Cody and her cattle dog Reb, she still devotes part of her life to the outdoors.

CPSIA information can be obtained at www.ICGtesting.com
Printed in the USA
LVOW011008120413

328838LV00003B/245/P